Was Ty the kind of person who would put an untrained woman—a woman he loved—into a position of fear and to possibly become a target?

The idea was a surgical assault. It required data and planning.

He would keep Kira safe. If he wasn't going to Tanzania on that plane, neither was she. He'd figure out how to preempt her trip if and when the time came. If he was on that plane, getting the details his team needed, then he'd make sure Kira was clear before she was anywhere near a Delta operation.

Had he just thought "the woman he loved"?

He did *not* love Kira, he worked to convince himself.

It was a mirage, not a future marriage.

Just psyops fiction.

Ty had been warned to keep that both within his awareness and tucked away so that gentle, soft, intelligent, empathic Kira didn't sense his duplicity and steer clear of him and his goal to get to the compound.

Ty needed to keep his head on straight.

Fiona Quinn is a six-time *USA TODAY* bestselling author, a Kindle Scout winner and an Amazon All-Star.

Quinn writes suspense in her Iniquus world of books, including the Lynx, Strike Force, Uncommon Enemies, Kate Hamilton Mysteries, FBI Joint Task Force, Cerberus Tactical K-9 Team Alpha and Delta Force Echo series, with more to come.

She writes urban fantasy as Fiona Angelica Quinn for her Elemental Witches series.

And, just for fun, she writes the Badge Bunny Booze Mystery Collection of raucous, bawdy humor with her dear friend Tina Glasneck as Quinn Glasneck.

Quinn is rooted in the Old Dominion, where she lives with her husband. There, she pops chocolates, devours books and taps continuously on her laptop.

Facebook, Twitter, Pinterest: Fiona Quinn Books.

A GUARDIAN'S DUTY

USA TODAY Bestselling Author

FIONA QUINN

Previously published as *Danger Signs*

This novel is dedicated to Ciara Noelle, with gratitude.
An inspiration, a muse, a teacher, beloved.

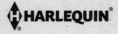

ISBN-13: 978-1-335-50839-3

A Guardian's Duty

First published as Danger Signs in 2021.
This edition published in 2023.

Copyright © 2021 by Fiona Quinn

Recycling programs
for this product may
not exist in your area.

For questions and comments about the quality of this book, please contact us at CustomerService@Harlequin.com.

Harlequin Enterprises ULC
22 Adelaide St. West, 41st Floor
Toronto, Ontario M5H 4E3, Canada
www.Harlequin.com

Printed in U.S.A.

A GUARDIAN'S DUTY

Acknowledgments

My great appreciation:

To the real-world Christen Davidson for our decades of friendship.

To my editor, Kathleen Payne.

To my assistant, Margaret Daly.

To my Beta Force, who are always honest and kind at the same time, especially M. Carlon and E. Hordon.

To my Street Force, who support me and my writing with such enthusiasm.

Thank you to the real-world military and CIA who serve to protect us.

To all the wonderful professionals whom I called on to get the details right. Please note: this is a work of fiction, and while I always try my best to get all the details correct, there are times when it serves the story to go slightly to the left or right of perfection. Please understand that any mistakes or discrepancies are my authorial decision-making alone and sit squarely on my shoulders.

Thank you to my family.

I send my love to my husband, and my great appreciation. T, you are my happily-ever-after. You are my encouragement and my adventure. Thank you.

And of course, thank *you* for reading my stories. I'm smiling joyfully as I type this. I so appreciate you!

Chapter 1

Ty

As soon as Ty heard D-Day's high-pitched gasp, he knew they were in big trouble.

A nanosecond later, he sucked in his own gulp of air. Sudden sharp pains snapped over his body.

Ty's brain scrambled to understand their situation—to make sense of whatever was happening. And to find a way to survive it.

One minute they had been dangling peacefully from his parachute harness, floating through the night's sky, and now—completely blinded in the pitch-black night—their situation turned dire.

Time slowed—what operators called *vapor lock*—the point where the brain knew for a fact that the situation was desperate and dumped adrenaline into the body's systems, not only powering up muscle strength but focusing the mind sharply on the immediate threat.

Everything physical felt like pouring cold molasses; everything mental sped forward at warp speed.

Ty's senses expanded, clawing the environment for information to tell him how best to endure the next moments. But in the darkness, Ty Newcomb—Tier One operator with Delta Force Echo—had almost nothing to go on.

It was zero-dark-thirty along the Kenya-Uganda border in central Africa.

Up until this moment, the jump had been textbook. Getting down was supposed to be a cakewalk for him, even if he was jumping tandem with D-Day attached to his chest straps.

Ty hadn't been worried about getting them on-site for this mission. He'd steer for the IR illuminator that marked their landing zone with practiced efficiency.

When Ty had run off the back of the plane a few minutes before, with D-Day tethered to him, the *only* thing Ty had worried about had been the landing. Murphy's Law meant there was a high probability for skidding along the grassy meadow only to discover he was dragging through some wildebeest excrement—or whatever herd of wild animals had grazed the grasses down.

After Ty's parachute thwacked open, and he'd descended in the pitch black, there had been peace. Weightless, visionless, with a slight woosh of wind, heard through his helmet, Ty had split his attention between situational awareness and a moment of joy.

He imagined himself a space explorer, gliding into a wormhole to come out the other side on some strange new planet.

He'd enjoyed it.

Always did.

A moment of indulgence, and he was back on task,

focused on the Ugandan soldier ally below them, waving his red lights in sweeping arcs to give Ty a bull's-eye to aim for.

Ty began to repeat his list of landing protocols aloud to remind D-Day what she was supposed to do as they hit the ground. "Hands crossing the chest, legs lifted from the hips…"

A gust of wind suddenly dragged their canopy higher in the sky and blew them off course.

Way off course.

Past the field out beyond the range of the light source.

Yup, he'd been worried about buffalo dung.

And to say they were in the shits would be putting it mildly.

This was life or death.

They were slicing through a tree in the thick canopy of what Ty assumed must be Queen Elizabeth Park's northernmost edge. If not, they'd blown into the Congo, and that would be a whole other SNAFU layer to be dealt with.

First, Ty had to survive the next thirty seconds.

The velocity of their descent pressed the smaller branches away only to have them whip angrily back in stinging rebuke, leaving vengeful welts on their skin as Ty and D-Day fell from the sky.

Ty tipped his chin down to his chest and protected his eyes in the crook of his elbow. "D-Day, cross your ankles, press your thighs together, soften your knees!" As he yelled out, he tried to maneuver his own body into this safer configuration.

Getting stopped by a branch between his legs would make the rest of this mission a nightmare.

That was *if* they survived this fall.

His head jerked backward as his night-vision goggles snagged and ripped from his combat helmet.

"Arms protecting your face!" Ty hoped D-Day could hear him bellow as they crashed past limb after limb.

The branches dressed in thick foliage grappled with his equipment, yanking at the closures and straps until the sheer weight and speed of the operators' slide ripped them free of the branches' grasp.

Down, down, down, they careened.

Without the full canopy of their parachute capturing air and drifting them safely to the ground, they had no brakes, no control, and Ty had no idea how far they were from the ground.

If they continued to fall like this, they were going to die.

Up in a tree alive was better than down and dead.

Ty reached into the stygian night, not seeing even an edge of a solid object, completely blind to his surroundings. His knuckles grazed along the bark of a limb to his left. Ty flexed his hand to grab at it.

The weight of the two operators, their equipment, plus speed tore the branch from his fingers.

He tried again.

And again.

And again.

Each time their descent noticeably slowed.

Tunnel vision—especially in a pure black tunnel like this—meant he had no concept of what D-Day was doing below him. But she was a pilot for the SOAR 160th—an elite Army special operations unit. She was used to working in scenarios of sensory deprivation and high stress. Surely, she was doing something to help.

If Ty could just get their chute to tangle up in a branch that was strong enough to support their weight, or he could find purchase on a stout limb, they could survive.

Hoping to affect either of those options, with Ty's next grab, he tugged hard to the side where he thought the trunk might be.

Their abrupt halt was teeth jarring.

"Hang tight," Ty called down to D-Day as soon as his lungs were working enough for him to form words.

"As if I had a choice," she choked out her response.

"Give me a minute to assess."

"Yeah, you do that," D-Day called up to him.

The last time Ty had seen D-Day, her helmet was just below his chin. Ty patted her head to see if she'd managed to keep her night vision goggles. His hand landed on her hair, cut in a short pixie style. She'd lost her whole helmet; that must have hurt like hell. But the only sound she'd made through all this was that initial gasp of surprise.

She was lucky that losing her helmet hadn't snapped her neck.

Ty gave himself a moment to regroup.

It had been a while since Ty had parachuted with a human attached to his straps.

Typically when Ty jumped with Delta Force Echo, he had his Military Working Dog, Rory, in a pouch as they headed down to whatever off-grid mission Fort Bragg's JSOC—Joint Special Operations Command—sent them on.

Rory loved to jump; it was like sticking his nose out the window during a long country car ride but on steroids. Rory was a K9 that could best be described as a dog on steroids. He was all go-mode when he was on a task but a dork when he was hanging out at the base.

Luckily, this time, Rory was left behind—asleep in his kennel.

Hanging out in a tree until an Echo brother could get them an assist, yeah, that could take hours.

Rory in a tree for hours, dangling from his pouch, mad, with his sharp teeth inches from Ty's jugular?

If this had to happen on a tandem jump, selfishly, Ty was glad he had a human—who understood the concept of patience—strapped to his front.

Delta Force Echo missions were always high risk. Any damned thing could go haywire at any point. It was expertise built on training and experience that kept everyone operational.

But Ty had *never* landed in a tree before—with or without a tandem partner. And certainly not on a night so dark that it seemed to sponge up any possible trace of illumination. For him, this was all theoretical. Something they'd talked through in jump school.

Rule number one, stay calm.

"Well?" D-Day asked.

"Working the problem," Ty said. He'd managed to keep his radio on him—small miracle. He adjusted the channel then tabbed the mic. "Echo-zero-two for Echo-zero-one." He directed his communications to their team leader, Master Chief T-Rex. Since T-Rex was second out of the plane, Ty hoped he got down before the winds kicked up.

"Go for Echo-zero-one," T-Rex's voice came over his speaker.

"Echo-zero-two and D-Day are sitting in a tree."

"K-I-S-S-I-N-G," T-Rex sang.

"Funny," D-Day muttered.

"I was wondering where the team took off to," T-Rex

said. "We had a designated landing spot. You didn't get the memo?"

"Sorry, I must have been getting a coffee while you went over that part of the mission."

T-Rex went through the Echo roster, using their team numbers to check on their situations. As it turned out, T-Rex and Nitro were the only ones with boots on the actual ground. The rest of Echo were up in the trees like a troupe of monkeys.

"Echo-zero-one to Echo-zero-two. Did either you or D-Day sustain serious injuries?"

Before Ty depressed the button to answer T-Rex, he asked, "How are you doing down there, D-Day?"

"Hard to tell," D-Day answered. "It feels like I have most of my body parts."

"This is Echo-zero-two. D-Day and I will need to assess once we're on the ground. We're both conscious."

"We'll take what we can get. Any idea how high up you two are?"

"Standby."

Ty's mind spun through the situation. For sure, he had no idea how high they were up off the ground.

Five feet? Fifty?

And if it were fifty, would their chute hold fast?

Silk ripped easily, and their combined weight was a lot to ask for the fabric to hold. Ty was two-ten. D-Day was tiny. But she was also solid muscle. Looking at her, he'd guess one-ten, one-fifteen? But when he caught her under the arms and lifted her briefly up onto a platform back at the base, he'd say with her clothes and boots she was a good hundred and fifty.

Besides their personal weight, the tandem team had carried their share of equipment and provisions in their drop bag that weighed a hundred and forty-two pounds when Ty had put it on the scale.

The equipment bag hung between their legs on a twenty-foot cord with a bungee shock absorber. During a normal landing, the jumper detached the load before performing the parachute landing fall; this kept the bag from causing the jumper injuries.

Now, if a jumper saw they were headed into a tree canopy, the instruction book said to get rid of that bag lest the jumper lands in one tree and the equipment in the other.

Of course, if you kept it attached, it could provide an exit strategy. Tie the top in tight and simply climb down along the cord.

"D-Day, the provisions bag, does it reach the ground?"

"Nope," she exhaled. "But I'd like to—"

Ty heard the rip of parachute fabric written large against the otherwise silent night. They dropped about six inches before Ty's boot found a limb. His weight hung from the parachute ropes, but even having the tips of his toes on a surface made him feel better. He hoped his stomach would settle. Puking down D-Day's back would make him the butt of bar jokes for years to come.

D-Day's feet dangled over nothingness.

Ty could feel her weight dragging at him. Sweat formed on Ty's upper lip and chest as his body processed their life-threatening situation. "We have to get that weight off. Moving very slowly, D-Day, can you unclasp the supply bag?"

"I believe so, let me just feel… Yup, got it."

"Here's what we're going to do. You're going to count down your release, then we're going to listen for the bag to impact the ground. From that information, we're going to take our best guess at how high up we are.

Hopefully, you release the clasp, and the bag hits the ground. Twenty feet, we can work with."

"Wilco," D-Day said. "Three. Two. One. Release."

As soon as D-Day freed the weight, the tandem partners flew a good foot up in the air. Ty landed back with his toes on a branch.

With the strain on his back somewhat eased, Ty reached under D-Day's arms and tried to haul her up to the branch beside him. Even though she was positioned inches lower than he was in the restraints, he towered a good foot above her when they stood side by side on the ground. Here in the tree, her feet couldn't reach the branch Ty stood on. He lowered her back to dangle from his chest rigging.

In this configuration, Ty had his boys pinched down tight. He needed to get the weight off. How exactly he was going to do that, he wasn't sure. Getting castrated from the harness strap wasn't on his happy list.

He wanted to be a dad someday.

Maybe even someday soon—*if* the right woman walked into his life.

Ty had been thinking about this just the other day, how suddenly the timing seemed right to form a family of his own.

It would suck if he had to explain to his potential future Mrs. Newcomb how his nuts got crushed in a parachuting catastrophe.

It would suck even more if this was how things ended for him, and he never got the opportunity to love a woman, commit his life to her, and know the depth of feelings that came with being a dad.

The longer the webbing was cutting off circulation, the more worrisome his situation became. Ty thought about going to his uncle's farm and wrapping the calves' balls with bands...

He remembered asking his uncle how long it took after he'd put the band around the bulls' scrotum until the testicles fell off. As Ty remembered it, the amount of time depended on the size of the bull, but the testicles would fall off somewhere between ten and fifty days.

He had time before he castrated himself.

Yeah, maybe change the subject.

And all of those thoughts whipped through Ty's mind *before* the supply bag crashed to the ground.

"Whew!" D-Day said. "That was a long way down. Did you hear it?"

"How far?" Ty asked.

"Going out on a limb here, he-he-he. I'm guessing we're at the top of a very tall tree."

"Funny."

Three stories up in the air—that would be broken ankles and legs...if they were lucky. At forty feet—which was Ty's best guess at their height based on the equipment bag's thud—there was a fifty percent chance of death. Over fifty feet and that stat went up to a hundred percent dead—no shot at surviving.

He toggled his mic. "Echo-zero-one, Echo-zero-two is over twenty feet. Zero visibility. No light source or night vision available."

"Are you lashed in?"

"We seem stable," Ty reported.

"Echo," T-Rex spoke to their entire team. "I have your GPS coordinates. Our forward team and I are headed your way." T-Rex's voice was staticky in Ty's headset.

"Looks like the wind action we had hoped to avert was in play," T-Rex continued. "The team was blown about three klicks off target." Three kilometers—not quite two miles. That would have all been fine, except for the trees.

Ty called down to D-Day. "T-Rex is one of our fastest runners. It's only three kilometers. He'll be here soon."

"Soon would be awesome."

Chapter 2

Kira

Kira was halfway up the brick stairs to her porch when she saw the brown-paper-wrapped box leaning against the front door of her little Cape Cod–styled home. She stalled as she took in the Arabic writing at the top left, fluid and beautiful. Colorful Qatari stamps covered the top right. And in the center in block letters, less sure and comfortable, "Shakira al-Attiyah" was written atop of her Durham, North Carolina, address in the Latin alphabet.

Kira had been waiting expectantly for this box.

"A treasure," she whispered to Princess Beatrice, the King Charles spaniel who sniffed at the thick bank of ruby-red geraniums that lined her walkway.

Beatrice was her friend London Davidson's dog. Kira was working for London this summer—the time between walking across the stage to collect her doctoral diploma and the beginning of her next chapter. Her summer job was not so much about the need for money—Kira had inherited from her father and didn't need to work at all—it was more about quieting her family's concerns.

Kira was an unmarried female, and her father was dead. While she lived in America—she was, in fact, born and raised an American—the whole of her surviving family lived in Qatar, where by tradition, her life would be defined by her male protector.

Since her father's death, there was no male head of household who took responsibility for Kira in the United States. This traditional duty landed on her father's oldest brother's shoulders. Uncle Nadir had told Kira that as long as she was enrolled at the university, she could continue along her educational path. Qatar held education in high regard, and even among females, most everyone in the small peninsular country, jutting like an egg into the Persian Gulf, had a college education.

Her family obligation to follow the dictates of her uncle was ultimately why Kira had obtained her PhD. It was sort of like the men during the Vietnam era who stayed in school for as long as possible to dodge the draft and thus dodge Viet-Kong bullets.

The bullet Kira dodged, for the time being, wasn't as obviously lethal.

But with her graduation, her uncle Nadir had called Kira back to Qatar, where Kira's widowed mother now lived with her deceased husband's family. Her mother, Hamina, too, was under the "protection" of Uncle Nadir.

The difference was that Kira's mother was happy for the arrangement, and Kira most decidedly was not.

Stepping into Kira's melodrama was Kira's friend London. London was able to give Kira a little more time to make up her mind—would she move to Qatar and do as she was told? Or, would she refuse and thereby give up her relationships with her mother as well as her beloved aunts and cousins?

Family or Freedom?

The choice had tormented Kira since she was eighteen, and her dad's freak slip on the ice, the blow to his head in the fall, and his ultimate death when no one realized he was outside in the winter storm for hours.

Looking at her life, Kira could say that there were many times when fate seemed to step in and change her future's trajectory—even if fate was working one degree away from her.

London Markle was a perfect example.

London had been Kira's randomly assigned roommate freshman year at Duke. The two women had always gotten along and had lived with each other through undergrad. When Kira went to visit her family in Qatar, London often accompanied her there. Together, London and Kira had enjoyed the fantastic museums, the cultural foods, art, and music, the tableau of international glittery people.

During their last visit to Doha, Kira introduced London to Uncle Nadir's friend William Davidson, an energy industry billionaire—a man who was easily as old as Kira's dad would have been had he lived.

That age difference didn't matter to London; when she met William, she was agog. If Cupid had been flitting around and shot off his arrows, that was the only way to describe what Kira witnessed. When London shook William's hand, her eyes stretched wide, and she stared at him as though her brain had stopped processing. London shook herself free, but the spell had been cast.

Love at first sight?

Kira hadn't believed in it. She had thought London merely star-struck, or maybe that she'd eaten a bad oyster, and it was making her hallucinate.

But no, London was *smitten*.

It was a May-December romance. Though London was younger than William's Army-pilot daughter Christen—which was gross—and this was actually William's fifth attempt at conjugal bliss, London and William decided their love was fate. After a three-month whirlwind romance, they tied the knot.

Kira had been fascinated by London's stepdaughter Christen, her ability to thwart the family's expectations and desires for her to be a pampered socialite. Christen simply did what she wanted, going off and joining the Army to become some hotshot pilot with the radio name D-Day.

Kira couldn't imagine wanting to be in danger—going out and looking for dire situations, flying helicopters into the deadly scenarios. Though, there was the perk that Christen flew with special operator teams—the best of the best of *hunky* heroes. Kira wouldn't mind having her own hunky hero—the kind she'd read about in her novels.

She sighed noisily. "Come on, Princess Bea, time to go in." She gave a gentle tug on the lead, which Beatrice ignored. "Spoiled thing." Kira smiled at the pup with a bit of indulgence and a bit of impatience. Kira wanted to open her box. But Beatrice looked like she might potty. That would give Kira some time between the constant in and out, in and out of Beatrice's routine.

Kira moved into a shadow to wait and think. Yes,

Kira had spent long hours thinking about London's step-daughter Christen. It was brave of her to strike her own path through life. Was she happy? And did Christen have a price that she paid for her choices? One that hurt, like Kira's would?

London had made her life's choices, too. And she paid a price for them: London got a fair amount of blow-back being called a trophy wife, a gold digger...

Kira was selfishly glad for London's union. The fact that William and Uncle Nadir were in business together was the single reason why Kira had this tiny little wiggle room in her uncle's proclamation that she should return to Qatar following her graduation, where he would find Kira an acceptable husband.

Kira would push the inevitable decisions out as far as she could into the future.

William Davidson had told Uncle Nadir that he would tuck his "dear wife's friend" under his wing and act as Kira's protector this summer.

Granted, Kira was twenty-eight years old.

She was quite comfortable on her own and had been since she graduated from Patrick Henry High ten years before.

Kira felt no reason whatsoever for her uncle to pressure her the way he did.

Except—

If Kira was to stay in America, unwed and without "male protection," she would bring shame to her family. Her family was part of the extended royal family. *She* was part of the royal family and could prove a "diplomatic challenge" should anything go wrong.

Uncle Nadir was playing hardball using Kira's close relationship with her mother, aunts, and cousins as a cudgel. Did she want to bring dishonor to her family?

Make her cousins unmarriageable in the view of polite society? Because, just like in the 19th-century novels that Kira studied, the morality of an individual reflected on the entire family. Brought disgrace to the whole family. And that shame would have to be punished.

Kira didn't think it would go that far, but it was always a possibility that she could be disposed of by honor killing. Dozens happened every year right here in the United States. The borders wouldn't protect her.

A shiver raked Kira's body, and she quickly looked over her shoulder and up and down the street.

For now, for today at least, as long as Kira worked for London, she had a reprieve.

And working for London meant doing fairly mindless tasks like dogsitting Princess Beatrice the Spoiled.

"Come on, Bea." Kira tugged at the leash once Beatrice lowered her leg and started nibbling at the flowers.

Beatrice disliked change and had been rather punitive toward Kira in both big ways and small. That had been tolerable up until Princess Beatrice spun around at Kira's command and saw the package at the door. The spaniel darted up the stairs ahead of Kira and lifted her leg toward the box.

Kira plunged forward and snatched the package up. "Are you kidding me right now, Bea? You would do that? You just went."

Princess Beatrice pouted while Kira inserted her key into the deadbolt lock. "I'm going to tell London that you've been extra destructive since you've been here. You know," Kira said as she pushed the door open to the cool dark interior of her entry hall. "Your momma is heading to Tanzania. And in Africa, there are lions." She elbowed the door shut, clicked on the hall lights, and moved inside, glad to be out of the intensity of the July sun and North Carolinian humidity.

Beatrice toddled along behind her.

"Lions are huge cats. As big as…oh as big as my couch. And a lion would eat you as a snack, lick its chops, and search for another bite to eat." Kira placed the package on her entry table, clanged her keys into the key bowl, then bent to unhook the lead from Beatrice's collar. "So you *should be* grateful that I let you come here as my house guest. And you *should be* more considerate about where you pee and what you chew up. If it wasn't for my willingness to take care of you, you'd be heading out on safari and fending off the wild animals." She scooped Beatrice up, tucking the furball under her arm, and walked toward the kitchen. "I'm going to put you in your kennel and let you think about your bad behavior and how you can improve."

Beatrice actually loved her crate, loved the soft blankets, loved her chew toys. And she loved to nap.

Kira gently closed the door and flipped the latch. "I'll come back and get you at dinnertime."

Butterflies flitted in Kira's stomach as she stood. She rubbed at the goose bumps on her arms. "This is so exciting!" she told the robin sitting on the bird feeder outside of her kitchen window.

Two months ago, a cousin of her aunt Fatima in Qatar had written her a letter. "I have a friend who found something in her grandmother's trunk that you might be interested in studying," it had begun.

Kira's specialty was rare book collections and, more specifically, women's writing from historical times and from geographical locations where it would have been improbable for women to be writing anything at all.

These women shared the commonality of women's

struggles worldwide. Their fiction intrigued Kira, the bittersweetness of family life—being a mother, wishing more than anything that they *could* be a mother, the people they loved, the devastation they survived. It was all so raw on the page when a woman thought that no one would ever see the stories she'd created.

The strength and honesty of these women, Kira believed, should be honored and elevated.

And *she* was the one to do it.

Kira moved to her little guest bathroom and thoroughly washed her hands and arms, dried them, and went back to her office.

Imagine, she thought, putting such a rarity in a box and sending it across the ocean as if it were a sweater that she'd bought online.

Kira took the package from the entry hall to her office to unwrap the covering and pull open the cardboard top. With the end of a clean paintbrush, she gently lifted the tissue paper and peered down at the nineteen-thirties-styled photo album. The padded white satin on the cover was rusty and yellowed with the acid of aging materials. Dapples of mold marred the bottom corner with ugly dark gray splotches. "Our Wedding" was written in Arabic across the top in navy blue.

Kira had been told that the wedding album was used to hide the secret writings from male eyes.

She pulled open her desk drawer, full of snowy-white cotton gloves. She pulled on a pair before touching the treasure, protecting this artifact from any oils or dirt that might remain on her hands, lest it further degrade the book.

Tenderly lifting the album from the box, Kira moved the gift to her work table.

She took a deep breath and opened the cover.

Chapter 3

Ty

"How many Russian helicopters have you stolen in your lifetime, D-Day?"

"This is a first for me." Christen Davidson—known by the call sign D-Day—with her massive flight expertise, had attached to Echo to figure out next steps on their mission. They were tasked to sneak into Uganda at the northern tip of Lake Edward and steal the latest in Russian helicopter technology.

"I'll tell you what, Ty," D-Day said, "you break my legs on this jump, and no one is flying out of here on that bird."

"Wind is wind, ma'am."

"I hear you." D-Day reached behind her, grasping at Ty's arms as a gust blew her out over the abyss. Her cry of distress was held back behind clenched teeth.

Briefly, Ty considered unclasping D-Day; they'd both be more comfortable. But then, she'd have nothing tethering her to the tree. She'd be on her own if she were to lose her grip.

D-Day was *his* tandem jumper. Ty was responsible for her safety.

It would suck if Ty broke her on the way to the big event.

This was only step one of their mission. Get on the ground, then hoof it fifteen kilometers through the wilderness along the Congolese-Ugandan border to the strip of meadow and the helicopter.

Why had Russia abandoned its helicopter?

Could be it was out of fuel.

Could be that it had a major malfunction.

Or the pilot had been killed or captured. Maybe he fell in love with a local girl and decided to live in a round hut and herd cattle.

Maybe the pilot just decided fuck-it-all and walked off into the horizon.

Or maybe—and this was Ty's bet—Russia had tucked the helicopter away for some upcoming event... Oil had been found under Lake Edward, and there was an international scramble turned to massive unrest around the rights to that oil.

Already big oil out of England was making the locals' lives miserable—damaging Lake Edward's waters and causing the already difficult existence of those who survived on its shores for food, hydration, and sanitation that much more challenging.

Unrest.

Echo certainly didn't want to get swept up in that.

Sure, Echo had the permission of the Kenyan government to fly over their airspace. And yeah, Uganda had specifically rung up the Pentagon with an invitation for the United States to come and take the abandoned helicopter away as quickly as possible, *pretty please*, before the tribal factions discovered it.

The reason these two governments had called on America to show up and take over the situation was the need to preempt any number of less-than-optimal outcomes that could manifest on the world stage by leaving the heli in place.

JSOC absolutely did *not* want the Unit to run into any Russian operators. "Keep a tight lid on this mission, boys."

Yep. America had stepped warily into the situation. If Echo got this right, they'd have their hands on the latest and greatest technology that Russia was employing. The engineers could study the systems and decide if any of the features were useful in updating America's fleet. It would also show America where the Russian copters' weak spots were and how they could best be exploited.

That sounded like a win.

But if they were caught red-handed by tribal leaders or failed at remaining covert... The Somalian FUBAR mission Black Hawk Down came full-blown to Ty's mind. Yeah, their being in Uganda could piss off a bunch of people who might just want to turn this into a geo-political crisis.

It *might* even spark a war.

Stealth in this situation had been Echo's go-to crisis management tool.

When the jump plane took off an hour ago from a Kenyan military base, it flew through a thick bank of clouds that blanketed the sliver of new moon light.

Delta Force Echo had waited three days for these near-perfect weather conditions for the mission.

They'd been jazzed by the circumstances. Now? Ty tipped his head back as he heard the parachute silk rip—not so much.

"Don't move," Ty gasped out, tightening his grip on the branch above him. He tried to stop their swaying to get a new foothold. He'd guess that they just slid another ten or fifteen feet before he could once again get the parachute lines tangled and supporting their weight.

"That's not me. That's the wind." She didn't sound like she was freaking out.

Ty had been on a couple of missions where D-Day was the pilot. She seemed to be the one JSOC sent in when they needed someone to white-knuckle fly a bird mere feet off the ground, at high speeds, and even higher external pressure of enemy attention.

A blink of the eye could leave the heli and all the passengers in a ball of fire.

D-Day had ice running through her veins.

She liked to be balls to the wall. And she liked control.

Hands on the stick, managing a situation was a far cry from their present circumstance.

"Yo, D-Day?" A voice boomed from about twenty yards to their five o'clock.

"Is that you, Nick?" Nick of Time was D-Day's co-pilot. "Are you okay?"

"When they said they wanted my expertise in the air, I had no idea I'd be here hanging around like a banana on a tree."

"Don't talk about food," she called back. "I'm starving, here."

"You're *always* hungry," he said with a laugh.

"We should probably exercise noise discipline, ma'am."

"Oops. Sorry."

Once again, the night turned silent. It was eerie to be in the jungle with no sounds around them, save for the rustling leaves.

"Since we're hanging out..." Ty wanted some quiet banter to take his mind off the pain from their second brutal fall. "Anything exciting happening in your life? You still stationed in the sandbox?"

"I'm heading stateside after this mission."

"Training?"

"My wedding and honeymoon."

"Yeah? Anyone I've run across?"

"Gator Aid Rochambeau? He's an operator for Iniquus's Strike Force. Retired Marine Raider."

"Yeah, I know the guy. A few months back, he had a mission inside Fort Bragg and did the Unit a solid. We've got his back."

"Good to know. Hey, I think I figured out a way to get down."

"Ma'am, we're hanging about four stories over the ground."

"Yeah? Maybe. I think that last slide took us considerably closer to the bottom of this tree. Look, I'll go first, and then if it turns out okay, you can follow me down."

"D-Day, ma'am, I'm responsible for your safety. And," he stopped to chuckle, "as ridiculous as that sounds, given our predicament, you're considered our VIP at this time. None of us can do what you can. If you're out of the game, the game is over."

"If I lose my legs because the straps are as tight as a tourniquet, I'll be useless, too."

"All right, just for giggles, how about you talk me through how you're going to get down."

"In daylight, I'd just unstrap and go down. I'm a parkour champ."

"I heard you did that. Matter of fact, isn't that how you met Gator? The bar story I heard was that your dad hired him to be on your protection detail, and you weren't down with the intrusion into your personal space. So you Spidermanned your way up the side of a building and ran the roof lines?"

"That was the day I met Gator, yes." Her voice was tight.

"Seems like it didn't rub his ego the wrong way. You're getting married and all."

"Was he laughing when he told you the story?"

"Chest puffed out with pride, ma'am. But I had no idea you two were a couple. He was just telling a story."

"What was the topic, most onerous security details?"

"I believe it was a time when he got outmaneuvered. He said he went out with his principals for a jog, and you ran to an apartment and three stories up the wall. He'd seen it on YouTube but never imagined someone doing it in front of his eyes."

"Yeah, well. Jogging's a bore."

"Yes, ma'am."

"All right, listen, in that it's dark as sin out here, this is my plan. You release your emergency chute and let it fall toward the ground. I get myself out of my rigging, wrap my leg around the parachute cords and crawl down. Boom. Simple."

"Which would be fine, ma'am. But even hanging from that and jumping down, you're still only about halfway to where you need to be."

"Did Gator tell you I dove off the roof of that building, tucked, and flipped to disperse energy, hit the ground—"

"He said when you came off that building even though you somersaulted to disperse your momentum, that his second surprise that day was how much energy was in play from that dive."

"A body in motion…physics is a big part of success."

"He said when he tugged your hand, you sprang into his arms—"

"And straight into his heart."

Ty threw his head back and laughed. "Now that part, he left out."

"Natural born storyteller, possibly a tad of hyperbole in his word choices."

"In this case?" Ty asked.

"Nah, that's how it happened."

"The difference being, you were on a grass slope, clear of obstruction and most importantly, lots of sunlight so you could tell what you were doing."

She huffed a breath.

"I get that. Believe me. I am as uncomfortable as you are."

"Probably more so. I don't have balls in a vice."

"Yo!" A voice called from below them. "Anyone need an assist?"

Maintaining light discipline, T-Rex assessed D-Day and Ty's position in the tree through his night-vision goggles. He determined that D-Day's suggestion about climbing down the reserve chute was a good one. Holding the line taut, T-Rex talked D-Day down. Followed quickly after by Ty.

"Congratulations, Ty," D-Day said as she moved to pick up her helmet and pulled her own night vision into place. "You were able to execute that landing without a single cuss word."

"I'm not saying I wasn't thinking them, ma'am."

D-Day spotted Ty's night vision goggles lying in a pile of debris and retrieved them. "But you had a *lady* dangling between your legs?" she asked with a laugh.

"Not touching that," Ty said. "No derision affixed to being a lady. I get that you're a pilot in the field and a woman when off duty. Just…"

Nitro went over both of them with the red-beamed flashlight. "One head and four limbs each, no blood, I'm saying good to go." Nitro slapped Ty on the back and moved on to check on Nick, who dropped from a bottom limb on his tree.

Ty adjusted his goggles. "Old habits, ma'am. If we get to the place where I'm cussing in front of a female, let alone an officer, I think we can pretty much conclude that things have spiraled out of control."

They were late checking boxes on this mission. The wind had blown them further off course, and soon the sun would brighten the horizon. At first light, they were supposed to be standing beside the Russian helicopter.

Echo put the supplies on their backs, and they were hot footing it behind their Ugandan counterparts who had done the original recon and set up the team's intended landing zone.

D-Day had asked to take some of the weight, but she'd been turned down. They were the beasts of burden, and she was the talent. That, from T-Rex, hadn't made her happy.

She wasn't even winded from their run.

Nick fell in beside them. "You do a full body check?" he asked. "You good?"

"Good enough. I might have some interesting bruise marks around my thighs on my wedding night."

"She's hitching up with Gator Rochambeau," Ty clarified.

"Good man. Echo owes him a debt," T-Rex said. "If you're planning on still being bruised, seems there's a clock ticking on you being single."

"There is, indeed. I need to go ahead and steal this heli, then jump a commercial flight back to Washington, D.C., in time to slide into my wedding dress and traipse down the aisle. It's planned for the end of this month. And since you all seem indebted to my betrothed for whatever reason, I'm just going to say, no dicking around. He wouldn't be very happy to be left at the altar."

"Hard to plan a wedding from the other side of the world. Is Gator putting it together?"

"Gator's mom and sisters are planning the wedding and the reception. My stepmother London was ticked that it was going to be a family and close friends—only event, so she's planned some shindig for that Thursday to invite my father's people. If y'all can keep me tucked tight so I miss that one, well *that* I wouldn't mind so much."

"London Davidson? *That's* your stepmom?" Nitro asked. "Christen Davidson, that was you? I'm used to calling you D-Day, so I didn't put it together." He let out a low whistle.

"You saw in the paper." D-Day's voice turned cold.

"It said there was a hunting accident, and you shot your brother."

"Hunting, yes. The only accident was with the angle of my shot. I could only get a clear bead on his leg."

"Huh. Dangerous woman to know." There was a smile in T-Rex's voice.

"Damned straight," D-Day said.

"Your brother must have deserved it. I've flown enough missions with you now to know butter wouldn't melt in your mouth," Nitro said. "You're cool under pressure. Ice in your veins."

"I have a warm heart," D-Day said. "How about we find a more interesting subject."

"You shot your brother in the leg, and now he's an amputee. You don't think that's an interesting story?" Nitro asked.

"Sure, you want the story of family dysfunction? I'll share. My dear old friend, Johnna White of the CIA, dragged me away from our mission—the one when we were saving her colleague John Grey from his prison—because she wanted to use my connections to overhear a conversation at my father's party. I found out my brother was going to kill my father, so I shot him," she said matter-of-factly. Her shrug didn't break her jog pace.

"Oh, is that all?" Ty asked.

"Shit happens," Nitro said.

"Amen to that, brother," Ty said. "Speaking of—" He slowed to a stop then bent to put his hands on his knees and catch his breath. He pointed with the blade of his hand at the monstrosity looming out in the distance. "There's the heli in all its glory."

Chapter 4

Kira

Kira reached out her foot to snag her tall stool and drag it over to her. She rested her thigh on the cushioned top, steadying herself and dispersing her weight to be more comfortable, but she was too jittery with excitement to settle in.

She exhaled through pursed lips and opened the cover of the gifted album, carefully adjusting a support that would protect the spine.

There, on the first page, listed the bride and groom's names and the date of the marriage, July twentieth, nineteen thirty-two.

She turned the heavy cardboard page to a photograph. The bride was in traditional Bedouin tribal wear, the groom in impeccably pressed robes. They looked… shell-shocked.

In Qatar, at the time, marriages were arranged by the male charged with the female's protection. Oftentimes, the couple met on their wedding day when they each signed the contract that bound them, transferring the responsibility for the woman from her male relative to the new husband. The woman could expect that she'd be supplanted from the family household she'd always known to live in her husband's family compound. There, multigenerational branches of the families all worked together to keep the home and raise the children.

It wasn't so different today.

Kira peered into the bride's eyes. Had this woman even met her husband before that moment? Did she like him? Find him sexually attractive? Kind? Intelligent? *Safe?* Kira read trepidation and resolution in the woman's eyes.

Kira had seen that look in many of her cousins' faces as they walked toward their new destinies with the men chosen by their fathers.

Born in the United States to an Iraqi mother and a Qatari father, Kira was an American. She liked the life here. The personal freedoms. Heck, she *really* liked sex. A lot. Had she lived in Qatar, she would have been held to those relationship standards. If she hadn't been married off, she'd be a virgin now, never having had the opportunity to experiment with different men to see what appealed to her—what her body wanted.

If her uncle knew that she was an experienced woman, it would bring great shame to her Qatari family. Punishment for such a lifestyle would be severe.

If they found out.

They could *never* find out.

Turning the heavy cardboard page, the next photo

showed the bridal gifts arranged in a sitting room. That was the last photo.

Under that page, presumably hidden from male eyes, four leather-bound books lay flat, side by side in a square, perfectly fitting underneath the first two photo album pages and between the covers.

She breathed out and delicately lifted the first volume.

Kira's eyes traveled from right to left along the small neat words written with a pen dipped into an inkwell. Tiny flecks of the India black ink, now faded with age, stippled portions of the text. The words—even here on the very first pages—were richly poetic and evocative.

Kira was hungry for them. This was an amazing gift that she'd received.

While removing the books from within the album, so she could better understand their condition and what might be needed to preserve them, Kira's phone buzzed in her pocket.

She slid off her cotton gloves, turned off the light that was shining on the artifacts, and swiped the cell phone screen to answer the video call. "Hi, London."

"How's my baby?"

"I'm assuming you're talking about the princess? She's moping in her crate. She didn't like that I wouldn't let her pee on my mail."

"Awww." There was a maternal smile on her face. "Sweet girl."

"How's your real baby?"

London moved the phone down so Kira could see Archie's cherubic cheeks pressed against London's chest as he slept. "He's perfection." London petted her fingers over the sparse silky strands of his tiny three-month-old head. "So I'm calling for a couple of reasons."

Kira slid over to her desk and sat down, moving her notepad and pen closer.

"How are things going for Christen's pre-nuptial cocktail party?" London asked.

"The RSVPs are flowing in. Looks like most of your guests will be able to attend."

"Oh, good."

"I can't get in touch with either Gator or Christen." Kira turned her head to clear her throat. "Excuse me." She reached for her bottle of water and took a swig. "You said if I couldn't, to just go ahead and approve at will."

"Yes, they're not necessarily being difficult." London paused with a pursed-lip frown. "I choose to believe that they *do* want to be involved with the Davidson side of the family and not just Gator's family." She dipped her head to kiss Archie. "But their lack of communication can be written off as legitimate. Gator, I don't even know what he does for a living besides his working for Iniquus. I looked up their website, and well, it all looked dangerous to me. He's probably off saving the world. That's how they met. I think I told you this."

"No."

"Gator picked up a security contract with William because someone tried to kidnap him."

"Whom?"

"William. Someone threw a bag over William's head." She stopped and shuddered. "Gator was on R & R in Tanzania and happened to be there and see it. He beat up the bad men and saved my William. William introduced Gator to Christen. Anyway, Gator is probably out of the country on assignment. I'm just guessing. Christen, we know where she is—sort of. Off on some Army base, we're not allowed to know where. All we know is she's to be on leave the week of her wedding. She said she and Gator will show up when and where I tell her to on that Thursday. I wish we'd been given more time. I guess Christen had to wait to get permission from her superiors. I think that's a thing in the military. Taking leave, especially when you're overseas..."

"That's probably it." Kira rocked back in her seat. "I'm bringing up the fact that I haven't talked to either of them because I don't know their tastes and special moments—songs, what have you. So I just built the evening around what William would like for his friends and associates. Your guests are sending gifts to your Dallas address."

"Good."

"I asked your head housekeeper to store them in the blue room."

"Lovely, though, you and I will probably need to open them, catalog the gifts, write the thank you notes and have them lined up for Christen to sign them. I'll have her father tell her she has to do it. Few people have any sway over that woman, but surely she's not rude enough to not show a basic level of etiquette. If it's too much, we may need to just sign them ourselves. After the niceties are done, I can get an address and ship the things—maybe we'll need to have a mover take them. I guess that depends on the amount of space they take up. How is the menu coming?"

"I'm flying up to D.C. to have a tasting and final approvals this week."

"When this week?"

Kira shifted her pad around to see her calendar. "Friday."

"No. That's not going to work. You'll need to put that off."

"Okay…?" Kira watched out the window as a mother pushed a baby carriage down the sidewalk and sighed. "The caterers aren't going to love that."

"You may have to just make decisions remotely. There's some big project concerning Tanzania that's afoot. World players. William has invited them to Davidson Range for a six-day retreat."

"Tanzania with you? Are you there now?"

"Not yet. There's been a change of plans. We aren't going to go there as a family to relax. Instead, William's changed this to a business retreat. Something's come up that has him very excited. A new colleague. The change of plans poses a few problems."

Kira took another sip of water while she listened to her friend.

"Neither of us enjoyed the tastes of the food from that French chef William had living there. He cooked a little too…"

"French?"

"Exactly. Small portions and too rich for my waistline and William's heart. He was let go. Anyway, William says this is an extremely important meeting, and he wants no glitches, so he's asked for me to arrange things and then leave them to their 'male space'—my words, not his. But truthful. You know how men are in this part of the world."

"Yes, that I do."

"And since I'm in Qatar and busy with Archie, that means I'm asking you to arrange things."

Kira focused back on her phone and her friend's face; she looked tired. "Whatever you need, London."

"Here's my plan. I've called my chef at our Dallas home. He's my favorite among our houses. Chef Bruno says it's no problem. He can handle the situation just fine. Bruno's constructing a menu for nine days. It can't go beyond that because we have Christen's wedding. The men won't be at the Range that long, only the six days. But, things happen, and I don't want the party to be without provisions. I'm being extra careful. It's so beautiful at the Range, and the animals are amazing—just…incredible. The party might wish to extend their stay. And again, I want no glitches. It's important to me that I do a good job for my husband."

Kira picked up her pen and rested the point on her pad, scribbling: "Bruno" with an arrow then "Dallas."

"Breakfast, morning snacks set out to be available for nibbling—I'm thinking fruit and cheese kinds of things. Different each day. Then lunch. Hors d'oeuvres and cocktails or other drinks for the non-imbibers in the mid-afternoon. Evening dinner, say around eight. And finally midnight chocolates and nibbles, champagne? Yes. I think champagne and brandy."

"Bruno knows this already?"

"Yes. Like I said, Bruno is developing the menus and will pass them on to you for approval. Once they've met your standard—like the profusion of generosity I experienced with your family in Qatar, that's what I want it to feel like—refined decadence."

"Okay." Kira scrawled reminder words on her pad.

"Bruno will then prepare everything and freeze them, or otherwise make them storable. He'll develop an instruction sheet that will need your translating."

"For Tanzanian nationals? London, I don't speak Swahili."

"Oh, isn't that the same as Arabic?"

"Close, but no," Kira said.

"Well, find someone who is educated enough to know what these items are and have them write the instructions. The help, as you remember, speaks only a little French and a couple words of English, though the property manager and the head of security speak English well enough. If you can't get this translated, we'll just depend on them. Okay, so you'll look over Bruno's work and fix any issues you see. Also, I need you to get in touch with a florist and get arrangements made. We'll have eleven guests, plus William and I, and you. Each bedroom should have a lovely arrangement, smaller ones in each bath, one glorious one to set on the entry table as a statement piece, a low spread for the dining table. Et cetera. Use that local place—the one down the road from your house. They do a beautiful job."

"All right. And what do I do with all of the products?"

"I'll send the jet to Dallas to pick up the food. Then to you in Durham. From there, the pilot will fly you to Dar es Salaam for refueling, then on to the Range." She paused and tapped her bottom lip. "Maybe I should just have Bruno come along to…no, I can't do that. He reminded me that he has a vacation on the books to go to Antarctica on a cruise of all horrible things."

"Wait, you want me…?"

"The plane will land at Davidson Range. You are to direct the staff on how to set everything up. I need you to make sure everything is clean, attractive, soothing, and calm for when we get there."

"How are you going to…?"

"The jet will leave you there to get things in place while the pilot comes and picks us up. We'll be a day behind you."

"But…"

"Now, once our party arrives at the Range, we'll refresh ourselves then join you for a welcome cocktail party. You'll hostess the first evening. I will be William's dutiful wife and will also care for Archie—his nanny is having an operation. I wish she could have put it off until after all of this. It makes my life complicated. But I have you!" She stopped and smiled at Kira. "Cigars! And whisky. I'll text the contact information for the shops William uses for that. Just have them charge it to William's account and have it sent over to Bruno to go on the plane with you."

"I…"

"Now, the next morning, the three of us—you, Archie, and I—will get back on the plane, fly back to Dar es Salaam for refueling, and then home. Well, to D.C. so you and I can finish arrangements for the wedding reception. So pack accordingly. Mmmm, not the 'reception,' what would you call this?"

"Maybe call it a celebration?" Kira drew in a breath. That had all been a lot to take in. "London, there are holes in this plan. It's usually frowned upon for people to bring food products and fauna into a foreign country. And I need a visa to go, don't I?"

"Yes. Yes." She waggled a dismissive hand. "That's all been arranged. I have the proper letters for you. I'll attach them in an email. The official one with the stamp is being overnighted to you."

"What about Princess Beatrice?"

"I hate for her to go to the Range. There are all kinds of horrible things that could befall her. Poisonous snakes and monkeys. At the same time, she gets neurotic if she isn't with either you or me."

"You. She's still neurotic with me."

"Less so than other places. She simply cannot be put under the psychological torture of being placed elsewhere. So she'll have to come and be on her lead. Besides, I miss her. It's been too long since I got to cuddle my little sweetie-peetie."

"I'll only be there for two days?" Kira glanced longingly at her new project.

"Fly all day Friday. It's twenty hours. I know. Dreadful. Hopefully, most of the time, you can sleep. I'm not sure what to do about bathrooming my princess, perhaps puppy pads in the bathroom? I'll let you figure that out. Get things set up Saturday. We arrive Sunday. We fly out Monday morning for home—well, home enough. We'll be in D.C. to go over the venue and make adjustments for the wedding celebration. We'll stay at our Arlington home while William finishes up his business. I need to send the jet straight back to the Range—after the pilot gets some sleep, of course. Do you see all of the details I have to keep straight? Archie's nanny will meet us in D.C. that Wednesday morning if all goes well with her medical issues." She stopped to hold up crossed fingers. "A whirlwind tour."

"And we have permission to have the dog with us?"

"Yes, that's on the list. I'll send you the paperwork, and you can look it over and plug any holes. But it says staff and companionate K9s. Can you imagine Princess Beatrice being called a K9?" She laughed. "So macho for my delicate princess."

Kira paused to see if London was done.

"Okay?" London asked.

"Yes. Okay," Kira agreed on a sigh. Her project would have to wait. This was the price she was paying to keep her independence for another couple of months. The last thing she needed was for William to rescind his offer to be her "protector." Who knew, maybe she could convince William, by jumping through last-minute hoops, that she was a good person to keep around. And her uncle would leave her alone.

London grinned. "Excellent. Yay!" She dipped her head and kissed Archie. "Oh, and Kira, your uncle Nadir will be there. That should make you happy."

Uncle Nadir?

No, actually, that didn't make her happy. At. All.

Chapter 5

Ty

The men of Echo held the perimeter around the helicopter. The Ugandan special forces team spread out amongst the trees, keeping a close eye that there were no surprises.

No bands of extremists or guerillas amongst the gorillas.

The team had no eyes in the skies with overwatch; they'd left any support back in Kenya.

Uganda was worried about the ramifications of Russia knowing America was after their helicopter. The Ugandan military wouldn't even okay the team's flying their own little bird into the area, necessitating their jump.

This was a probe to see what needed to be done. Was it a quick fix?

That wasn't for Echo to decide. The deciders were

D-Day, Nick, the heli repair tech Jojo, and the engineer guy they called Snacks. Each member of the 160th SOAR team had been strapped to an operator and dropped from the sky. D-Day and Nick had been just fine with their time playing Tarzan in the trees. The other two didn't enjoy it as much. Ty ducked his head to hide his snicker. Probably once they got home again, this adventure would become one of the great heroic tales of their lives.

But now?

Now, Nitro was swatting the engineer to get him to stop sniveling. "Cowboy up, dude. And if you shit your pants, you're on your own walking out here. Dawn's breaking. That's when the predators wake up and want a snack, Snacks." He plopped a hand on Snacks's shoulder, making him jump.

As a soft morning glow meandered through the thick canopy surrounding them, the team snapped their night vision back on their helmets and out of their way. The Ugandan team of four recon specialists—trained by the Green Berets—put their hands on the helicopter, looking it over. Their excitement was palpable.

This was one of the most technologically advanced systems owned by a frenemy state.

A darling on the CIA wish list.

The Mi-25 was a Russian gunship designed as a super-speed attack and transport helicopter.

Without hesitation, D-Day called out, "Let's get to it, gentlemen." She pointed to Snacks and Jojo. "Jojo, check under the hood. Snacks, check the blades and exterior. We're looking for any mechanical reasons this bird might have been left to roost." She swiveled her head searching out her copilot. "Nick, I want you to check the fuel. See if the tank's empty. If there's enough go-juice for us to fly out of here, I want you to use the kit to check the fuel's viability. We don't know how long this beast has been sitting here. If it's months, the fuel might have gone bad." She smacked her hands together then looked over at T-Rex.

"We're at your service, ma'am. We'll secure the area unless and until you need us for something else." He pointed at Ty then pointed at D-Day.

Ty stayed put while his teammates spread out, slipping seamlessly and noiselessly into the foliage.

D-Day gave Ty a curt nod and climbed into the cockpit.

Snacks stood at the tail and called forward to D-Day. "How did Uganda expect us to get this out? Did they think we'd dismantle this beast and hump it out on our backs?"

"I guess if it comes to that." Having settled into the pilot's seat, she pulled what looked to Ty to be a pre-flight checklist out of a cubby. She shook her head at it. "Russian, of course."

"That's why I'm here, ma'am," Ty said, reaching for the clipboard. "Though some of this vocabulary is probably job-specific, and I wouldn't have run across it in language school." His eyes scanned down the Cyrillic letters, letting his brain switch gears from English to Russian.

"Hear me out," Snacks said as he walked toward them, running his hands over the skin of the copter. "It's the quicker picker-upper plan of helicopter thievery."

"We were invited," D-Day said. "It's not thievery. It's more like accepting a sweater from the lost and found bin when suddenly the air conditioning is blasted, and management sees you're cold."

"Okay. But listen, we get the air force to bring in a pair of twin-rotor MH-47 heavy lifting birds."

"Uh-huh." D-Day tipped her head at Ty and raised a brow.

He held up a finger as he continued to read through the Russian words. It had been a while, and his brain needed to shift gears.

"The MH-47 has the fuel range to get us out of here," Snacks said. "It has a night-vision-compatible cockpit. Come in low, dead of night. Run some straps under this baby and fly it off."

"Any body damage?" D-Day asked him.

"None," Snacks said. "I'm checking rotors now, but from a casual glance, I don't see anything that makes me nervous."

Nick slung himself into the helicopter. "Fuel tests fine. No adulterations."

She tapped the fuel gauge. "This looks like we have plenty. Why would they leave it here like this?" She swiveled to face Ty. "Under your elbow, there's what looks like it might be the flight log. That might be the best place to start. The instrument panel looks intuitive. For a short, non-combat flight, I think I can feel my way around piloting it. But maybe the Russian crew notated the reason it's here."

Ty handed her the checklist back and pulled out the log.

"Look at the last entry, maybe two," D-Day suggested. "We need to stop and eat." She put her hand to her mouth and called, "Eat. Now," before returning to her conversational tone. "It's bad to make decisions on an empty stomach."

"Agreed." Snacks pulled a cloth from his pocket and wiped a smear of grease from his hands.

"This log says they put down here June twelfth—so four weeks ago—per their orders."

D-Day's brows drew in tight. "That's it? Where did the pilot go? We're in Nowheresville."

Ty shook his head, reaching out for an MRE that Snacks handed him. D-Day accepted hers.

Nick and Jojo came around and climbed into the fuselage to accept their meals. None of them took the time to heat them. They poured some water into the packets to rehydrate the freeze-dried scrambled eggs and bacon, rolled the tops, and opened their accessory packets.

"Have you spent time in Africa before?" Snacks looked at D-Day as he poured water over the powdered orange drink in his cup.

"Yeah, she has," Nick said over his shoulder. "Tanzania just south of here on Lake Victoria. Her family has property there, some big safari lodge, right, D-Day? Davidson Range?"

"That's what I'm told." D-Day's lips pinched. "I've never been there, myself. My father bought it when he wanted to make nice with the government about energy contracts."

"Yeah?" Jojo asked. "Why haven't you gone? I think it would be cool to see the wild animals in their natural habitats. I mean, I've been to the zoo. It wasn't a very fulfilling experience. An elephant in the wild? A rhino? Hey, maybe your dad would let you bring your friends to go hang out."

"Yeah, maybe." D-Day sounded like she'd like to change the subject.

"I wouldn't mind being on a guided safari. But I'm down with not seeing anything staring back at me," Jojo said. "Come to think of it, I haven't seen or heard a single animal. Seems a little freaky doesn't it?"

"They saw your ugly mug and decided to lay low until you get yourself gone." Snacks shoveled up a spoonful of granola with some purple "blueberry" milk. "If I could go to a safari lodge, I'd do it. I've seen photos of those places. Swanky. You lay on a sofa and watch the sunset. Get you some good Scotch whisky. A servant with a flower behind her ear, swayin' by with something good to nibble."

"Heh, heh, heh," Nick said.

"Don't be conjuring your porn scenarios," D-Day said. "I can't say if there's a view like that or not. Somehow, I doubt it. My stepmother, London, says that she feels wonderfully safe there. The place is a fortified compound. Tall walls, covered walkways, it doesn't sound to me like they have much of a view to anything. Nick, can you move your keister over? You're blocking the light coming in the door."

"Were you born with a silver spoon in your mouth, D-Day?" Snacks asked.

"I was born." She bit into her tortilla. "I think the only thing in my mouth at the time was my tongue and perhaps some mucus and amniotic fluid."

"Her dad is William Davidson," Nick said. "*The* William Davidson."

Jojo whistled low under his breath. "And yet you're here hanging around with us lowlifes."

"I prefer living with my head in the clouds," D-Day said. "Literally. To change the subject back to the mission. What do you think? Why is this bird here? Anything stand out to any of you? Should we see what happens when we get the motor whirling?"

"Let's eat and then give it a go," Nick agreed, sticking a spoonful of eggs in his mouth. He tapped his MRE packaging with the spoon as he swallowed. "And to

D-Day's point, there's some good in knowing that having money doesn't solve all your problems. You know, figure things out with your brain instead of your wallet." He skated a hand out. "I'm not saying *all* rich people feel they're better than those without a fat bank account. But I think that a lot of them look down on us lowlifes that sweat and bleed to eat."

"We don't sweat and bleed to eat," D-Day said. "I don't. I sweat and bleed to fight for a bigger cause. For the safety of my country, and by extension, the greater world."

"Nothing like dangling from a tree in Uganda to make one philosophical about stuff," Ty said with a grin.

"Still, where are the animals?" Jojo pulled his shoulders to his ears. "Isn't this weird?"

"Afraid some silver-backed ape is gonna think you're cute and drag you home, Jojo?" D-Day asked.

"Well, if one showed up and—"

"Don't even finish that sentence," D-Day said. "I don't want to hear about your animal fetishes."

The group flinched and ducked when the echo of a rifle shot cracked in the distance.

The crew looked around as if to ask if the others had heard that, too. Their brains sifted the new information. Then there was a mad scramble as the crew gathered up their food and thrust it away from them.

Pistols, pulled from chest holsters, were held in the low ready position.

Ty dragged his rifle around as he jumped out into the tiny clearing, searching the foliage for an explanation.

"Echo-zero-one, we have contact." There was squall and static then T-Rex's voice came back over the airwaves. "D-Day, is there any way you can get that bird in the air?" His breath came heavy as he ran.

The background noise sounded like he was crashing through the brush.

"On it." She glanced around. "Any reason that you've found that this flight is a no-go?" she asked her men.

There was a rat a tat tat as rifle fire strafed the forest, and return fire sounded very close.

Ty handed Nick his rifle, then climbed into the helicopter to assist D-Day if she needed a label translated so she could get them in the air.

"I'd say there's every reason to make it a go even if it just gets us a couple kilometers away."

"Fireballs of an exploding copter or gunfire. I'm not a fan of either," Nick said, eyeing the copilot seat where Ty had sat down, then turned his back on the helicopter and lifted Ty's rifle to his shoulder.

"Careful there, cowboy." Ty's voice was calm and steady. "We have friendlies heading toward us. Both Echo and the Ugandan operators." Ty turned his attention back to D-Day to see if he could help her with the Russian tabs.

As her eyes scanned the instruments, she placed her fingers on different buttons and was muttering under her breath. Finally, she reached out and pressed a button, turned a knob, stilled, and listened.

A whop, whop, whop started up.

The line of gunfire was getting closer as the teams backed their way toward the helicopter.

"If this doesn't work, what's our fallback plan?" D-Day asked as she focused on the gauges.

"I'm thinking your parkour abilities might be something you might be leaning on. It might come down to which team can run the fastest."

She turned toward him, her eyes stretched wide. "Well, shit."

Echo team poured out of the forest. Blood seeped from a hole in Nitro's shirt sleeve.

"Good?" T-Rex called forward to D-Day.

D-Day gave him a thumbs-up and a tenuous smile.

"In. In. In. In. In," T-Rex called—his knee on the ground, his rifle molded against his cheek.

Men poured out of the brush.

"In!"

"Dear God, let this work." D-Day exhaled as she laced her fingers and turned her hands inside out to crack her knuckles. She pulled on her seat harness.

Nick stuck his head into the helicopter and counted Ty and D-Day, "One. Two." He slapped his hand on Nitro's shoulder as he climbed in. "Three."

Nitro sat in the back, pulling his first aid kit from his thigh pouch.

"Four. Five." Snacks and Jojo were on.

"How do the systems sound to you?" D-Day called back to them.

"It sounds good to me. I love the sound of rotor wash in the morning," Snacks called back.

Ty figured it didn't matter how bad it sounded. If it could get them up, over, and down, that would be good. If they had to shoot to kill, not just suppress—well, leaving nationals dead in their host nation was contrary to their orders to make this a clean mission with no footprint.

"Who's doing the shooting?" Ty asked Nitro. He lifted his chin toward Nitro's arm. "Need any help there?"

"Flesh wound, it'll need stitching. It looks like it's probably a local paramilitary group. That's what the

Ugandan guys are saying. They had what might be the Russian pilot at gunpoint. I think they were heading here to steal the helicopter themselves. They might be a little ticked that we got here first."

"Do you think they had kidnapped the pilot?" D-day asked. "Can we get him back?"

As Echo operators crashed out of the tree line, they turned and took a knee, pointing their rifles into the foliage.

"The Russian-looking guy?" T-Rex asked. "Hard to tell what was going on. I let a bullet wing past the ear of the man holding a gun on him. The Russian took off running. No idea where he thinks he's going to go."

Nitro looked through the opening to the clearing. "Come on. Come on. Who's missing? Let's get gone," he muttered under his breath.

T-Rex suddenly popped up. "Load up."

Nick patted shoulders, counting off as the men climbed past him into the Russian copter. "Six. Seven. Eight." As the rest of Echo climbed in, they threw down the gear bags they carried on with them.

Jojo and Snacks pulled the equipment out of the way, making room for the rest of the team.

With the last Ugandan soldier accounted for, T-Rex strapped himself to the runner and dangled out the side, putting down suppressive fire. "Get us out of here, D-Day."

D-Day worked her magic and the bird lifted straight up. When they were just over the tops of the trees, she rocketed them away from the fighters.

Ty looked over, and though her facial features looked cool as a cucumber, sweat dripped from under her helmet, down her face.

* * *

When the team landed back at base in Djibouti, they arrived as victors with the spoils of war.

A cheering crowd of fellow soldiers had gathered to watch D-Day expertly land the beast.

Ty's Russian had been minimally helpful. Still, the thrill of victory tasted sweet in his mouth.

As they made their way past the high fives and fist pumps, Ty watched the grin on D-Day's face fall off.

There, CIA agent Johnna White was clapping her hands over her head. She brought her pinky and index finger to her mouth and sent out a shrill whistle. Her sleek black hair in a low ponytail, her intelligent almond-shaped eyes squinting against the bright sunlight.

D-Day threw her hands up like a sentinel signaling to stop. "No!" She barked out the single word emphatically, coming to a dead stop.

White stood about the same tiny height as D-Day. "Well, hello to you, too." White's smile, by contrast, was friendly and relaxed. "Fancy meeting you in a place like this."

"Unless this is about your dress fitting for my wedding—which you should take up with Gator's sisters—I don't want to know why you're here. I'm not going anywhere with you. I don't care about anyone's orders. Throw me in the stockade."

"Don't get your panties in a bunch. I'm not here for you." White looked Ty dead in the eye. "He's the one I want."

Chapter 6

Ty

D-Day turned and tipped her head with her brows raised in surprise.

"Gentlemen," White said. "I know you just got in, and I'll let you get to your hot wash to debrief your last mission momentarily, but you're going to like this." White's smile broadened into a grin. She clapped her hands together, then rubbed her palms back and forth like she was in Vegas getting ready for the roulette to spin. "Let me get you briefed, then Ty and I are going to head out on the new mission."

Ty glanced toward T-Rex.

T-Rex gave him a slight shake of his head and a pop of his brow to say 'no clue'; this was going to be interesting.

D-Day scrambled to get away—their celebration cut short.

The men filed into the command tent, down the corridor, and into a room that was set up with a screen and computer ready for a presentation. Metal chairs scraped against the plank floor as the men took their places around the long table. They crossed their arms over their chests and tucked their chins.

The CIA was filled with good idea fairies. They didn't much care what was said by boots on the ground about how practical those ideas were to their execution.

White moved to the front of the room. She nodded at T-Rex. "Master Chief."

"Ma'am."

Without ceremony, she reached over to her laptop and said, "Johnna White, CIA." She pointed toward another woman in the corner, dressed in tactical khakis and a V-necked t-shirt. "My colleague, Angela Reston." She paused and scanned the room. "Some faces around this room I've met in person, some not. But here's a face I think you will all recognize." She tapped a button, and a man with a thick beard, unruly eyebrows, a turban, and tribal robes glared down at them.

The mood in the room shifted.

The Echo operators leaned forward, forearms on their thighs, their eyes intent, nostrils flared.

"See? You do know him." She gestured toward the screen. "This is Abu Musab al Khalil."

"Shit yeah, he is," Nitro said under his breath.

When Ty was new to the Unit, Abu Musab al Khalil was the jack of clubs in the card deck that portrayed the most wanted terrorists sought by the U.S. government. The cards were developed so troops could learn the most wanted faces and recognize them should their paths ever cross. Abu Musab's claim to fame was propaganda. He didn't want to kill Americans as much as he liked to capture them and put them on camera, doing horrific things that turned Westerners' stomachs and at the same time recruited others to the radicals' team.

Seven years ago, Abu Musab al Khalil's men attacked a convoy. The terrorists kidnapped the four American soldiers not killed in the blast, including a female counterpart named Storm Meyers, who had not only served as a translator for special operations forces but also happened to be engaged to an Echo brother.

Echo put their noses to the ground and didn't let up until they found the terrorist enclave. When they raided the camp, Ty had been first into the tent where Storm Meyers was held.

And though she lived, she was never the same.

Echo had wanted to be the team that took down Abu Musab al Khalil. But he had disappeared after that branch of his followers was eliminated.

Echo had been led to believe this terrorist had been vaporized in a bombing.

"Not dead then." T-Rex leaned back in his chair—a monster-sized man, glowering at the tiny woman.

Ty was surprised that White didn't flinch or even take a step back.

"*Not* dead?" T-Rex repeated.

For the first time in Ty's time with Echo, he heard menace slide into T-Rex's low rumbling voice. A vein throbbed at the master chief's temple.

The rest of Echo shifted around in their seats. Antsy. Ready to throw themselves out the door and onto this man's track.

"Not dead," White said, then took a breath. "We have DNA. We have fingerprints. It's him."

"Where?" Ty asked.

"He's all cleaned up and hiding in Qatar as home

base. New papers. New name, Omar Mohamed Imadi."
White pronounced the name slowly as she tapped the
computer again. Up came a much different-looking man
dressed in pristine, snow-white robes. His beard was
groomed. He looked pampered and cosmopolitan. "I'll
be referring to Abu Musab al Khalil from now on under
his adopted name. Omar has been rehabilitating himself as a Qatari businessman. Sort of."

The men squinted at the image.

"An amazing transformation, isn't it? DNA is the
same," White responded. "His ambitions are the same.
He's still the same level of crazy. But he's accepted into
polite society like this."

"You're sure. A hundred percent?" Ty asked.

"A change in appearance, grooming, styling, and
with years having passed, a change of features. But no
matter how much money you have, you can't change
your genetics. We have his right pinky in a deep freezer
somewhere." She lifted her brows and let them drop.
"And among other forensic evidence, Omar is missing
his pinky on his right hand. We're a *hundred* percent
certain it's him."

"Where is he now?" Ty asked.

"Who knows—he's off-grid. Why? Because he's
back to his old tricks. But we know where he'll be next
Sunday." A new slide showed on the screen. "This is
Davidson Range on the western border of Lake Victoria in Tanzania. Omar was invited to join some busi-
nessmen for a retreat to discuss the future of fossil fuels
and helium amidst the global environmental crisis. We
just need you guys to be able to go in and surgically remove him." She rolled her lips in and let her gaze move
slowly around the room.

"Surgically," T-Rex said. "We'll need the intel to make that happen."

White looked over at Ty. "Yes, I'm trying my best to get that for you."

"And when you say surgical," Nitro asked.

"No one should know you were there. 'Good morning, have you seen Omar?' 'No. No, I haven't. What could have happened to him, poor bloke?'" She stopped to grin, then let the smile fall away. "We'd like him alive so we can ask him some questions. But if that's not possible, then he needs to be terminated with extreme prejudice before he follows through with his newest plot."

The men were sharply focused.

She tapped her computer again, and another photo came up. "Momo Bourhan."

"Is dead," Nitro said.

"That's right." White nodded. "Last summer, he was orchestrating quite the string of terrorist attacks. Momo kidnapped and held the Helston oil CEO and his wife—found and recovered by Iniquus and the Navy. Then he moved on to part two of his plan. With his attack on the hotel in Ngorongoro, Tanzania, Momo hoped to destroy international business in the area and thus any further prosperity. But he got dead." She shrugged then beamed a smile around the room. "And the international community was released from his crime streak. He had big plans for effecting terror strikes around the world to push power into the hands of a few."

Ty said, "Can't do much, moldering in the grave."

"Well—in a way he can. His silent partner was—"

"Omar Mohamed Imadi," T-Rex growled.

White put a finger on her nose and pointed her other hand at him like he'd gotten the answer right playing at charades.

This wasn't a game. This guy came after and hurt one of their own. Whether he was the one who put his hands on Storm, or it was just one of his knuckle draggers, made no difference to them.

They were all in.

"The Tanzanian government would very much like to avert terrorism in their country. They have been so good as to welcome our operation on their soil and offer to turn a blind eye. We have not told them where we think Omar is heading or when. We simply have an agreement in place for our actions. And, unless absolutely necessary, they'd rather not be part of any of it. Just come in, get what we need, and get out again. On tiptoes." She held her hand out to her colleague. "Angela, if you'll continue with the brief for Echo. I'm going to go ahead and take Ty out of the group. He'll be working one on one with me."

"I—" Ty gestured angrily toward the screen.

White held up her index finger. "I assure you, you're part of this mission. I know why this man would be particularly important to Echo and to you specifically. Storm, am I right?"

Ty was silent.

"You will be the lynchpin, but your work happens elsewhere." Satisfied that she'd said what was necessary, her gaze took in each of the men. "We're going to do this. This man is my white whale. I trust that you're the right team to accomplish the mission."

Chapter 7

Kira

As much as Kira wanted to lie low and not communicate with her family right now, she needed to let her aunt know that the package had arrived safely.

Closing the album cover, she draped the top with an acid-free cloth that would block light and other environmental contaminants from damaging the books further.

Kira sat back with a frown dragging at the corners of her mouth, thinking jealously about the pleasurable hours she had in front of her, reading, translating, and studying the text. But that would have to be put on hold while she dealt with the demands of her situation.

If she didn't have the pressures from her family, she would politely have said no to London, had a cup of tea, and gone back to the project.

Just this morning, in the European news—and then

picked up as gloriously scandalous across world news outlets—had been the story of a princess in Bahrain. She'd tried to leave the country without her male protector's permission. Having boarded a yacht in the Persian Gulf, the princess had been heading toward India, where she hoped to seek asylum. That was two years ago. The princess's father sent armed men to "rescue her from a kidnapping attempt." That was the picture the royals had painted of her attempt to leave. She hadn't been heard from since.

Until now.

The princess, crouching low and whispering into the camera, had made a video in her bathroom. She told her story of how she was held against her will in solitary confinement, bars on her windows, locks on her doors, no visitors, no medical help.

Horrible.

Terrifying.

Real.

Many countries in the Middle East were making strides toward some independence and autonomy for women, but being under the thumb of a male protector was onerous.

Kira had cousins whose father died about the same time her own father had passed away. The power went to the next male in their household—an eighteen-year-old boy who then had control of his mother's and his sisters' daily lives. He was an evil kid. He did terrible things to the family, spending the money that the women made at work on whatever he wanted while he played video games all day. Kira's cousins' only hope was for them to marry a good man, but their marriages were up to that brother. That, or wait until she was twenty-five years old and could travel without a male guardian's permission, and then they could escape. As a child, Kira's female cousins had, in secret whispered conversations at night, talked about turning that magical age and then going to Kira in America.

And now, Kira was coming to them instead.

It was a mess.

While the lack of personal agency was hard on the women who fell under the guardianship laws, Kira could only think how much *more* difficult it would be for her to live full-time under such a system. Kira's whole life, she'd experienced a Western lifestyle. She could wear what she wanted, go where she wanted, speak to whom she wanted, have sex with whom she wanted.

This article about the princess had been a gut punch.

Kira had become physically ill reading it.

Now, Kira sat in her office, staring at the wall, her hand resting on the phone, willing herself to dial her aunt Fatima.

Long minutes must have passed. She was revived with the sharp pitched bark from her kitchen where Princess Beatrice was caged, followed by a mad series of squeaks from Bea's favorite rubber chicken-shaped toy.

Kira pulled the phone closer, pressed the buttons, and took a deep breath.

"Aunt, it's Kira." She belatedly glanced at her clock. Doha, Qatar, was eight hours ahead of Eastern Standard Time. Luckily, it was just now turning three in the afternoon in Durham; it was eleven there. Aunt Fatima liked to take a nap in the heat of the day, so she was up late into the night to enjoy the cool air. Kira would have caught her aunt reading on her bedroom balcony and drinking a nighttime cup of jasmine tea. Any later, though, would have been rude.

"Did the box get to you safely?" Her aunt's words came in an excited rush.

"It did. When it's a more reasonable hour, and I won't disturb her sleep, I'll send a text to Sheikha Sara to let her know that it is safe with me."

"Does it look interesting to you?"

"Immensely." Kira tried to pull up the enthusiasm that she had felt earlier, so her aunt wouldn't be concerned by her dour tone. "I promise it will be well cared for."

"I know this to be true, or I would not have suggested it be sent to you." Aunt Fatima was warmly generous.

Kira wished she could confide in her aunt, but her uncle Nadir would know of every word that they exchanged. Kira always had to be on guard. "I'm surprised that—" Kira's words were cut off when she heard a man's voice near her aunt.

"Kira, your uncle wishes to speak to you."

Cold washed over Kira. She could tell from the sudden change from excitement to trepidation in her aunt's tone that her uncle didn't wish to say hello; how are you?

He never did.

Her uncle left familial wellbeing and gossip to the women. When he spoke to Kira, it was as the head of household. The man of the family.

Kira had been born to a Qatari man and an Iraqi woman. They had both arrived in the United States on student visas and had been attending Penn State when they met, fell in love, and married. Kira's dad got a green card when he was hired as a chemical engineer for a small start-up, and her mother stayed home, following the traditional roles of even educated Middle Eastern women. Life had been fine. Living on her father's salary instead of his inherited wealth, to prove some point to himself, they weren't rich, and they weren't poor. They weren't particularly happy, nor were they burdened. Kira had been raised in a solidly, decidedly unexceptional way.

She wasn't brave enough to forge new pathways.

She wasn't so malleable to let life just pass her by.

Kira, too, was an in-between.

In her youth, Kira had found the perfect way to survive the banality of her existence through stories. She adored Jane Austen as an author. Her biting wit. Her profound intelligence and skill with words.

Trying her own hand at writing, Kira found that her life's ordinariness and predictability didn't offer much fodder for stories. Even on the subject of love, she didn't have much to say. She'd had lovers, but no abiding loves. She'd had infatuations, a handful of boyfriends, but those relationships felt dry as time passed, and were never anything that felt like love.

All of it—her whole life was just kind of...*normal*. She moved from one decision to the next, led by circumstances more than an innate desire to head toward any given destination.

The thing that made her different was that her dad died, and there were ramifications to that death.

Kira and her dad had never been that close. And if Kira was being honest, she didn't think about him often. When he brushed into her consciousness, it was with a handful of sentimental images, but she didn't miss him. Not really. Men lived in a men's world. And women? They lived in a women's world directed by those men. And because the men were separate, they had very little idea about what it was to be a woman.

Kira knew why her uncle wanted to speak with her.

"My dear, I must congratulate you," came her uncle's voice without even the traditional greetings.

Kira remained silent.

"I have found you a husband."

While Kira's parents had met and fallen in love in America, that was not the tradition in their Qatari family. All of her aunts, on both sides of her family, were in arranged marriages. Some of her uncles had more than one wife. Kira was too American to think that was okay.

"You will be his first wife."

That meant she wasn't coming into a family and encroaching on some other woman's relationship—though, of her aunts who were in families with other wives, those aunts seemed contented to either share the marital sexual duties or be done with them altogether.

Kira *liked* being in a sexually active relationship. She had what she considered to be a very healthy sexual appetite. To share her husband with other women? That was a terrible thought. Unless, of course, she didn't like the guy. But if you didn't lie with a husband, you weren't getting laid at all.

Death could well come to a woman who took even the most innocuous step toward a man who wasn't her husband.

"Uncle…"

"You asked that I would wait for you to be finished with your education."

"Yes, sir."

"I allowed you to go all the way through the doctoral level. At least you chose a more feminine study. One that you will be able to pursue in your leisure time once you have established your household here in Doha."

Kira was silent.

"You will have a home within a walking distance of our family's compound."

It had always been her family's plan for her, and now here it was.

Kira thought back to her last visit to Qatar. It was beautiful there. Kira loved the water and the architecture. She loved the music and food. She loved the traditional Bedouin belly dancing that the women performed in the women's area of the compound—undulating hips, chest pops, and snake arms were fun and athletic in a graceful, joyful way. It was hard to be sad when you shimmied.

Perspiration shined her skin. Her heart was beating so hard in her chest that it took up the space that would allow her lungs to expand with oxygen. Her lips began to tingle.

This was it. This was what she'd thrust off into the future, hoping to find a way out.

Kira had hoped to fall in love. If she had a reputable husband here in America, this phone call would never happen. If she were married to an upstanding American, she could stay here and pursue her career and interests.

She didn't want to marry a stranger.

But to thwart her uncle would mean censure. At the very least, she'd be cut off from her family—her Qatari aunts and cousins that she loved so dearly. She'd also be cut off from her mother, who was traditional through and through—except when it came to her own love and marriage. Kira's mom would impose on her daughter what she had rejected for herself. And that felt unfair.

While losing her family would be devastating to Kira, she might still consider that as a course of action. There was always the possibility that Uncle Nadir would have her captured, brought to Qatar against her will, and imprisoned like the Bahraini princess was if Kira spoke the one word over the cell phone that she desperately wanted to—*no*.

Chapter 8

Ty

White pushed through the door, leaving the meeting room, and started at a fast clip down the hall.

Ty trailed along behind her. He wanted to be back with Echo listening to the other CIA officer's presentation about the mission to capture Omar Mohamed Imadi.

He wasn't thrilled to be singled out.

Through the next door, they were back outside. With a quicker pace than he might have imagined from someone of White's stature, they headed past the helicopter. Though it was hidden under camouflage netting, the service members gathered around, curious to see what had just arrived at Camp Lemonnier in Djibouti—the only permanent U.S. military base in Africa.

As the two reached an open space where they

couldn't be overheard, White's boots kicked up dust as she came to a sudden stop and spun toward him.

Ty had to shorten his stride as he came to an abrupt halt.

"I know you don't want to be here, but you're the only man for this job."

Ty stood with his hands at his sides, not exactly standing at attention, but certainly not casual.

"You've been chosen for a psyops mission."

"Ma'am?"

"Psychological operations."

Ty reached a hand up and rubbed his neck, still sore from his Tarzan act, swinging from his parachute ropes. "Yes, ma'am. I'm aware of what psyops means." He put his hand on his chest. "I'm a Military War Dog handler. So if the psyops has to do with training a K9…"

"Well…" She stopped and shook her head with a wry smile. "I was going to say it has to do with training a bitch. But that would be wholly inaccurate in any sense of the word. Sorry." She reached up and tucked the strand of hair that was blowing across her face back behind her ear. "My tired sense of humor." She offered a tight smile. "I'm running on fumes." She shielded her eyes as she looked up at him. "This has to do with a woman who is the complete opposite of a bitch. She is almost Disneyesque, as a matter of fact. A Qatari royal family member. *Also*, an American citizen. She is attractive, intelligent, modest in all the meanings of the word, accomplished in her own right. I could easily imagine that if she held out her finger and sang into the wind, small woodland animals would come to clean her house."

Ty wasn't clear what was happening. Was this sarcasm? Disdain? Was this an accurate reading of some woman's character? He didn't like this game. *Psyops*. "Ma'am?"

"Fatigue. Look, there's the plane." She pointed down the runway at a private jet. "Grab your..." She turned back to him and waggled her hand. "Grab anything you might need for the next two weeks for you and Rory. I'll be providing your wardrobe, so no need to worry about that."

A private ran over to him with a clipboard. "I need a signature, Sergeant."

Ty took the pen, glanced over the sheet, and tried to sign. The ink failed. He shook the pen down and tried again.

"Here." White handed him a ballpoint from her pocket.

Ty signed his name, the private took off at a jog, and Ty held the pen out to White.

She batted her hand. "Keep it. It's a gift." She pointed back at the plane. "Load up there. My pilot will help if you need it." White turned back to him. "I think I ate all the peanut packs on the way here, so if you wouldn't mind grabbing a bunch of MREs for the four of us— you, me, and the crew... Good boy treats for Rory. Or tranquilizers—I'm not sure what's best. It's a twenty-one-hour flight if we have the right wind conditions. I don't know how Rory bathrooms under such circumstances." She offered a smile in which Ty could easily read exhaustion. "You know what to do. I'll let you figure it out. I'm going to find a couch in a dark room and take a power nap, then slug an espresso. Thirty minutes, and we need to take off. Every minute counts to get you on your target. I'll be prepping you for this mission as we get going."

He turned on his heel and fell in step with her as she

moved back toward the guest area. "Where are we flying to, ma'am?"

"Durham, North Carolina."

"United States? Posse Comitatus, ma'am. I can't operate on American soil."

"For the first stage of your mission, you can." She came to a stop and turned to him. "And you *will*." She lifted her extended pointer finger and stabbed at the air to emphasize each word as she said, "Because this is a big fucking deal." She turned and strode away.

Ty put his hands on his hips and watched her go. Then set out at a jog to grab his Dopp kit and a quick shower.

He was still covered in filth from the last mission.

She called herself Johnna White. This wasn't the first time she'd shown up in an Echo briefing room. And when she did, the thing that was about to go down was always big and hairy.

Her power and position within the CIA were enormous, and in stark contrast, she was physically tiny—a hundred pounds of athleticism. Her physical and mental strength was evident. It was in the way she moved and the tight muscularity of her frame. He could almost see the thinking cogs whirring when he looked her in the eye. She made him think of Olympic gymnasts. Power. Focus. The ability to be still one moment and explosive the next. Of course, he knew her name wasn't Johnna White.

It had been a while since he'd last seen her. Based on what D-Day had said when they arrived here in Djibouti, Ty could surmise that D-Day and White had a long history. A friendship.

D-Day and Ty had run into White in the hallway at

a FOB—forward operating base—on the Syrian border. Yeah, that had been a year ago, almost to the day.

Ty flipped his bag open, grabbed what he needed, and headed to the shower, half focused on getting mission-ready, half focused on bringing up his mental Johnna White file, so he was primed for dealing with next steps on this new operation.

The mission last year had been about rescuing White's colleague, John Grey—also CIA. The plan that the good idea fairies had come up with was the kind of thing you'd see in a spy movie with highly choreographed stunt doubles. Without practice or input from the Unit, they were handed their orders and loaded into D-Day's Little Bird with a Black Hawk watching their six. The operation window had been a narrow one. The consequences of delay too dire to national security for hesitation. It had been the very definition of "a wing and a prayer."

D-Day had flown her bird up the main street of the Syrian city. A street! A street that had been edged by buildings that towered over their helicopter and stood mere meters on either side of the blades.

It was one hairy flight plan.

She'd flown to the prison. Hovered outside of the correct cell. The right face pressed pleadingly against the glass.

Thumbs up.

It was Ty's responsibility to get Grey from inside that cell to inside the heli.

D-Day held the bird still. But man...that was a mission for the books.

Ty still couldn't believe it wasn't a dream. A nightmare.

And he'd done some crazy-assed shit in his day... Nothing like that.

He'd pushed a ladder out the side opening, knelt, then positioned himself on his stomach. Only his boots were still inside. His Echo brothers held his ankles tight, so he didn't plummet the number of stories to the ground.

Sure death.

His mouth and lungs had been full of rotor blast debris as he choked his way through cutting the thick metal bars with his plasma torch, broke the window, and grabbed hold of Grey.

Ty had been absolutely sure that at any moment one of two things was going to happen—some prison guard was going to come up under the helicopter wash and shoot him in the gut while he dangled between the helicopter and the prison, or two, the helicopter was going to shift a few inches left or right, the blades would catch on the building, and they would all explode in a hellish ball of fire.

Either way, Ty hoped it was fast.

A sentient being on a mission one second, pink mist the next.

If he was going to die, he'd prefer not to take the scenic route.

Had Ty failed to get Grey out, he had a second set of orders. Orders whispered in his ear with a knowing look by the CIA officer who explained the mission: "Triple tap, make sure it's a final good-bye." It couldn't be official, but everyone on the mission would understand his actions.

It sounded cold, but it was for sure what Ty would have wanted for himself. Ty had seen what happened to Americans when they were held and tortured.

Ty set his gear on the stool next to the shower stall and reached in to get the water warmed up while he pulled off his clothes, filled with a collection of twigs, leaves, and red soil.

A triple tap from a buddy? Ty thought, pulling his shirt over his head. He'd beam blessings from Heaven down on the guy for helping him get to the Pearly Gates with all of his fingers and toes still attached and his balls free from electrical burns from the car battery encourager.

In *The Last of the Mohicans*, Ty's mother's favorite, the movie portrayed a scene differently than the book. In this scene, Major Duncan Heyward of the British Army traded his life for that of strong-minded Cora after the tribal elder sentenced her to burn at the stake for her dead father's actions. The captors raised Heyward by his tied hands until he hung over the woodpile, then they lit the fire. Heyward was roasting over the flame, screaming high and shrill. To save him from the pain, Hawkeye ran out into the tree line, loaded up his rifle, and shot the tortured Heyward in the head to put him out of his misery.

That scene was impactful to a young Ty Newcomb. He had promised himself that even if it brought him dire consequences, he'd do what it took to save a compatriot from an excruciating end.

And he trained hard every day so it would *never* come to that.

Ty stepped under the showerhead. With his forearms braced against the wall, he bent his head and let the hot water sluice over his aching back and shoulders.

"Lula," that name came back to him now.

When D-Day had landed at the base with Grey, she'd walked in and seen White and had called her "Lula." Lula? Yeah, that name seemed lyrical and happy. It might well be who she was when she was functioning as a civilian, but White—cold, hard, bright—seemed a better fit when she was serving as an officer for the CIA.

Ty probably wasn't supposed to have heard the name, Lula. It sounded like the women were old friends, life-long friends. White had called D-Day "Christen." And White had used their relationship somehow. Exploited their connection. White pulled some hat trick that had made D-Day go as ballistic as Ty could imagine D-Day acting.

D-Day was a cool operator. And whatever it was that White wanted her to do had been a big ask.

And it had gone very badly.

D-Day had told them, while they were jogging to the helicopter just this morning, that White wanted to get into a meeting. And that somehow, along that time-line, D-Day found out her brother wanted to kill her dad. Ty assumed this was her older brother Karl. That she'd shot her brother, and her brother had lost the leg as a result, was mindboggling. Something you heard on a cable news show, not something that happened to someone you knew.

His mind flitted to his own sister, Molly. Ty couldn't imagine a scenario—even the one painted by D-Day— in which Molly would lift a rifle toward him and shoot.

Was D-Day on site of that mission a blessing because she was able to thwart the patricide, or was her being there the catalyst?

A lot of questions about those events. The thought processes...

Personalities and thinking styles made a difference in the outcome of a mission.

Ty would never get his questions answered—he wasn't in the loop of "need to know." But it made him wonder if White was going to be forthright with him or if this was going to be a replay of the Ugandan mission, the part where he was left dangling in the dark, uncomfortable, and yet also responsible for the outcomes.

As he soaped his hair and lathered his beard, Ty thought about that. White was effective. She went after the biggest and baddest around the globe and her intel made it possible for people like him to operate successfully. He respected that. What he wasn't so jazzed about was that White didn't seem to mind using people in any way she saw fit in order to accomplish whatever goal she was after.

That made him edgy.

He rinsed, shut off the water, and grabbed his towel. From this assessment, Ty concluded that he needed to stay on his toes when it came to operating with White.

She wanted him to do something in Durham, North Carolina. He needed to make sure that her "ask" didn't put him in the stockades for breaking U.S. laws.

He lifted his briefs, got them turned the right way, then stepped in, adjusting himself into place, then reached for his T-shirt.

The one thing that made him a little easier was that D-Day was marrying Gator, and if Ty heard D-Day right, White was going to be in their wedding party.

You don't ask someone to be part of your wedding unless you love and trust them, right?

That thought calmed Ty's mind a bit.

He tugged on his camouflage tactical pants while balancing on his flip-flops to keep his feet dry for his socks.

Ty had so many questions.

Here was the biggest one, though: What could White be cooking up in Durham that allowed the CIA to function there and to need a tier-one operator involved?

Chapter 9

Ty

White was gone for an hour, and it was just as well.

Ty had hustled to get everything squared away in the thirty-minute window he'd been given. That was what the Unit did: A call for help went out, they grabbed their gear and rode into the storm, no dithering around.

That extra half-hour gave Ty an opportunity to run off some of Rory's energy. Ty whipped the Frisbee out, and Rory leaped high to snatch it from the air. The athletic grace of a Malinois was glorious. Ty still felt awe when he watched Rory in action.

Ty thought he could never get tired of being a handler for military working dogs. It was hands down the best job in the world.

Feeling White approach, Ty turned her way. It looked like her speed nap had done her some good. Her shoulders were square, and she looked more relaxed.

It was going to be interesting to find out how he and old Rory fit into this picture.

White lifted her paper coffee cup toward him, then climbed onto the plane.

"Last one, Rory," Ty called as the Frisbee sailed into the distance.

Rory bounded, jumped, then pranced back with the toy clamped between his teeth. He followed along behind Ty as they climbed onto the jet. After sniffing the ⬛ and giving everything a quick assessment, Rory walked right over to his crate, stepped in, and curled up with his blanket, only releasing the toy when Ty issued the command.

White watched them closely.

Putting a Malinois in a crate for twenty-plus hours was never a great idea. As a breed, they were too high energy. Ty had some doggy pills from the vet stashed in the front pocket of his tactical pants for later. Right now, with Rory's tongue hanging long, contented from his playtime, he was good to go.

While Ty pulled a black-out blanket over the top of Rory's crate, White was getting herself settled in. "Have you ever been in love, Ty?" she asked without preamble.

"I can't say that I have." He took the seat across from White and beside Rory.

White reached into her briefcase, pulled out an 8 x 10, looked at it, and then handed it over.

The picture portrayed an older man, a pampered-looking woman in expensive clothes and jewels, D-Day, and White.

While he recognized D-Day, this picture was the first time he'd seen her with makeup and formalwear. The date mark at the bottom of the photo put it in July of last year. This must have been the mission that had turned calamitous.

D-Day stood in the center of the group looking as uncomfortable as he'd ever seen her. Heck, she was much more at ease stealing the Russian helicopter while under paramilitary fire than she was in that photo.

"You know D-Day pretty well," he said. "Should I recognize the others in the picture? Besides you, of course." He balanced the photo on his knee where White could take it back once she'd made her point.

They both stalled to pull on their safety belts at direction of the pilot.

The jet engines sparked to life.

"That's William Davidson, D-Day's dad. And the blonde is his newest wife, London Davidson." White took a sip of coffee, then checked the lid and set it in the cupholder. "London and I became besties last year as part of a wider op I've been working."

"Does this have something to do with Omar the White Whale?"

"Exactly. But what I need you to know here is that I was Christen Davidson—D-Day's pal when we were growing up. I still am. As a matter of fact, she's getting married at the end of the month, and I'm her bridesmaid. There's nothing that would make me happier than to serve in that role with the whale no longer on my catch list."

"Yes, ma'am."

"I'm not the friend adopted into the family—the extra daughter if you will. It's not that warm of a family. Christen's sort of arm's length from the Davidsons."

"Was this before or after she shot her brother?"

"Ah, you heard. Before *and* after."

"London refers to Christen as her daughter? They look the same age."

"Christen's older. As you can probably see in the photo, London isn't a Christen fan. She rarely refers to her at all. Not important at all to what we're talking about. But what you need to know here is that the Davidson family knows me by a different name. If you were to see a photo of me or hear a story—let it go. That person is a stranger to you."

"Got it."

White took the photo back and replaced it with another. Their conversation paused as she gave Ty a moment to look at the image.

Though his eyes were on the photo, he could feel White's hope. Wasn't that an interesting thought?

He focused on the clues that he might find in this image. The woman was dressed in yoga pants and a hoody. Protruding from the striped canvas bag, slung casually over her shoulder, was a yoga mat and a bunch of flowers. They were his sister Molly's favorites, blue hydrangeas. The woman in the photo's black hair was pulled back into a sleek bun at the nape of her neck. It was a graceful neck. Yes, grace was the word he'd use to describe this woman. A dancer-like quality to her long tight muscles. She seemed like she was engrossed in thought with a little worry line between her carefully plucked brows. Somehow pampered and approachably comfortable at the same time. He thought this woman probably had a lot of nuances. Depth. He bet she would be interesting to have a conversation with.

Ty lifted the photo to look closer, wondering what White wanted him to see here. It intrigued him that this woman, who had a soft vulnerability to her, had anything to do with D-Day, White, or Omar.

She lived in the wrong part of the world for her to have much of a connection. This scene looked like an American suburb with a line of Cape Cod houses. But by her apparent ethnicity, she could well be Saudi like Omar was. A relative?

Ty scowled at White.

"Her name is Shakira al-Attiyah. People call her Kira." White tipped her head at the picture. "Pretty, don't you think?"

Yeah, he did. But that question sounded like a trap.

"She's an INFJ on the Myers–Briggs assessment," White leaned back in her seat. "Very unusual that. The guess by researchers is that only about one percent of the population is an INFJ. They're considered the diplomats."

"Is that what she does?"

"Diplomacy? No. She's a PhD. in humanities. But her life has had to be very diplomatic."

Cryptic, but he'd wait and see what White wanted from him.

"The interesting thing about the INFJ personality is that they are the most intuitive personality that psychologists have studied." White leaned forward, her forearms on her thighs, her hands clasped. She nodded toward the photo. "You and Kira will hopefully be spending a great deal of time together over the next few days. When you do, you must always remember, Kira will know if you're lying to her. *Don't* lie. It's better to say you don't want to answer or to distract her than to lie. She must trust you a thousand percent."

Ty's brows drew together. So this was going to be a meet and greet assignment. He wouldn't just be monitoring her movements. The Unit was trained for that by the FBI and CIA. He had some theory and some practice under his belt. But why had White's opening bid been to ask if he'd ever been in love before?

"You're an ENTJ. The nice thing about INFJ and ENTJ, along with other psych tests that you've both taken—"

He raised his eyes from the photo to focus on White's face to see if he could read anything there. "Remind me again, Myers–Briggs test?"

"Myers–Briggs has distilled brain function/world views down to sixteen variants. You and Kira are both highly intuitive. That's the 'N.' 'F' is feeling. J is judging. Where you differ is she is an introvert 'I' and you are an extrovert 'E' and 'T' thinking—ENTJ. That I and E change a lot in how you interact with the world. For example, what Kira has, that you most decidedly do not, is her intuition and introversion, meaning she feels people's judgments, and she has a high internal pressure around expectations. She *hates* to let anyone down. Kira is her own worst critic and never wants to be unethical or to disappoint. You don't have that particular brand of punitive inner critic. Also ethical, also highly intelligent and intuitive, you don't much care what others think of you. That small change makes the world of difference in, say, career choices." She batted her eyelashes. "I got to paw through your files."

He tipped his head. "Did you like what you found there?"

"For this mission? Yes." She paused. "The nice thing about your personality tests is that you and Kira have a high level of compatibility in the two ways that are meaningful to this assignment. One, you will 'get' each other in an effortless way. If I'm right, when you meet, it will feel like you've always known each other. And two, where she is weak, you are strong. She is the yin, and you are the yang, which should make her feel that where she doesn't have the skills, she'd be willing to defer to yours."

Ty rubbed his finger and thumb across his brows. He did *not* like where this was heading.

"She's feminine, and you're masculine. She's intellectual, and you're brawn and action." White paused. "Not a stereotypical dumb jock. I get that the Unit only has brilliant tacticians. I'm speaking in an erudite white-tower way. Nope. That's wrong too, she doesn't act like an erudite or someone who lives in the white tower. You get what I mean. She's theoretical, and you're applied."

Ty dipped his head to show he got the gist of what she was trying to express.

"She's holding down the homefront. You're 'take me to the action.' It's good. I think it will work."

"Think what will work exactly?"

"I want her to fall in love with you. And we have five days, including today, to make that happen."

Ty looked White in the eye for a full breath, then threw his head back as laughter erupted from his belly. He laughed until tears dripped down his cheeks. He sobered again when he saw White's face. *Shit.* She wasn't kidding.

"That's…not something I have any experience in at all," Ty said. "I've actually made it my brand to be anti-love/relationship. If you think I can somehow swoop in and be Casanova, you definitely picked the wrong man. I'm plain and easy. I love my country, my brothers, my job. I like a cold beer and hanging out with Rory. Simple. Uncomplicated. A relationship would pull me away from the things I love. And I say that with self-awareness. It sounds selfish, but honestly, I think it's the opposite. I'm not searching for someone to hitch onto my wagon. Ha. That was a long explanation of—I haven't got those skills."

Though, yeah, Ty had recently realized he'd like to change all of that. Maybe he could find a good woman and settle down—a couple of rug rats. But looking for love to turn into a life commitment wasn't what White was aiming for here.

Make a woman fall in love in five days?

With him?

And *then* what?

"You don't need those skills. Your psychologies line up. Your looks line up. I've scripted your meet-cute to perfection. She's going to fall hard. We need for that to happen because she is your vehicle into the compound where we will find Omar Mohamed Imadi. Believe me, I've tried other avenues. This is our last hope for a surgical outcome. And surgical is what the Tanzanian government requires of us if we're going to operate in their country."

Ty nodded. Just thinking about getting this terror leader sent his heart racing. In his mind, Ty was back in the tent in the middle of the rock-strewn desert, the sour scent of sweat, the tangy coppery smell of blood. A terrorist lay crumpled and lifeless with Ty's bullet in his brain. But that guy wasn't the ringleader—Omar was.

Ty wanted justice for so many like Storm Meyers.

"We get you in." White's eyes drifted to where Ty's hands had made fists on the armrests. "You do the recon for Echo and Foxtrot. Once they have the information they need, they get in and get out with Omar in shackles."

This sounded like what spooks did—honey pots and

all that emotional drama—and that wasn't Ty's career path *at all*. "Okay, I'm listening."

"Falling in love 101."

Ty rubbed his hands over his face. He'd rather be in a gunfight with a terrorist than sitting on this jet with the air conditioning blasting, learning about love. It seemed…juvenile. Like his birds and bees class back in fifth-grade health.

"I can practically hear the primal scream in your brain," White said. "I'll keep it to the basics, but you need this. First, studies have shown that women tend to pick a mate that closely resembles her brother."

"Okay, well, I can't imagine I look anything like her brother. Nitro has a more Middle Eastern look than I do."

"Yes, but Nitro's married. Also, Kira doesn't have a brother. What she does have is a best friend next door growing up who had a brother, Ben, seven years their senior, who doted on the girls. He called them his princesses, pretended to be their Prince Charming, putting them on his back and riding them around like he was their horse. Ben was much beloved, breaking Kira's heart when she was about to turn ten years old, and he joined the Marines and moved away. Kira's father played a shadow figure in her life, he was never around, and she was a girl, so he didn't pay much attention to her. This is important because Ben created the paradigm for Kira of how a man should behave when he cares for her. She's wanted a relationship with someone who thinks of her as a treasure and precious, and for whom she feels the same—only, you know, in a brave, manly kind of way." White popped her brows. "Ben set that high standard that, up until now, ruined her for all men after him. No one treated her with such adoration and

well, for lack of a better way of putting it, chivalry."
She stopped and smiled. "Fortunately for our endeavors, that serves us well."

"And how do you know this?"

"She talked about his importance to her in Ben's
eulogy. Not in those words, but one could easily read
between the lines. He was a Marine, killed in a training mission."

Ty gave her a thoughtful nod as he absorbed that
information. "So she knows about military lifestyles
and the possible consequences. Will she know I'm a
soldier?"

"Yes, a K9 trainer out of Fort Bragg. You look
enough like Ben for her brain to think in terms of her
youthful adoration and conviction that she would grow
up and marry Ben. But you also look different enough
that hopefully you won't trigger her grief and make her
want to keep her distance."

"Tightrope walking."

"Exactly." White held out her phone where she'd
been scrolling and showed Ty a picture of a man in a
Marine uniform that could easily have been Ty's brother
if he'd had one.

Uncanny was the word that came to mind.

"You're four inches taller and have a lot more muscle," White said, accepting her phone back.

Ty didn't say anything.

She turned the screen toward her. "It's the eyes where
I see most of the resemblance. The shape. The chocolate brown with depth and warmth." She pursed her
lips, pulling a deep, noisy breath through her nostrils.
"Yup. Your eyes were the clincher and why you were
chosen." She dropped the phone into her bag. "Check
your stereotypes and prejudgments at the door."

He looked at her blankly then shook his head.

"So here's the thing, we will be getting off this plane and right into action. You've already had a full day. You're going to be exhausted with the jetlag. This is to our benefit and to our detriment. Over the next week, you will be mentally exhausted by this process because you're going to be watching your every move and every word, and it's fatiguing to be that focused. You need to be ultra-careful of what you say and how you say it. When you're tired, that's a harder task."

"Okay."

"Here's another piece of psychology. Mentally fatigued people are perceived as less prejudiced and more direct."

"Prejudice against her?"

"She's of Arab descent, so from a different ethnic group."

"You're from a different ethnic group. Do you find my behavior to be prejudiced?"

White blinked.

"Look. I'm in the United States military. My fellow soldiers are from every possible ethnic group. They're my brothers and sisters. I judge people on their character, whether they've got my back in a life-or-death situation. We all bleed red, white, and blue."

"Kira's not in the military. She's yoga and chai. She's books and daydreaming while looking out the window. She's a cat resting in the crook of her knee while she's curled up poring over her translations—actually, she's allergic to cats, so nix that image. Starry nights. Rainy days. Fires in a darkened room. Whispered conversations."

"A romantic."

"A romantic, yes, but not syrupy. She will not bleed

for you in any color. You won't have that ethos to lean into. You won't have the shared background of physical pain and deprivation. She's not pampered, but she was raised upper-middle class. Fine wine. Sometimes-foody. Flexitarian."

"Flex-a-what? Should I be taking notes?"

"No. Just listen. Get a feel for this. It's not academic. It's—" she wiggled her shoulders as she looked at the ceiling, searching for the word "—natural. Flexitarian means she tries to eat mostly vegetarian, but she won't argue with you about your choice to eat meat, and she might even eat it herself on occasion. But no pork."

"Does she eat Halal?"

"Not that I know of. Just she doesn't eat pork—well, meat. She doesn't like it. She eats fish, though, and animal products—dairy. Why?"

"Just gathering data points. Okay. You're trying to make the case that we're opposites? Opposites attract or something. Uptown girl who falls for the guy from the wrong side of the tracks."

She paused to consider him. "Is that how you see yourself?"

"Not at all. I'm just trying to understand the situation and your thought process because, as you said, this is a psyops, and that's not my specialty."

"Right, well, psyops, to get you onto the compound so you can do what you do best, take down Omar Mohamed Imadi."

Chapter 10

Kira

"Wow, you're up early, or late... What time is it there?" Kira looked over at her clock and did a quick computation. "It's one in the morning in Doha."

"Archie needed a bottle. I tell you, doing this mothering thing without a nanny is exhausting. I'm not used to having to do nighttime feedings." London leaned toward her computer screen, where she had the video chat running. "You look terrible."

"Gosh, thanks." Kira smoothed her hair back.

"Didn't you sleep? You don't have an infant screeching you awake. And I will tell you, I'm glad that William uses hearing aids and can put them on his bedside table, or he'd be awake too. There are things to look forward to later in life."

"I assume there are things to look forward to now. I'm just hard-pressed to think of any of them."

"I heard." London sighed.

"Have you met him?"

"Your intended? No. Tell me, what's his name? What does he look like? What does he do for a living? Is he independently wealthy?"

"Uncle Nadir didn't say anything about him, only that the decision has been made. Did Uncle Nadir say anything about it to William?"

"No. Only that the guy is Saudi by birth, and he's in Saudi Arabia with William's son Karl right now. Apparently, Karl and this man are good friends. If they're friends as well as business partners, I'd guess they're about the same age, wouldn't you think so? Karl is five years older than we are."

"How's Karl doing?" Kira asked as she brought her cup of tea to her lips.

"William is trying to decide if we need to fly into Riyadh on our way to Tanzania."

Kira paused, teacup mid-air. "Why's that?"

"Karl's having trouble with his prosthetic leg. After he was shot, the security people put the tourniquet on him way up high on his leg—which I'm told is the thing to do, 'high and tight' is supposedly the mantra. Anyway, the tourniquet position meant that by the time they finally got him to the mainland, too many hours had passed for them to save his leg—well, and the gun was a rifle with those big bullets that splintered his femur." London stopped to give a little shiver. "Horrible. Anyway, the way they cut off his leg makes everything hard to fit and makes rehabilitation so much more difficult for him. I tell you, it's a rotten time for this to be happening. It opens old wounds."

"From rubbing on the prosthesis?"

"No, I mean old emotional wounds. The wedding

coming up and all. When the bad men were trying to hurt William—" she stopped to clutch at the top of her robe "—Christen tried to save her father by taking that shot. She's a pilot, not a—what do you call them, infantry? Not a soldier that shoots people. She's trained to fly helicopters. So it's tragic that she made that mistake. Worse, William feels horribly conflicted. His son was wounded and left behind by Christen when she flew them off the island. And her leaving Karl there is why he lost his leg. But Christen saved William's life and her own, of course. It's just a lot for William to know that his children were endangered and that now Karl wants nothing to do with Christen. The family is always on tenterhooks around her. She's a difficult child who wants her own way no matter how it impacts her family." London sighed. "I guess I just need to stay out of it."

"Lula was there on the island when that happened. What is she saying about all that?"

"She said that the helicopter was full, that there was a lot of shooting. Christen did what had to be done. Lula says that Christen's decision-making was based on what she was trained to do for the army. We can't really fault her. She did what she learned as best practices. Selfishly, I'm glad that she did what she did. I got to keep my wonderful husband, though his heart is broken. He's such a good family man." She lifted Archie to her shoulder and started patting him on the back.

"Oh, dear." Kira drew in a deep breath as she looked up to the ceiling, then focused back on London's image on her computer screen. "That's a piece that I hadn't considered."

"What's that?"

"I wasn't thinking about last year's fiasco when I

was working with the venue for Christen and Gator's celebration. Since I know so little about the couple, we just took a stab at the decisions. We picked a 1940's kind of a World War II pilot theme for the party. I hired a swing band. I had the designers do little wooden planes to add to the centerpieces outside of the ballroom. You know how cute they used to paint the old warplanes with the ladies' pin-up images and names on the side. 'Betty Blue,' and what have you. We were having 'Uncle Sam Wants You' and 'Rosie the Riveter' kinds of war propaganda posters in the corridor on the way into the ballroom, and then inside it was sort of the Hollywood glam look. Think Rick's Café in Casablanca—romance and military. But now that seems really wrong since there was aviation involved in the tragedy last summer."

"No. No. I like that idea." She lifted Archie when he belched. "Does that feel better, lovekins? Let's finish our bottle, and then we'll go back to sleep." London looked back at Kira. "Can you arrange for a casino? William loves to play roulette and poker. We could have them play with fake money and their winnings donated to the charity of their choice in Christen and Gator's names. Oh, I really like that idea. Keep going with those plans."

"Okay."

London pulled her brows together. "You really don't look like yourself. Why don't you go to the spa and get a little pampering? Relax a little."

"I have a lot to do before I head to Tanzania. I'm supposed to talk to Bruno here in a minute. I should probably go to the bathroom and get myself another cup of tea, so I'm ready."

"All right. Thank you." She looked down at her infant. "I think Archie's fallen asleep." She smiled. "I'm going to go lay him in his crib and try to get some shut-eye, myself."

"London?"

"Mhmm?"

"Do you think you could try to get some information about this man that Uncle Nadir picked for me? His name? Maybe even a picture?"

"Kira, you know that's men's business. I rather like how the male and female roles are separated out here in Qatar. I think I'd like to live here most of the time. It's freeing, isn't it, to be unburdened by responsibility and under the protection and guardianship of my husband? And, now—" she smiled "—you'll have your own husband-protector when you move here, then we can see each other *all* the time."

Kira swallowed audibly. "I have to go. I'll send you an email about what I find out from Bruno about the food I'll be bringing to Davidson Range. Sleep well."

When the screen went black, Kira sat very still, feeling fragile, as if she moved too quickly right now, she'd shatter into a million pieces.

Chapter 11

Ty

"**I**s he okay in there?" White asked, backing away while breathing out forcibly to clear her lungs.

Rory was snoring loudly and had just gas bombed them, completely oblivious that his crate balanced on Ty's shoulder as Ty navigated from the jet to the pickup truck, waiting for them at the hangar.

"It's the meds. He'll be up again in a couple hours, right as rain."

"Good. He's a huge part of the next step, and we need him bright-eyed. Our clock is ticking," White reminded him. "We have four days for Cupid's arrow to pierce the fair maiden's heart."

Ty squatted as he lowered the crate down to the open tailgate and slid Rory into the back.

"Are you ready?" She clambered into the back of the

rented pickup and over to the integrated attachments that would keep Rory safer should there be an accident.

"I'll follow your directives. Four days… It'll be a trick shot to pull this off." He moved along the side of the truck bed to inspect her work and make sure Rory was secured. "You have a backup plan, right?"

White crawled back out like a crab. "This is the backup plan. If you fail at your mission, soldier, our only recourse is to storm the castle and hope that in the mayhem, Omar doesn't slither through the cracks and disappear." She accepted Ty's hand as she jumped down from the bed. "No pressure, though." She brushed her hands off on the back of her pants.

"Yeah, right."

"If you can keep it together to maintain your cover story while you were put through SERE—your survival, evasion, resistance, and escape training—and torture sessions, then I don't think that Princess Shakira will be your undoing." She leaned over to grab a set of keys from the side pocket of her briefcase, tossing them to Ty.

Ty repeated, "Princess?" as he snatched the keyring from the air.

White shrugged. "Royalty, like we discussed, but not a direct line to the throne."

"We were counseled about this when I was a Ranger. Foreign royalty is a no-go."

"How's that?"

He sauntered toward the driver's side of the truck, using the key fob to disengage the locks. "There was a Marine—a Mormon guy—who met a woman while he was on tour in Bahrain. I don't remember the specifics. This was years back." When White opened her door and climbed in, he did the same, leaving the door open for a moment to let the built-up heat rush out the door. "She wasn't allowed to leave the country because she didn't have her father's permission. But the guy's Marine buddies helped him sneak the princess out of Bahrain. He was in love with her—it's not as clear if she felt the same." He pressed the engine button to get the air-conditioning started. "They eloped—against both of their faiths. He got in big trouble with the military, especially since it caused an international stink. A cautionary tale—stay away from foreign royalty, or I too will find myself in the stockade with my rank and pay stripped. And I'm not really down with that."

White fluffed her shirt, dissipating the sudden heat from inside the sweltering cab. "So that was a personal relationship, personal choices, and personal ramifications. This is not. You need to remember that. I'm setting Kira up to fall enough in love with you so she will trust and lean on you to help her feel safe at Davidson Range. This relationship is going *nowhere*. It has an eight-day expiration date. Keep this at the forefront of your mind. She's Qatari royalty."

"And a U.S. citizen, you said." He adjusted the hot blast of air from the vent away from White and then him.

"She is *Qatari* royalty. Your relationship will be lab engineered. I'm being as upfront with you about all of this as I can because the science that I'm applying to make her feel she's falling in love with you will also impact your brain." She paused. "What was that look that just crossed your face?"

"Nothing. I was just thinking she sounds like a mess. Ladies in distress aren't my type. It's a psyops mission. It doesn't matter what I think about her as a person."

"Oh, but it does matter," White said forcefully. "I told

you, her psych eval shows she is highly, highly, *highly* intuitive. She'll know if you're just playing a role."

"You expect me to fall in love with her?"

"Let me go back and tell you, no, she's not a damsel in distress. She's a woman in conflict. She's a woman who has an enormous amount of pressure on her shoulders put there by everyone she holds most dear. But she has thwarted those demands for a decade to live her own life and pursue her own objectives. You happen to be walking into the picture as this situation in her life comes to a head. We're actually very lucky. If this operation took off just a week from now, it's very likely we'd fail on this front, putting everyone in a lot more danger." She reached out and pulled her door shut. "I chose you specifically for this mission because I believe you *will* fall in love with her, and she will perceive your emotions as authentic. And, if and when you do fall in love, you can remember this is a science experiment. Your emotions are being manipulated. It's *not* real. And, when this is over, I can help you undo it." She reached for the briefcase at her feet.

"How's that?" he asked as she dug around the bottom of her bag.

She pulled out a pharmacy bottle, gave it a little rattle, then extended it to him. "There are studies that find if we start you on an antidepressant medication, that will help. Granted, it takes six to eight weeks to get the medication fully into your system," she explained as Ty accepted the bottle and read his name on the label. "This assignment will last approximately eight days. So there will be an uncomfortable period. Think about it like you were shot, and you need to rest and recover." She reached over and tapped the bottle. "If you start now, then any continued lovesickness might only last for a couple of months. Then you'll be okay."

"That's kind of cold." The Velcro closure rasped as Ty pulled at the flap on his thigh pocket and pressed the bottle inside.

"I'm a frosty bitch when it comes to saving the world from terrorists." She shrugged. "Sue me."

His mind was whirring, thinking of the ramifications of this mission. "Did you list these meds in my file?"

"I did *not*. I know how something like that could affect your future military assignments."

"Career."

White acknowledged that with a nod. "You follow the label as it's typed up. When that one's done, we'll start weaning you off, depending on how you're doing. It's our little secret." She winked, then pulled on her seat belt. "I have a warm spot in my heart for you, Ty." Her voice turned serious. "One of my best friends, John Grey, is alive today—survived the attempt to torture and kill him—because you dangled out the side of a hovering helicopter and put your life on the line for him. I will *always* have your back. I think you can see that's true. After all, there are a lot of teams I could have chosen to take down Omar Mohamed Imadi. I'm paying part of my debt by choosing Echo."

"Thank you," Ty said with conviction.

"And as we move forward, the least I can do is try to give you a bandage for the wounds I anticipate I will be inflicting."

"Staunch the bleeding. I appreciate your candor." He put a hand on the steering wheel, sent a glance out the back window at Rory's crate, then put the truck in gear. "Side effects?"

"Maybe. Everyone's different. If they become intrusive to your work, let me know, and we'll quietly find a solution. I'm not throwing you to the wolves. You're essentially my asset, and I will protect you. And that includes your heart."

He dipped his head. "Thanks." The way he said it was a throwaway phrase. He didn't mean it to show gratitude. He just wanted to move the conversation along. Ty had zero interest in taking the drugs. He'd been in the military for almost half his life—sixteen years. He'd been through all kinds of horror and near-death situations. He'd experienced the broadest spectrum of human emotion. A scientifically devised crush on a woman?

Yeah, that didn't worry him at all.

He could handle it.

White pulled out her phone and tapped the directions app. "I have an appointment for you at the salon. We need to get you cleaned up. While your long hair and beard work for you in the Middle East, they won't work for you on this assignment. I'm saying mani-pedi, probably a facial. You're looking scuffed up from wherever you came in from before I found you in Djibouti. You need a clean-cut military look. You're not a special operator. You're a K9 handler and trainer up at the fort. Sometimes you handle the K9s overseas if needed. You go where you're told. If Kira asks, tell her the truth, you live on base. But right now, you're staying at a hotel up the street from her house because you're training Rory for a mission where he'll be doing close protection for a VIP. Since Rory has been off working on missions with special forces, you want to give his polite-company skills a polish. All of that is true. But you should phrase it in that way, should she ask."

Without comment, Ty followed the map out of the parking lot and down the street.

"I need you to open your mind as you drive. This assignment is going to be a crash course in psychological manipulation. You're to take it in. Other than my specific directions, I want this all to just kind of free flow in your subconscious as you interact with Kira. Nothing plastic. Over the next four days, you will be working Kira's emotions with specific tasks and, at the same time, be fluid and natural. INFJ, she's intuitive like your brothers on a mission when everything just flows because you can taste the wind."

"While poetic, that's not really how that goes. We flow because we've trained day in and day out."

"—to know intuitively what the other will do. Now imagine someone with those same capabilities, which didn't need the gazillion hours of training time to do the same thing, and you'll have Kira."

Ty kept his eye on the road. He had to do his share of soul searching throughout his career with the military. It was important to his ethos—his code—that he be personally squared away with the ethics of his actions.

This felt like it was treading a very thin line. There were ramifications to playing with someone's heart, especially in bad faith. He'd never done it. He was always straightforward with the women in his life. But then again, they had been part of his personal life, and this was a job.

Did that distinction make a difference?

"What about sex?"

"You went right there, didn't you?" White chuckled.

"I'd say it's a fair question. A moral question."

"Don't get wrapped up in the ins and outs of this—

and that would be an example of a poorly worded response. He he he."

Ty glanced at her and saw a faint blush on her cheeks.

"If Kira wants a roll in the sack and you want to, then go for it. If she wants to and you don't want to, figure out a way to use that desire to your advantage without things becoming physically intimate. You're not ordered to sleep with the woman." White focused on him. "But do you find her attractive?"

"I think she'd be seen universally as a naturally beautiful woman. She looks like she's very nice."

"Nice?"

"What do you want me to say, White? Yes, she appeals to me. Yes, from the photo, she's my type. Happy?"

"Very. Thank you. But I've placed you in a scenario that you've never been in and aren't trained for. You're having moral questions about getting a woman to fall in love with you to expedite a mission. What if we threw into that thought pile the idea that her falling for you and leaning on you could save hundreds if not thousands of people from horrific ends when we capture Omar Mohamed Imadi?"

"Yeah," he said noncommittally. A little bit depended on why this woman Kira had anything to do with Omar. White certainly didn't paint Kira as having terrorist sympathies. But White could well be manipulating him by sharing what she wanted to share and hiding the rest.

"All right, how about we start?" he asked as they rolled to a stop at the light.

"I've been developing Kira for just over a year now. This meeting and Omar as a player are a new twist. A happy and unexpected boon from other work I was doing. Back in their university days, London and Kira were roommates. They continue to have a close friendship. That's D-Day's stepmother, London Davidson, I'm talking about. This summer, Kira is doing some work for London. My befriending Kira was originally meant for me to get a better standing in the Davidson social circle. It's borderline for me because the Davidsons, as we discussed, know my real name. So all I can do is gather intel and direct others to follow up on it. This all happened on foreign soil—and I say that because you mentioned Posse Comitatus. I don't want you to think we stepped on Kira's constitutional rights. Recent conversations directed us to a specific event at Davidson Range."

"Kira's planning to be there?"

"London wants her to fly to Tanzania with food and flowers, welcome the guests, and leave the next morning with London to move on to their next social event."

"Getting ready for D-Day's wedding."

"Yep. Busy. Busy. Busy. I need you on that plane to the Range. And for you to use your time there gathering what you need to best strike at Omar."

"Got it. But why does she have to fall in love with me? That's so—"

"Necessary. You'll have to trust me on this. It's the only way—especially with the new circumstances—that this will work."

"Are you going to share?"

"I'm not sure yet. I need to think on that a bit." She sat quietly for a moment, then continued. "It's a last-minute meeting at the Range, and we're scrambling to take advantage of it. I originally thought I could go in, but my superiors correctly pointed out to me that would be a no-go. While I'm trained to assess a structure and a security team, I would be a woman in a Muslim area of the country and so not able to wander around to all the places that a man could without raising suspicions. Second, I think like a 'good idea fairy.'"

Ty turned to catch her wink, then pressed the gas down as he moved with the traffic.

"And you think like 'boots on the ground,'" she continued. "There is no room for missteps. We need someone in there that can plan the mission, communicate that plan to his team, and the team can execute that plan."

"I won't be executing it?" Ty's scowl was fierce. He wanted *his* hands on Omar.

"To protect Kira, you will leave with her once you have your information. Things you should know about the situation—"

Ty's scowl hadn't fallen off. He was drumming his fingers on the steering wheel as he drove, trying to disperse his agitation.

"Kira is American born and American educated but has one foot in the West and one in the East. Every one of her living relatives is in Qatar. And you already know she's from the royal family. To be clear, we do not associate this case with the royal family. We associate this case with corrupt individuals from various countries, including Kira's uncle, and including her dear friend London's husband, William Davidson."

"Okay."

"America has a good relationship with Qatar. They're our strategic allies. We have a military base there, which is important to global security. It's imperative that we don't upset the royal family. Our diplomatic stance is that we see some Americans who are making pretty big waves."

"Kira is one of those Americans?"

"She's a bystander in the vicinity, not a problematic player on the board. It's her uncle who's the terrorist sympathizer. There will be millions, possibly billions in his pocket, and foreseen prestige in the Middle East if he pulls this off. What I can tell you is, if he pulls this off, the entire world will turn on Qatar. We *must* stay on top of this. And that's the full background that I can share right now."

Ty spun the wheel, rolling the truck into a parking space out front of the salon where he could keep a close eye on Rory. He'd move Rory to the cab and leave the engine running with the air conditioning on and have White keep an awareness for his safety.

White pointed toward the building. "We're going to style you the way Kira prefers—grooming and clothing." She undid her safety belt and swiveled toward Ty. "This is not the kind of assignment where I think you're in mortal danger. But—" She stopped and pressed her lips together.

"That's a mighty powerful 'but,'" Ty said. He'd admit it, his stomach clenched. He'd known White on previous missions. It wasn't at all like her to grapple with language choice.

She swatted his leg. "Come on. It's time to get you in there and transform you into Kira's heartthrob."

Chapter 12

Ty

Standing outside the hotel, Ty petted over his face and the back of his neck. He'd grown his hair and his beard for his work overseas. It felt strange to be this groomed, but he preferred it. He wondered what kind of impact this would have on him when he was working a mission overseas. To that end, White had agreed that he didn't have to be clean-shaven.

The stylist removed the bulk of his beard. He was groomed like some pretty boy in a magazine, with products applied that made his beard soft to the touch. He'd have to grow it back when this was in his rearview mirror.

One mission at a time.

Right now, Rory was sniffing at some bushes, trying to decide which one he'd honor. He was still a little groggy and stumbly. Ty thought some food in Rory's stomach, a bowl of water, and a little more time, and he'd be okay.

They still had just over an hour before they went to what White kept calling the "meet-cute."

"No idea what that means, ma'am."

"It's a literary phrase, it's the point where the hero of the book—that's you—and the heroine of the book—that's Kira—meet. And it's so cute and memorable." She clutched her hands under her chin and batted her eyes.

"And this has to do with Rory?"

"It does. Now, I know you have a Harley. Have you ever driven one with a sidecar?"

"You want me to put Kira in a sidecar? Why wouldn't she just sit behind me and hold on?"

"Oh," White said. "That would be wonderful. But for today, I just want Rory to ride along with you."

Ty looked down at Rory as he lost his balance midstream. "I may need to rinse him off first."

They walked through the lobby to the elevator.

The valet was dealing with the bags and Rory's crate. Ty was used to sleeping outside with a rock as his pillow. Even Rory was impressed with their new digs. His nose was busy as he walked to the elevator.

White and Ty were silent as they made their way up to the third floor and through his door.

"Nice," he said. Walking farther into the room, he saw that there was already clothing hanging in the closet. "I'll keep the lead on Rory until the bellhop's brought our things up." He moved over to the window to get the lay of the land—habit.

Out in the parking lot, he saw a cherry red Harley with a black sidecar. That must be his ride. He'd already spotted the black helmet sitting next to the TV. He let the curtain fall back into place. "That's for me?"

"What do you think?"

"Looks like a good time in terms of riding around. Looks like a spider web for your fly. Not sure how I feel about all this."

"It's your job to protect America. And as such, making the princess fall in love seems the easiest of assignments."

"Hold up now. Let's discuss this. I mean, I've got no qualms about catching the lady's eye, getting her to trust Rory and me. I'm not clear on why love needs to be in the picture. That's a psychological attack on an American."

"She's an asset."

"She's a lady. An American citizen."

"Suck it up, buttercup. Your assignment is to get to the Range in Tanzania by hook or by crook. Map it, plot it, prepare it, and get the vulnerables out of the way."

"Right."

"Rory already knows how to wear dog goggles. I have some for him here in case you didn't have any in your pack."

"Yep."

White had a drawer open and was laying clothes on the king-sized bed. A pair of jeans with a rip on the left knee, a pristine white t-shirt. She looked up and caught his eye.

Ty looked into the opened drawer. "You must not trust my ability to put on clothes."

"The sticky notes are a step too far?"

"It's like my mom getting my six-year-old self prepped for overnight camp."

She pulled out a pair of black socks and a pair of boxer briefs.

"Seriously? You bought me underwear?"

"And washed it a few times too, so it would be soft for you." She moved to the closet and pulled out a pair of leather biker's boots.

"She didn't look to me like the kind of woman who would go for a biker."

"She wouldn't. You're right." White placed the boots at the end of the bed. "But we are recreating a scene for her." She stepped back until she could lean her hips into the lowboy. "Are you ready to learn the fundamentals of quick rapport building as it is viewed from the perspective of the CIA?"

"Is anyone ever ready for that? Should I get dressed?"

"Time's of the essence."

He gathered his costume and headed toward the bathroom, bringing Rory along with him.

Rory looked like he wasn't feeling great coming off his plane tranquilizers. If he was going to puke, Ty would prefer it happen on a hard surface. He signaled Rory to jump into the bathtub, giving Ty room to get ready.

Ty left the door open a crack, so he could listen to White while he changed.

Rory lay down on the cool surface of the bathtub ceramic and looked much happier.

"I'm listening." Ty sat on the toilet and unlaced his boots.

"We're using a bunch of known psychological techniques to help ensure we get you where you need to go. We're putting behavioral psychology in play with a lot more strategies than usual because we're on such a tight timeframe."

"What are we talking about here? I'm uneasy about manipulating a civilian, pulling them into the terrorist's sphere of influence. That's not what I do."

"Me either, but to keep American soldiers safe, wouldn't you try to befriend an informant?"

"That's not what you're talking about here." He pulled off his combat boot and started untying the other, wiggling his newly pedicured toes. It was weird having a stranger touch his feet. He didn't like it. "You want me to show up and sweep this woman into my arms."

"Yes." White projected her voice so he could hear her. "It's the best way, and she's particularly vulnerable to that right now."

He set his second boot to the side then stood to take off his pants and shorts. "Why? Did she just get thrown over by some turd?"

"Not that I know of. She has an uncle that's decided to get involved in her life in a way that Kira doesn't welcome."

He folded his clothes, put them on the counter, and took a minute to look over his body.

Standing naked in front of a mirror in bright light, now he could see how beat up he was. If he did end up in bed with this woman, these bruises and welts would be hard to explain for a dog handler at the fort. He looked like some guy who was into heavy bondage. And she didn't seem the type that would be down with that kind of scene. He'd have to finagle some scenario where she couldn't see him to ask questions about the strap width bruises around his thighs. If she was as intuitive as White had been insisting, she'd know if he was making stuff up, and he couldn't exactly explain getting blown into a tree in Uganda.

Ty stepped gingerly into the black shorts then turned this way then that. Ty had to admit, they looked pretty good. Well, better than his Army-issued boxers. White knew what she was doing. About this anyway.

"Is everything fitting?"

Ty pulled on the T-shirt. "I'll be out in a second, and you can see for yourself. So tell me why this uncle is getting involved."

"He became the traditional male guardian after Kira's father died. In Qatar, there's Sharia, and she falls under her uncle's mantle."

"She's an American. And she looked mid-twenties? She's not subject to that." After zipping up the jeans, he sat down to put on the socks and biker boots. Should it make him trust White more that she got his clothes size to a T?

When Ty put his foot on the tub to do the closure, Rory reached his nose over and sniffed at the new leather.

"What do you think, buddy? You like how they smell?"

Rory thumped his tail, obviously coming out of his fog.

"Kira's twenty-eight years old. If she lived in Qatar, she could travel without male permission since she's over twenty-five. But Sharia law would apply to her while she's in the country. Life's complicated. She has choices to make, but all of them have consequences. Right now, she sees two possible roads into the future, and both are dangerous. She needs to pick the one she thinks she can survive."

Ty swung the door open to find himself face to face with White. "Do you have information to help her find the safest path forward?" Ty had never met the woman, but already he was ready to go to the mat for her.

"Okay, how about this, boy wonder?" She smoothed her hand over his T-shirt and sent a critical eye front and back. "This will do nicely." She smiled and took a step back. "What if I promise you that I'll make sure she's given an intelligence briefing after the mission is complete?"

His brows came in tight. "Are you in a position to make that pledge?"

"Yes. I believe I am." She plopped onto the corner of the bed. "Okay, time to brief you on your assignment. Step one. You will come into her sphere of awareness in such a way that she's intrigued, and you are *unaware* of her. This allows her to observe you from a comfortable distance."

"What if she doesn't like what she sees?"

"Oh, she will. That's a given. Well, it is when I teach you the scenario. Ready?"

Chapter 13

Kira

Princess Beatrice plopped her tiny bottom on the slate floor of the foyer and looked up at her leash.

Her sharp, insistent bark dragged Kira's attention from her job of photographing each page of the first novel found hidden in the wedding album. This would allow her to start translations as she worked on the painstaking steps of preserving the delicate parchment. The date on the first page of this incredible treasure was April 10, 1800.

This gift was a treasure.

Beatrice saw Kira turn to her and stopped her summoning, only to start up again when Kira's attention went to turning off the light on the platform camera and securing the work for the day.

"I hear you, Bea. I'm coming. I just lost track of time." She glanced at her phone, and sure enough, it was three o'clock on the dot. "You are better than an alarm clock when it comes to your schedule. Pretty uncanny." She closed the cover and pulled the protective cloth over it. "Are you sure you can't read time?"

Beatrice responded by grabbing the tail end of her lead and trying to pull it from its hook.

"I'm coming, Bea. Let me get my shoes on." After pulling on a pair of ballet flats, Kira stood and headed into the hallway. Stopping at the mirror, she poked at her messy bun, pulled at the oversized shirt she wore over a pair of black capris, and decided it didn't matter what she looked like.

"So what shall I bring with us to play with today?" She reached into the basket next to her key bowl. "Ball or throw bone?" She held one in each of her hands, wiggling them around until Beatrice jumped for the green ball on her right. "Good choice." She tossed the throw bone back where it belonged and grabbed her keys and her striped hobo bag.

Princess Beatrice was supposed to have stayed with her for a week. That was two months ago. Once William was over in the Middle East, he got involved in his business and didn't want to come home to the States.

Since London got pregnant with Archie, she'd changed. She sort of collapsed into the world-of-William. Everything he wanted, he got. And William wanted London with him. So Princess Beatrice had remained with Kira.

That had been all right. Kira preferred big, muscular dogs. And wasn't a huge fan of the yipping and the destruction, but soon enough, the two of them had fallen into a routine that worked. Part of that was that Beatrice accompanied Kira on her daily trip to the coffee shop.

Three o'clock was when Kira's energy flagged. In

the winter, a cup of hot coffee, in the summer a glass of iced chai at the cute little woman-owned coffee shop worked out perfectly as a way to get her blood flowing, free her thoughts, and get her through her afternoon work until she called it done around dinner.

Once Bea came on the scene, Kira sat outside at one of the café tables. She followed her drink with a walk up to the park, two blocks away. At that time of day, there were few, if any, others in the fenced area for dogs to play off lead. Kira could be sure that Bea got the exercise she needed.

Beatrice scampered down the front steps with her lead clipped into place, pulling at Kira to come along.

"Okay, Princess Impatience, wait for a second. I need to lock up." Keys, ball, wallet, and phone were eyed and verified in her bag, and Kira set off.

It was a beautiful day. The humidity was a rare low, and the temperatures were still cooler from last night's rain shower.

Kira let Beatrice set the pace as they headed down the street and toward "their" table. Before she sat down, Kira stopped to look through the window until the barista spotted her and raised her hand in salute.

Kira tied Bea's lead to the chair arm then reached up to adjust the umbrella.

The barista leaned out of the door. "Usual?"

"Thank you," Kira said as she took her seat. Typically, she had a paperback in her bag, but today she'd left it behind in Beatrice's insistence to get going. Kira decided to play a game instead. She'd watch people, pretending they were fictional characters, and make up a genre and backstory for them.

A worried-looking man was rushing out of the pharmacy next door. Sweet Romance: He became a dad, scurrying home with the medicine he hoped would keep his son from the emergency room but would ultimately fail to help. Rushed to the hospital, this widower with his young son would run serendipitously into the dad's college girlfriend, who was now the specialist who could save his boy's life. As soon as the doctor-ex-girlfriend saw this man, her love sparked back into a roaring flame. She would not leave the hospital until the boy was cured. The two would eventually marry, and the family would live happily ever after.

And there was that woman directly across the road. She was sitting in her car as Kira had walked up the street. The engine on, her wheels turned as if she were about to leave. Instead, she scrolled through her phone. Genre, Mystery: She may look like a suburban mom in her minivan, but, in reality, she was the CIA. That van was full of sensitive tracking apparatus, listening devices, and people watching monitors, hidden behind the dark-tint windows. She was waiting for the international crime boss to show, then she'd use her subterfuge to follow him to the drop site. Eventually bagging her man.

And as she came to the end of the scenario, Kira heard the rumble of a motorcycle. She turned and smiled. "Look at that, Beatrice." Coming down the road was a cherry-red Harley with a sidecar. "This one is easy. It's just like in the movie *Pete and Me*. Only Pete was a lab, not a Malinois. Look how adorable. His little doggie goggles. Aw! So cute!"

The minivan pulled out and continued down the road. Kira's storyline was forgotten as the motorcycle turned smoothly into the empty spot right in front of the ice cream parlor.

Could this be happening?

"Lula has to see this," she whispered to Beatrice as

she pulled her phone from her bag, tapped on the camera, and started to video the scene.

The Malinois sat upright in his seat in the sidecar, looking very proud of himself in his mirrored dog goggles. His tongue hung out the side of his mouth in a dopey, contented kind of way.

And oh, my.

The man who had been riding the motorcycle stood and swung one long, muscular, jeans-clad leg over the seat. He must be six-one, six-two? And those shoulders! And his tight hips.

The guy reached up to drag the helmet from his head.

Kira found herself gripping the edge of the table. "Lula, do you see this? Is this crazy?" she whispered loud enough for her words to be caught on the video to be sent to her friend later when her pulse wasn't racing.

Black riding boots, trimmed beard, soft-looking brown hair cut in a short, almost military style. And that t-shirt, tight across his pecs and around his biceps.

Kira imagined him in her bedroom, reaching down to pull off that snow-white T. Under it, she was sure she'd find washboard abs. Pop the button on those jeans and follow the goody trail… Kira reached up and swiped her fingers around her lips to make sure she wasn't drooling.

"It's exactly like *Pete and Me*," she told no one in particular.

Kira knew that humans could feel eyes staring at them. She'd just used that technique to get the barista's attention. She certainly didn't want this guy to turn around and see her staring at his, mmmm, his yummy ass. "Look at that butt, Lula. That is a thing of beauty. How many squats do you think that guy does every day?"

The guy looked at his dog and gave him some kind of hand signal.

Kira ducked her chin, reaching up to pull the elastic from her bun and shake her hair across her cheeks so she could gawk from behind the curtain of black hair and the phone she was pretending to read.

Biker Boy made his way to the order window at the side of the ice cream storefront.

"Get the vanilla soft serve. Get the vanilla soft serve," Kira mouthed. *Honestly, when did something like this happen, when one of your favorite movies was played out right in front of your eyes?*

After a moment, the man turned. The white peak of ice cream in his hand, a napkin in the other. "Lick it." She sent the thought wave directives in his direction to keep the scene playing correctly.

Kira hoped she was capturing all of this. Her friend Lula was going to swoon. It was Lula's favorite film, too.

He. Licked. The. Cone.

Didn't just lick it. He *savored* it.

Kira squirmed in her seat as she watched the slow stroke of his tongue from the cone to the peak, and then another, and another. She blew her breath out slowly through pursed lips as her body tingled. Boy, would she like to be that ice cream right about now.

Now Studly was offering the cone to his pooch. *Pete and Me!*

Studly drew the cone away from the pup after his dog made a lunging bite like he'd like to eat the ice cream cone whole and possibly the hand that held it, too.

The pup's tail was thumping so hard it was making the bike shake.

Studly made a calming gesture and started to hold

out the cone. Another lunge, more hand gestures, more gentle commands, then the Malinois started licking it politely.

Suddenly, Stud muffin's gaze popped up. He slung his head to the side. He yelled, "Stop," with his hand up. He flung a "Stay!" over his shoulder as he leaped toward the road.

Just then, a shriek of tires.

High pitched yipping of dog terror rose from under the car wheels.

Bea! Kira had been so engrossed in watching Studly that she hadn't felt Beatrice pull herself free from the arm of the chair, and the little dog had raced out into the road.

Kira surged to her feet, clutching her phone to her chest. She ran three steps to the curb. Before she vaulted into the street, the light had turned green at the corner, and a stream of cars drove past, blocking her from helping.

Kira stood on her tiptoes, trying to see what was happening, her eyelids stretched wide, her eyebrows strained toward her hairline.

Studly squatted out of view.

Princess Bea's shrieking stopped.

He stood again, with Bea in one hand the ice cream cone in the other. He caught Kira's gaze. "Your dog's fine," he called over to Kira.

Kira stood there, immobilized with fear and guilt.

The woman in the car had rolled down her windows. She looked just as affected as Kira.

"She's fine, ma'am," Studly told the driver. "You caught her lead under your wheel. You can drive on."

The woman clutched her heart then gave a small wave as she slowly rolled forward.

Studly crouched again, and this time when he came up, Kira saw he'd grabbed Bea's leash and reattached it to her collar.

The next car in line on his side of the road was waiting patiently, and the vehicles on Kira's side of the road had driven by, so Studly walked over to her.

Beatrice had leaned over and was licking the ice cream cone.

Kira looked at the Malinois to see if he was jealous. She bet that dog could take Bea out in a single bite. He just sat in the sidecar, watching the scene through his dog goggles.

"Yours?" he asked.

"Goodness, thank you so much," she said, reaching for Bea and settling her under her arm. "Beatrice, how did you get yourself loose?"

"I think maybe she saw Rory having some ice cream and wanted some, too. I apologize." He held out the cone to her. "My treat."

Phone and Bea in one hand, dripping ice cream cone in the other, all Kira could do was stand there and blink at Studly.

With a raised hand, he turned and crossed the street again. She watched as he praised his dog for sitting there like a good boy. He lifted his helmet and was pulling it on as Kira's tongue untied enough that she could call out, "Thank you so much!"

He raised a hand in a nonchalant way that told Kira that he was the kind of man who dove toward oncoming cars to save dogs all the time. Her heart was thumping in her chest so hard that she thought she'd pass out. And she thought it probably had little to do with her fright over Beatrice's safety, though there was some of that in the mix.

Kira plopped onto her seat at the table as the waitress came out with her iced chai and a bowl of water for Bea. "Is Beatrice okay? I saw that from the window."

"She seems fine," Kira said, her lips buzzing. She put Beatrice on the ground with the ice cream.

Turning the camera toward her to tap off the video function, Kira saw her face. She left herself recording for a moment while she looked at her expression. It was the exact expression that had been on London's face when she shook hands with William the very first time and was shot through the heart by Cupid's arrow, smitten.

Sweat beaded on her nose and forehead. Kira picked up the chai and downed it in one gulp, trying to cool her heated system.

Smitten.

Surely *not*, surely it was the movie scene and the fear for Beatrice…

Smitten?

She looked around and was thoroughly confused that everyone was going on about their day as if the world hadn't stopped spinning on its axis a moment ago.

Smitten.

Wow, it sucked to be her. A man she'd never see again was now pumping through her veins, and a man she'd never seen before was waiting to marry her.

Chapter 14

Ty

When Ty and Rory walked through his hotel room door, he found White lying on his bed with her computer on her lap and a grin on her face.

"Well, well, well, lover boy."

"Don't call me that." He let the door bang shut then threw the security latch.

"Excellent job!"

"And how would you know?" He tossed the key card on top of the apartment-sized fridge in the room set up for an extended stay. Kitchenette, office space, and a seating area toward the front of the room meant it didn't feel like White was sitting in his bedroom.

"Well, the CIA officer who was saving your parking place at the ice cream parlor turned the corner and was watching out the side window of her minivan with her zoom lens."

"Don't do that." He unclipped Rory and gave him a good rub. "If I know you've got spooks around recording me, it's going to show up in my posture. Feeling eyes on the back of my neck is going to put me in operator mode, and that's too tense for what you want to happen."

"Okay. I'll call off the spooks. Happy?" She raised a single brow.

"Not especially. So your colleague has this recorded, and you thought it went okay?" He sat on the edge of the sofa to take off the biker boots that needed breaking in before they'd be comfortable.

"Better than okay. Kira posted to a select few of her friends on social media. It turns out that Kira was recording, too. I told you that I've been developing a relationship with her this year. One of the things that I have in common with Kira is a love for a film called *Pete and Me*."

"I've never seen it."

"That scene with the motorcycle and the dog, your clothes, the ice cream, all of it was exactly like that film. Rom-com, chick flick, I'm not surprised you haven't seen it. Anyway, your performance was pitch-perfect up until Princess Beatrice pulled her lead off the chair to get some ice cream, too. I could not have paced this scenario better if I had tried. Come look. She was taping this for me to see, so she narrates."

Not comfortable crawling up and sitting with his back against the headboard with White, Ty moved a chair from the dinette over and sat where they could both see the screen.

First, White played the relevant snippet from the movie.

Ty didn't think he looked anything like the actor.

Rory for sure didn't look like a blonde lab. The motorcycle, wardrobe, and ice cream were right. Yeah, he could see how she would have recognized this scene.

White went on Facebook. "Kira is extremely circumspect with this account. She mainly posts literary quotes and book memes. But occasionally she chooses a private setting and tags certain friends. Usually, London and I get a tag. It's interesting and meaningful that she tagged two other friends and me, but not London, in this post. Her husband William might feel obligated to show this to Kira's uncle Nadir, her protector. That would go over badly, especially when you see and hear her reaction to you. Before I play this, recognize that this is how women talk to each other in private."

Ty scratched under his beard. He'd admit it; he was curious about how Kira had seen him. His personal reaction to seeing Kira for the first time was off the charts. He'd never had such a visceral experience when meeting a woman, even a woman he was attracted to romantically. It was like he knew her already, and all he wanted to do was gather her in his arms and hold her tightly to his heart, where she belonged. *There you are. Welcome home.* It was such a strange, crazy-making feeling that he didn't know what to do with it.

He'd been irritated and prickly ever since he'd thrown his leg back over the motorcycle and drove away from her.

His stomach clenched as he was about to find out what Kira said about him to her friends. Could she have felt the same? That boded poorly for both of them. The last thing Ty wanted to do was hurt Kira in any way.

White tapped the screen, and the scene played out from her vantage point.

It was like being a voyeur, and he both wanted to see and felt like he was intruding on Kira's privacy.

On the screen, Ty offered a lick of ice cream to Princess Beatrice.

"That's perfect. I was going to save this technique for later but look at you, you're a natural manipulator."

"No, ma'am, I'm not. It was a moment of—I don't know—humanity? It was just being a person."

"You don't think people manipulate each other constantly?"

"I didn't, and if that's what we do, I'd probably rather not know about it." He stood and lifted the ladderback chair and turned it around to sit backward with his forearms resting across the top. Maybe he needed a bit of a barricade between him and this woman with all her theories. "Honestly, ma'am, your kind of thought process is screwing with my mind a bit."

"Look at the comments." She read from under the video post. "Look what happened today!"

"Oh, man!" White had posted as Lula. "It's like a scene out of that movie. When do I get to meet him?"

Kira responded, "Oh, I'll never see him again. No idea what his name even is."

"Did you catch his face? He's so cute!" Karen had posted. "His eyes are gorgeous."

"Face? I can't see his face. I'm transfixed by his body. Holy moly, come to mama, big boy," Barb posted.

"My god! He's an Adonis. And his pupper. Smooches!" Karen commented with a string of hearts.

"We need to find him," White said as Lula.

"No way to find him. Let it go," Kira had typed. "Besides, it looks like things have already been arranged as far as my love life goes :'(But it was fun this happened today."

"What does that mean? Have you met someone? Spill!" Karen wrote.

Kira didn't answer.

White tapped the screen and the video Kira had made played again.

He watched himself jog across the street to get back to Rory. He'd been worried that Rory would think that ice cream belonged to him, and as the alpha, he deserved all of it. There had been a good chance Rory might have just dashed over and retrieved the cone. But Ty thought the real reward for Rory was riding around in the sidecar. He'd had a blast. Ty might even consider buying one for Rory. It would also give him a place to put his groceries or an overnight bag if Ty decided to go on a bike trip.

"Ha, see here?" White stopped the video. "She thinks she's turned off the video as she lays her phone down. Watch what she does."

"She drinks her drink." Ty didn't see anything to get ruffled about.

"One of the chemical body things that I had hoped to take advantage of was that she'd be sitting there drinking her chai in the heat of the sun. She wasn't out there long enough to register that heat as having to do with where she was sitting and the temperature of the day. Instead, her brain would register the heat as having to do with the scenario that had just played out."

"What chemistry are we talking about here?"

"All right, another love lesson." White turned off the tablet and laid it beside her. "One of the most dependable neurotransmitter markers for love or lust is found in the skin. The water in a person's skin conducts electricity."

Rory jumped on the bed, walked over, and sniffed around White's face and hair.

White sat very still.

"Lay down," Ty commanded, and Rory complied, rolling on his back, belly up, looking from Ty to White to see if someone would rub his tummy.

Ty moved his chair closer to the bed, so he could comply. Rory had been a very good boy earlier. "I'm listening."

"When a human is aroused by something in their environment, the body pushes water to the surface of the skin."

"You mean sweat?"

"Yeah, as time goes by, but before you can actually see sweat." She tapped the tablet on a still picture of Kira. "No sweat." She tapped again at the end of the video. "Look at her nose and forehead. Sweat."

Ty had been sweating, too. He'd thought it was his fear that the dog was going to be run over. But yeah, he'd admit it, he'd had an immediate and profound body reaction when he stood beside Kira.

"With more water near the surface of the skin, there isn't as much electrical resistance."

"Applying that to Kira…"

"Looking at someone you love, for example, makes that happen. Also, see this little smile on her face. Kind of weird. She looks shellshocked and happy at the same time. That's what happens when you get zapped by the love bug."

"Stop."

"You think I'm kidding? It's the peripheral nervous system at play. The electricity makes the zygomatic muscles in the face tug the corners of the lips up like that. This is the look of love at first sight. Which is exactly what we wanted. And—tada! Exactly what you manifested. Kudos."

"Love at first sight is *not* a thing." At least he'd been trying to convince himself of that from the moment he got back on that bike, and everything in his system told him not to ride away without Kira.

When he walked up to Kira with the dog under his arm, his whole body lit up with…something. It was like recognition, like they knew each other, were friends, were more… He'd had to use his combat skills to lower his pulse and play calm and cool under fire.

The look of fear on her face from concern for the dog had made his heart bang and clang around in his chest, had made him feel like he was expanding to shield and protect her. It was a sensation he'd never experienced before, and he didn't know what to do with it.

White and her damned applied science.

Maybe this assignment wasn't going to be as easy as he thought it would be.

He knew he wasn't coming out of this unscathed.

"No, love at first sight isn't a thing. Science would agree with you," White was saying. "Relationship scientists believe in lust at first sight. And while you did great today, don't start fist-pumping. Cognitive research shows that the initial electrical whooptie-do that Kira wrote about, spoke of, and showed on her face isn't concrete. It could easily change to nothing the next time she sees you or on day five or on day five hundred. Every time you're together during this assignment, we will be applying science to keep you in play."

Rory rolled over and jumped off the bed, moving toward the air conditioning unit and lying down.

"You're a dangerous woman."

"And don't you forget it." She winked.

He lifted an eyebrow.

"That was the easiest part. Kira's watched this movie dozens of times. I was almost a hundred percent we'd get that physiological response."

"But we don't know why. This scene may mean nothing to her."

"I wanted her to see that played out in real life to set the tone of the trajectory. This is a happily ever after movie."

"T-Rex would have been a better man for this assignment." And while he said that, some Neanderthal part of him wanted to bang his chest and claim Kira as *his* woman. What a thought. He didn't like this feeling. In his life with the Unit, he trained every day to be in command of his body, his emotions, and his actions. White was blowing that all to hell.

White batted her hand through the air. "T-Rex's ears are too big."

Ty pulled his brows together with confusion. T-Rex didn't have big ears.

"My concern was over ear-to-eye ratio. Your ears and eyes are correct to show that you are prime for reproduction."

"Repro—You're kidding."

"I am not. I measured all of the non-married Echo and Foxtrot men on my possibility list. Foxtrot, by the way, is doing recon for you out at the Range as we speak."

Ty nodded.

She rubbed her bottom lip. "Do you want to know this?"

"Sure, why not?"

"In the most simplistic form. Our ears continue to grow throughout our lifetime. At some point, the eye-to-ear ratio comes into a phase where our caveman lizard brain picks up on that ratio to tell when a potential mate is in their age of procreation. So when you can physically create a baby, your eye and ear ratio will show you're old enough to do that safely. Ears continue to grow. When you get to the age when, meh, maybe you're too old to start making cubs, that ratio shifts, and a woman's brain would say—"

"Friendzone."

"Exactly. A nice enough friend but too old to protect and help raise the family. And before you start arguing that T-Rex is only a few years older than you, you must have been born with smaller ears. And I bet he got laid earlier than you did."

"Not going there."

"I'm not saying T-Rex is past his sell-by date. He's an appealing man. There were other considerations that put you in the hot seat."

"He knows more about long-term relationships. He was married, you know."

"I know. And I can almost see from a man's point of view why you'd say that. But it was another strike against using him. Even if he's widowed, that's not the draw that men on social media believe it is. When a woman finds out the man is widowed, the first question in her mind is—"

"What happened to his wife?"

"Exactly. Is this guy safe? How did she die? Anything odd there? Any reason why he wasn't able to help or save her?"

"That's a burden." Maybe that was why T-Rex hadn't dated since his wife was killed in action as a police officer.

"It's the truth. Margaret Atwood of *Handmaid's Tale*

fame said, 'Men are afraid that women will laugh at them. Women are afraid that men will kill them.'"

Ty's brow pulled in tight. "Is that true?"

"Pretty much." She reached for the mug on his side table, looked in it, then set it back down, empty.

"But we were talking about ear ratios. Kira couldn't possibly have seen my ears from across the street."

White reached over and tapped his knee. "You had these *particular* jeans on, chosen to accentuate your muscled thighs and butt. Yup, this is me objectifying you—scientifically and professionally, of course."

"Of course."

"Kira mentioned that in the video. You heard her asking about your squats. I picked your clothes to mimic the hero in the movie, hence the rip in the knee. But why do you think the wardrobe person chose that particular outfit for the character?"

"Why don't you tell me."

"It showed off the character's and your body ratios. Those ratios told Kira's brain that not only were you down for a good fuck, but you'd make beautiful babies."

"Jeezis, you're kidding, right?" He stood up, feeling self-conscious. "Speaking of clothes, I'm going to change into my own things. Unless you need me to go out again and show off my ratios in public."

"Go. Change."

Ty bent over his ruck and found a pair of old tactical pants and a comfortably loose T.

"This works both ways, by the way, the mathematical equation of attraction. People like proportion. The more symmetrical the face, the more beautiful they're considered. You have a very symmetrical face."

"You measured." He gathered his things and moved

into the bathroom, leaving the door open, so White knew he was still listening.

"Every single face on my possibility list, yes, of course, I did. Every tool is being applied to this event to capture the High-Value Target we're talking about here. Not Osama bin Laden high. But we've been putting blood and treasure on the line for a decade trying to get him. We're not messing up this opportunity by being lazy or sloppy."

While Ty wasn't a huge fan of how he was being psychologically manipulated or, in turn, how he was manipulating Kira, it was still kind of interesting. What Ty thought was random was actually his brain function on its own secret agenda. Well, it was true that animals had one task, species survival. So it made sense that impregnation was a major driver in the biological reasons for his unconscious choices and surely, to some extent, his behavior.

Look at him; somehow, his body knew it was time. Ty had come to the conclusion he needed to put forth some effort and find his future Mrs. Newcomb and start his family. And he'd thought only women had biological clocks.

In his mind, Ty pulled up the image of Kira's face just before she picked up her glass and slugged it down. She looked as shellshocked as he had felt. He could play it off as her fear for her dog, but Ty's gut said no.

He had affected her.

She had entered his bloodstream. It was like he could feel her as part of him.

"Let's talk about broad shoulders."

Ty didn't answer. He was knocking around the bathroom, getting the too-tight jeans off.

"For men, it's shoulder to waist ratio. For women,

bust to waist to hip. Adonis figures for men. Aphrodite figures, an hourglass shape, for women. Your golden ratio of broad shoulders to tight abs tells Kira that you're a strong, virile specimen of a man. And therefore, she will want to mate with you. And I wanted her to be very aware that you are an Adonis shape, so I dressed you to accentuate your innate traits."

While on the surface, what White said was repulsive in terms of body shaming and stereotyping beauty, Ty had to tamp down the inner voice that was jumping up and down, cheering the thought that Kira would want to sleep with him.

"Hey, I'm making another pot of coffee. Do you want a cup?"

"No thanks."

Ty could hear White get off the bed and move around the kitchen space.

"I bet if you think back," White said. "When you're in jeans and a T-shirt, you get the most female interest. The women are aware that you are proportionally desirable because you have the makings for fertility— making pretty babies for them and then being able to protect those babies into adulthood. Put on a jacket and confuse that Adonis measurement, and you won't have nearly the same success rate. I think that's why people fall in love in the spring. They're shedding their winter clothes that obscure their ratios. Meh, it's a theory." The water ran at the kitchen area's sink. "And also, for your awareness, Kira is an hourglass shape that closely approximates the golden ratio. So your procreative hormones should be egging you on too."

"I thought you said it was because I looked like her brother figure, that guy Ben. Kira doesn't look anything like my sister."

"Molly? No, the science doesn't support the theory. You just postulated that if a woman ends up with men who look like their brothers, that men in return will end up with women who look like their sisters. At least, I haven't seen any studies that support that. And since I'm of Asian descent and I'm dating a guy whose grandparents are still in Sweden, I'm going to suggest that I prove the point. Now, this is science, but this isn't the science that is consistent across all replications, obviously. And yes, I am slathering it on thick. Your ear ratio, your Adonis proportions, your brother-like face, the meet-cute that approximated a happily ever after movie."

Ty came out of the bathroom with his folded clothes.

"We let her marinate until tomorrow afternoon when you're going to happen upon her at the dog park. We just need to do what we can do based on available scientific data to make Kira fall in love with you by Thursday and invite you on Friday's plane ride to Tanzania."

"No pressure."

"Actually, quite the opposite. Everything depends on your success getting into that compound so we can capture Omar Mohamed Imadi and stop his crusade of terror."

Chapter 15

Ty

There was a knock at his hotel room door. Ty went over and squinted through the peephole—White.

He threw the bolt and opened the door to her. Ty was aware that his muscles had braced.

"Dinnertime," she singsonged. "I thought because of Rory, you might want to eat room service up here." She pushed past him. "And I thought I'd join you, so we can go over the plans for your second meeting with Kira tomorrow."

White walked over to the coffee table and picked up the room service folder, scanning down the page. "I'm going to get the Mediterranean platter." She handed it to Ty to make his selection. Instead of accepting it, he said, "That's fine for me, too."

He waited while White called down their order. She covered the receiver with the flat of her hand. "Thirty minutes. I'm ordering some red wine. Are you drinking that, or do you want something different?"

"Water for me."

Once White hung up the phone, she held out her hand. There was a little white vial resting on her palm.

What now?

"I'm going to jump right in because I don't want to forget these or misplace them."

He picked up the bottle and read the label. He didn't recognize the name printed there.

"You need to use these before you meet Kira in person. They're eye drops. They'll last for an hour."

"PCP?"

"Ha, you wish. No, these are mild dilators. They won't make you look like you've just been to the ophthalmologist. You'll still have visible irises."

Ty curled his hand around them and sent her a questioning look before he walked to the bathroom, placing them next to his Dopp kit.

"Why do you need them?" White called after him. "Because you'll be meeting Kira outside, and it's going to be a sunny day, your pupils will normally be constricted."

"The method behind the madness." He reemerged and headed to the kitchen counter to prep Rory's dinner.

"Unconsciously, the human brain is wired to look at pupil size."

"Is this like the ear thing?" He reached up and tugged on his ear lobe. "She'll think I'm fertile and ready to mate?"

"A little." White slipped off her flip-flops and curled onto the sofa, making herself at home.

Rory trotted over and sniffed her, then jumped on

the bed, thumped his tail a few times as he watched Ty scoop his food from the can.

"When someone looks at the person they care for—love—their pupils dilate. Your dilated pupils will tell Kira's brain that you like her. Humans are hardwired for reciprocity. The hope is, though I have no data to support my hypothesis, that when she sees your enlarged pupils—"

"That sounds politely erotic."

"Enlarged pupils can lead to engorged—"

"Yeah, okay." He put the bowl on the floor and looked over at Rory. "Chow now."

Rory stood up and stretched back into a luxurious down-dog, then leaped to the ground and over to his bowl.

"Say grace," Ty commanded.

Rory wrapped his paws around his snout for the count of three, then looked at Ty. Good enough?

"Okay, buddy. Dig in."

Once the dinner ritual was complete, White continued. "Enlarged pupils have also been shown to make someone trust the other person more."

"I guess that makes sense, someone who loves you should be more trustworthy."

"Should," White replied, and a strange light came into her eyes.

Something niggled in Ty's consciousness. He thought that White had more information about the situation than she was sharing with him. Was someone who supposedly loved Kira acting in an untrustworthy way? Besides potentially him—that was. "So if my pupils dilate, it tells her brain I like her, and her brain tries to like me back?"

"That's the theory. You know we use every tool in

the toolbox. Our lead time is so narrow. We need you in that compound. Today, our allies picked up a phone conversation that verifies that Omar will be heading for Davidson Range at the meeting we had hoped he'd attend. That's a go."

Ty pumped a fist.

"We need that extraction to be seamless. Our best shot at getting him away from his security and under our control alive is through intimate knowledge of the compound, the schedule, the security systems, the guards' actions, and the sleeping arrangements." She stabbed a finger into the air toward Ty. "That's on you. Use the drops."

"I am not sure love is necessary. I can just be friendly and offer her security in a strange land."

"No, soldier." White's gaze hardened. "That is *not* what you're going to do. You are on a mission to manipulate an asset to lead you to a man who means to do America immeasurable harm. You will say, do, look, act any way that is required of you to get Kira to take you with her to Tanzania. Knowing Kira the way I do, the *only* way you're on that plane is if she thinks she's in love with you and you with her, or she won't accept your chivalry. You will do whatever is required. If it means bedding her and giving her such a screaming orgasm that it takes her two days to get her toes uncurled, then *that* is what you'll do."

"Yes, ma'am." This psyops stuff was not his deal. Jumping out of planes and stealing Russian helicopters was how he spent his days. The Casanova shit should be CIA. But he could see the importance of getting a Unit boy over the threshold to see what was going on with security, make a plan, and pass the intel on to his brothers.

"Listen, tomorrow, your assignment is to run from here to the dog park. You passed it yesterday on the way to get ice cream."

He nodded.

"Jog from here to there. It's five kilometers. Take a toy to throw for Rory in the park. You need to be there at fifteen-twenty hours exactly. That's what time Kira gets there every day. I'd like you jogging in from the back of the park, so it looks like complete happenstance that you're showing up there. I want you to invite her to dinner. I've made reservations in your name at The Frog and the Good Ol' Boy."

"That's a restaurant?"

"Fusion southern cuisine with a French flair."

"I can't even imagine what that means. Frog legs and hush puppies?"

"Something like that. Kira loves that restaurant. She goes there when she wants to celebrate something. As far as I know, she's never been there on a date, so it's a clean canvas. You'll wear the outfit with the number four sticky notes—urban chic."

"Yes, Mom. What about Rory while I'm out on that date?"

White tapped her chin as she looked around his room. Her gaze landed on the crate sitting next to the sofa where she was perched. "Can Rory stay in his crate here at the hotel by himself?"

"If he absolutely has to, but Uncle Sam doesn't like the K9s of his caliber to go unattended. That's years of training costs. It's all about the bottom line. Along with public safety."

"I can dog sit him. I'll stay here and keep working. Just text me if you're bringing Kira back to your hotel room after your dinner, and I'll skedaddle. This next step shouldn't be hard. When you saved Princess Beatrice and gave her your ice cream, you created internal pressure for Kira to do something for you in return."

"I'm not trying to be a braggart, but it's rare that I get turned down when I invite a lady out."

"There are low stakes in your normal dating scenarios. There are the highest stakes in this one. And while I can easily see that you wouldn't have any issues wooing a normal lady on a normal day, Kira is not in a normal American woman's position, and this is far from a normal day."

"Are you going to flesh out why she's not a normal American woman?"

"No."

"That makes me uncomfortable."

"So be it. Now, getting to the restaurant. Once there, the lighting will help you make the sale."

"And by sale, you mean me. What has lighting got to do with anything? Forget it—I remember now. Big pupils."

"The Frog and the Good Ol' Boy is right off Route 85 on Falls Lake with huge picture windows. The boats will be sailing by at sunset. Very romantic. And yes, because of the dim lighting, your eyes will adjust by dilating. Her brain will read you as sexually primed, and if you're not a total goon—which you haven't been up until this point—"

"Things can change."

"Granted. Don't be a goon. Play the role of a gentleman. She's old-fashioned. She likes etiquette and chivalry."

"Huh." He reached past White to the side table to grab his water bottle.

"You're fine. I've watched video of you eating. Your

parents obviously made a point of manners at your house."

"Go back. You were going to tell me how to be sure she'd accept my invitation. I might as well get some of this science under my belt. It might come in handy on a mission down the line." He tipped the bottle back.

"Right. So we're going to lean heavily on two psychological knee-jerk reactions. The first one has to do with reciprocity. Before you ask someone for something, you have a far, far better chance of getting what you want if you give a small gift to the other person, then make sure they know you are giving them a gift."

"Shoot." He brought his wrist to his lip to catch a drop of the water, then screwed the cap back on the bottle.

"Why shoot?"

"You did that to me back when you wanted me to take on this assignment."

"You weren't really in a place to deny the mission. JSOC agreed to assist the CIA, so we could, in turn, assist you."

"You gave me the pen in Djibouti. You said, 'This is a gift.' And I thought it a bit odd at the time."

She winked. "And you felt compelled by brain biology to return the perceived debt. It's almost untenable for someone to receive a gift and then not do something reciprocal. Think how terrible you feel when someone gives you a Christmas gift, and you've nothing for them. It haunts you. It's part of our survival biology. You give your mark something—in general, it can be something small, so your target isn't overwhelmed and defensive. A cupcake. A single flower. 'I saw this and thought of you. I wanted you to have this.' You must be sure that they know it's a gift, so no matter how small—a pebble off the ground, 'Here is a gift.'"

"Got it."

"I'm circling around to that in two seconds. But I don't want to forget this part. The next step is to make an ask and add the word 'because.'"

"Because?"

"Exactly."

"No, sorry. I'm asking why I need to use the word 'because.'"

"Studies show that if you ask, you will often be turned down. 'May I go ahead of you in line?' If you ask and you give a reason—'May I go ahead of you in line? I'm meeting someone in the theater.' Still won't get you what you want. For some reason, study after study shows if you simply add the word 'because,' it's very hard for the person you're asking to say 'no' to you. So for example, 'Kira, would you join me for dinner *because* I found a restaurant that I think you might enjoy.'"

"All right, do I tell her the name?"

"Only if she asks at that time. I'd leave it alone. Show up and look surprised when she tells you it's a favorite. Then you need to add a reason you brought her there. Like, 'I read about the views, and I thought you might enjoy watching the boats at sunset.'"

"Got it. To get a 'yes' I simply give someone a small gift and make an ask, including the word 'because.'"

"To that end, at dinner tomorrow, you'll bring a single lavender rose and hand it to her. When you pick her up for your date, say, 'I saw this, and I thought of you.' Oh, before I forget, we had your Land Rover brought up. It's in the parking lot, and the keys are in your underwear drawer. Kira will be more comfortable if she's not riding in the sidecar—long hair and all. Back to the rose." White walked over to the fridge and opened the door, sweeping her hand so he'd look inside at the single rose, wrapped in floral paper with a delicate white ribbon.

"She likes lavender?"

"Maybe." White shut the fridge door and picked up her coffee cup to move over to the sofa. "She's a humanities scholar. She'll have studied the nuances of literature, especially love symbols."

"And so a red rose—"

"Would be cheesy and cheap. Kira probably wouldn't receive it in the way we want her to. On the other hand, lavender is unique, special, and she will know the meaning behind it."

"Which is?"

"Love at first sight. Also, they're called Sterling roses, not lavender. Sterling roses are the only thornless roses, or so I'm told. Double meaning."

"And she'll think this is the message I want to convey—I fell in love at first sight, and I hand you only beauty with no thorns?"

"It will be in her subconscious if not her conscious. I think she'll think it then talk herself out of it. Few men know the meanings behind the flowers they offer. But back in the olden days—the times that Kira focused her studies on—all of polite society would have understood the meanings and would read the offered bouquets as secret communications. People who cared for each other, at the time, weren't allowed to voice their emotions until they were betrothed. Anyway, you know the rose is waiting in your fridge."

He walked over and opened the fridge and lifted it out to smell it. Heady with perfume, Ty had never seen a flower like that, perfectly shaped, with a color he'd never seen on a rose before. He thought it was a good reflection of his first impressions of Kira, graceful, unique, and tender.

Ty caught himself. *Man, you need to get a grip on your inner dialogue. She is not for you. She's a mission. And then you get anti-depressants to get over her.*

Wasn't that a damned disheartening thought in and of itself?

He carefully replaced the rose.

"Good?"

"I think it'll work. All right. I meet her at the door with my gift. Once she accepts it, she owes me. Internal pressure. I wait until later and bring up my ask and use the word 'because.' But the ask is if I can come along to Tanzania."

"If it comes up and she invites you by some miracle. 'Yes, I'd like to join you, *because...*' For example, because you enjoy photography and would like to take some pictures. But other than her asking you to join her, just let that debt fester. It will grow in internal psychological pressure." White smiled.

"Man, that is so manipulative."

"Yup. Manipulation is the name of the game in my line of work."

Chapter 16

Kira

"Now, don't you look nice?" The barista set Kira's glass of iced chai on the table.

Kira smoothed her hand across her deep-rose-colored sundress. It had a tightly fitted bodice, spaghetti straps, and a full skirt that hit just below the knees. On her feet she had matching ballet slippers.

The barista stooped to give Princess Beatrice a bowl of water. When she stood, she looked up and down the street. "Do you think he's coming back today?"

Shoot, maybe she was being too obvious. Was her wardrobe choice too much for a stroll to the café and then the park? Probably. "Whom?" Kira asked innocently.

"Oh, you know, that 100% grade A prime beefcake that was talking to you yesterday. The fella on the cherry-colored bike."

"Oh. No. I don't know. I don't know him."

The barista tucked her tray under her arm. "Looked like he wanted to get to know you. We were all watching through the window." She lifted her hand to shade the sun's glare as she scanned up the road. "I thought for sure he'd be back today."

Kira had thought so too. She'd hoped so. Bobbling her head by way of response, Kira lifted her lips into a Mona Lisa smile. What did you say to something like that?

The barista held up crossed fingers. "You still have time."

Just because he was here yesterday meant little. She'd never seen him before, and she'd most likely never see him again. It made no difference that he had filled her dreams last night with the most erotic fantasies she'd experienced in her whole life. It was just her brain playing games with her now that she had been committed to some stranger. It was her body's way of having a last hoorah before she was tucked away, leaving a sex life behind.

She was twenty-eight and soon would be a dried-up, lonely raisin.

Maybe she'd like her husband, she thought as she sipped her chai. It could be that they'd get along. Kira simply couldn't imagine that to be true. Not someone her uncle Nadir had chosen for her.

This was silly. *She* was silly. Look at her dressed up like this in case a stranger on a red Harley wanted to buy his dog some ice cream.

Pitiful.

Kira downed her chai as quickly as yesterday, then stuck a five-dollar bill under her empty glass. "Come on, Bea. Let's go to the park and wear you out, so I can get my work done this afternoon."

Beatrice toddled happily ahead of Kira as she made her way two blocks up Elm Street, all while Kira was praying under her breath for the sound of a motorcycle.

When they arrived at the park, Kira pulled the latch on the gate up to release the childproof lock, swung the door open, and in they went.

They were alone.

Kira shut the door, then unclasped Beatrice's lead, sticking it safely in her straw bag. Since no one else was there, she dropped the bag by the edge of the eight-foot fence, retrieved Bea's ball, and walked away, leaving it there. "Ready, Bea?"

Beatrice was jumping up on her hind legs, trying to get the ball.

Kira threw it out and watched as Bea chased after it. As the ball hit the fence on the far side of the park, Bea stopped and barked. Kira held a hand up to shade her eyes and saw a runner in the distance. "Leave him alone, Bea. Come on and bring me the ball."

Beatrice grabbed the ball and raced back so Kira would throw it again.

Out went the ball, followed closely with a sprinting Beatrice on her tiny little legs.

Bea grabbed the ball and stalled at the fence, placing the ball down and focusing on the runner. Again she barked high-pitched "come here" barks.

"Bea! The ball!" This time when Kira brought her hand up to look at why Bea was so focused, Kira saw that it was a man running with a dog beside him.

From this distance, she couldn't see his face, but her whole system lit up with buzzing, tingling happiness.

Was it him? The motorcycle guy? She walked toward Beatrice.

The man was running with an athleticism that Kira didn't normally see displayed in this park of senior fast-walkers and a few portly souls who were trying their best. He wore a pair of running shorts and a sleeveless sports shirt. The dog was the right size. It *might* be him.

Kira smoothed her hand over her dress, then her hair.

Beatrice showed up with her ball.

There was a clank at the gate behind them. An elderly man in a Hawaiian shirt and white socks with his sandals was there with his black dog. The dog had a fat collar around his neck attached to his leash.

Kira glanced at her straw bag and decided that she was probably a lot faster than he was if the guy wanted to steal her things. She'd leave it. Her attention was on the runner who was coming up the path toward the dog park.

Was it him?

Bea jumped up and barked.

Kira realized she was holding Bea's ball over her head for the throw and was just standing there like an idiot. "Sorry, sweetie, here you go." She tossed out the ball, and Beatrice chased after it.

As soon as Beatrice had the ball in her mouth, a whir of black raced past Kira.

The Hawaiian-shirt man's dog was off his lead, and the beast was focused on getting to Bea.

Kira shrieked and chased after the dog, trying to outrace the charging dog. The closer she got, the bigger the dog seemed. What was she going to do? She spun around and didn't immediately see the old man. "Hey!" she yelled. "Hey! Call off your dog!"

"Stop running!" the athlete was hollering at her.

"Stop! Stand still!" His gait turned from jog to sprint as he headed toward her.

How could she stand still when the black dog had trapped Beatrice in the corner? Bea had her ball clamped between her teeth and was shivering against the fence.

"Rory, jump!" the athlete yelled.

His dog was already off his lead and was racing ahead of the man toward the fence. It was so tall that Kira couldn't reach the top of it.

Jump?

What was this man asking his dog to do?

Kira was still running for Beatrice. Beatrice was still whimpering in the corner.

The black dog had spread his legs wide and was crouched low, growling at Beatrice, when Rory leaped into the air, twisted, and flung his body into the dog's area.

"Rory, hold the fort! Hold the fort!" the athlete called. He was almost to her.

Hold the fort? What in the world? Kira slowed, gasping, trying to understand this scene.

Rory jumped between shivering Beatrice and— "Oh my goodness, he's a rottweiler!"

Rory pulled back his lips. His growl was ferocious. White foam bubbled along the corners of his mouth. Hackles up.

Breathless, Kira focused on Princess Beatrice. Bea was London's first baby. Her friend *loved* this dog. London called daily to Facetime with her pup. Kira absolutely could not allow anything to happen to her.

Sliding along the fence, she was desperate to protect Bea.

The rottweiler jumped forward, biting at the air.

Kira crouched over Beatrice, wrapping her body

around the quivering pup. She tucked her head and clung to the fence bars.

Rory held the black dog at bay, but surely this couldn't last. One dog or the other was going to lunge, and she'd be in the middle of a dog fight.

"Stay still, ma'am. Don't move," the man called out. He was right beside her now, but the gate was way far away on the other side of the dog park. One way in. One way out.

She hugged Beatrice tight to her chest.

Clanging had her peeping from under her arm, and she realized the man was simply crawling up the fence.

"Hold the fort, Rory!"

Was he coming to protect his own dog? That didn't make sense. He'd commanded his dog to jump over the fence. He must be coming to help *her*.

The rottweiler circled to the side to get around Rory.

Rory was having none of it.

For every step the rotti took toward Kira, Rory took two aggressive steps to stave him off.

The man jumped. As he came over the fence, he landed in a crouch, then toppled into a roll and up on his feet again like a Ninja. *Wow!*

Holding Beatrice tight to her chest, Kira stood, thinking if worse came to worse, maybe she could throw Beatrice to the other side of the fence, and the pup would be safe.

It was a ridiculous notion.

Kira wasn't equipped with the skills to throw fifteen pounds into the air. And Beatrice was not the kind of dog who could figure out what to do to land safely.

The man came up beside Rory, taking almost the same posture of wide-spread legs, crouching low. His arms were held wide on either side of him.

Now, it was Rory and the man against the rottweiler, and the rotti looked uncertain.

Kira pressed herself against the fence, trying to keep out of their way and not be a distraction. She was trembling as hard as Beatrice.

The teeth on that dog!

"Go!" The man shouted and smacked his hands together hard as he leaped forward.

The rottweiler circled away from him, barking in a low rumble of anger that Kira could feel in her teeth.

"Go!" He tried again.

Rory was fearless. Kira thought he was just waiting for the man to give him the directive, and this was going to turn into a full-pitched dog attack. Kira could do nothing to help except pay for vet bills. What a horrific thought. She didn't want anyone getting injured on account of her.

Kira focused on Beatrice and realized the pup still had her green ball trapped in her comparably itty-bitty teeth. Kira wrenched the ball from Bea's jaw, held it toward the rotti, and yelled, "Fetch!"

The rottweiler watched the ball sail over his head and turned to chase it down.

As he ran to the ball, the old man in his Hawaiian shirt showed up. "Hey, sorry about that," he called.

She watched the rotti go over and hand him the ball. He clipped the lead to his dog, tossed the ball back toward her, and they left. Just. Like. That.

Kira couldn't believe it. The nerve of that man!

"Hey, hey, hey." A warm male voice pulled her head around.

There he was.

He was even more gorgeous than yesterday. Kira

thought she was going to swoon in the most ridiculous Regency romance way.

"Hey, you're squeezing her too tightly."

Now Kira could hear the high-pitched rebuke that Beatrice was yipping.

The man loosened her arms, which was good, because her body had forgotten how to function.

He set Beatrice gently on the ground.

Rory came over and sniffed at her.

A warm hand was on her arm. "Are you okay? Were you hurt?"

She didn't think she was in shock from the dog attack, maybe a little. It was just that…

"Where are your shoes? This park is full of dog mess."

She looked down at her bare feet. She must have run right out of her shoes and hadn't even noticed.

Could she not get herself together?

"Stay put. I'll find them."

Off went Studly in search of her shoes, and Kira let out an exhale. With her hands on her head, Kira leaned back, looking at the sky.

How could this be happening to her?

She was gobsmacked. She was over the moon. She was an idiot.

Kira shook herself to break the spell and walked in the direction the man had headed.

Just over the rise, there he was with her shoes dangling from his fingers as he made his way back to her.

It was oddly intimate for him to have his fingers in her shoes.

He held them up so she could see. "Are you okay?" he asked again as he approached.

"Thank you." She looked back at the fence, taking in how high it was. "That was some heroic action. Your dog is…you are…" And for the first time in her life, Kira seemed to have lost her ability to speak the English language.

Studly stood in front of her, and she looked up into his eyes.

Beautiful eyes. Sincere, curious, concerned eyes.

They were a dark chocolatey brown made almost black by the size of his pupils. In them, she could imagine she saw affection and honesty shining back at her.

"I'm Kira." *Brilliant conversationalist.* "Uhm, thank you." She reached for her shoes.

"Tyler Newcomb," he said in return, lightly holding her elbow to steady her while she stooped to brush some of the dirt from her foot and put her shoe back on. She noticed that he had strange bruises on his arms and wondered how he had gotten them.

"Most everyone calls me Ty." He turned his head and chuckled. "It's like Lady and the Tramp."

Kira turned to see what had amused him.

Rory and Beatrice each held the end of a long stick and were running side by side. Beatrice running her little legs off, and Rory trotting gently by her side.

"Hold the fort?" Kira asked.

"I'm a K9 handler at Fort Bragg."

She nodded.

"The guy who handled Rory before I did was a SEAL who had decided that instead of training his dogs in German or another language, that he'd make up his own words. I had to learn all of Rory's quirky commands. 'Hold the fort' means to not let the enemy approach. Basically, *en garde*."

"Oh, clever. But why is Rory with you? Is the SEAL okay?"

"That SEAL is now a dog handler for a group called

Cerberus K9 at Iniquus. His SEAL days were cut short when he got sick, and it affected his lung capacity." His voice was so calm. And while he sent tingles up and down her spine with the newness of discovery, she also felt like she'd known him all her life. That he was safe. That she was safe *with* him. It was uncanny.

"It's hard to jump out of planes at high altitude," Ty said, "or swim long distances like SEALs need to on the job when you have a diminished lung capacity."

"Oh, heartbreaking." Kira turned her hand so that as he held her arm, she could hold him, as well.

"He's good. It all works out."

Suddenly, this guy felt ill at ease to her. The end of the small talk. Crisis over. Now they were just two strangers in a park.

She should let him go.

But she absolutely didn't want to. "I've interrupted your workout. But I'm so grateful." She stopped and blinked. She wanted to thank him. Two days in a row saving Beatrice and, by extension, her. She *owed* him something for his rescues, and she couldn't figure out how to repay him. But she certainly couldn't let him walk away again.

"I'm in town because old Rory is getting ready to go out on a personal protection assignment. He's been in theater—uh, out in the boonies working. And I need to make sure that he's practiced his good manners. So I'm here in town for the week."

Kira nodded. That probably explained his bruises. She couldn't ask him about that, it was too personal of a question. She needed to think of *something* to say. "I live a few blocks from here." Okay, that was something. Kira rolled her eyes at herself. She held an open palm in the direction of her house, thinking she could ask him for a glass of iced tea. But how lame was that?

They looked at the dogs, still running with their stick. "We don't eat that well at Fort Bragg. There aren't a wide variety of restaurants in my area. I was wondering, Kira, if you would keep me company at dinner tonight *because* I found a place up on the lake that looks like it's got an interesting fusion going on."

"Oh, yes." She sent him a radiant smile. "I would enjoy that."

"I'll walk you home then *because* that way I'll know where to pick you up. Will seven work? My reservation is for seven-thirty."

Chapter 17

Ty

When Ty saw White lying on his bed like yesterday, unfamiliar rage filled his system. He slammed the door shut.

Rory spun to look at him, startled and on guard.

"You did that, didn't you?" Ty pointed his finger aggressively at White.

White yawned and stretched, not giving two shits that he was *pissed*. "You'll have to be more specific."

"You had a hundred-twenty-pound rottweiler squaring off with a hundred-and-twenty-pound untrained woman and her twelve-pound spaniel."

White pulled up her legs to sit cross-legged, moving her computer to the side. "Surely, you saw the radio collar, and you knew the dog was following commands."

"That was a dangerous game you played." He felt his system expand. That damned scene was too risky, Kira racing to save Beatrice like that, both admirably self-less and naïve. "Rory is trained to kill. Can you imagine what would have happened if Rory ripped the jugular out of that dog's throat in front of Kira? Or worse, if something had happened to Beatrice? That would be the image Kira saw every time I was near, and she'd run for the woods. It was counterproductive and hazardous as hell—for K9s and humans alike. That could have become a shit show in the blink of an eye. Don't mess around in things that you obviously know nothing about, like K9 behavior."

"You have control over Rory."

"Look, I told you, if I hold someone or take care of someone, Rory sees them as part of his pack. He will protect them. Yesterday, at the ice cream place—you saw it on your videos—I picked up Beatrice and gave her licks off Rory's ice cream. What do you think Rory took away from that? Then I handed Rory's ice cream and the dog to Kira. Do you know how smart Rory is? Do you think that scene passed by him unnoticed?"

Rory was sitting by Ty's side glaring at White, adding his own disapproval, his lip twitching like he wasn't sure if he should growl at her too.

"At the time, I thought your plan was a good thing," Ty said. "It would make introducing Rory to Kira and Beatrice that much simpler. I had no idea you were going to pull that crap in the dog park. That could have gone FUBAR in an instant." He snapped his fingers.

"But it didn't."

"This isn't a game, lady."

"Oh, of that, I am very aware, thank you, First Sergeant Newcomb." She turned and punched up her pillows, shifting them around behind her until she was more comfortable, taking a moment, Ty assumed, to think.

"He had a zap collar, a radio collar, and a handler," she offered.

"Have you ever seen a Malinois train a takedown?" His bladed hands came to rest on his hips.

"Yes."

He held out the flat of his left hand and stabbed his index finger into his palm to punctuate each of his points. "Speed. Force of will. Single-minded focus. Your buddy with his shock collar and voice command would have zero—and hear me when I say this, White—he would have had *zero* shot of breaking up two dogs as powerful and as tenacious as those dog breeds are. Rory was guarding his pack—me, Kira, and Beatrice."

Rory decided he needed to add his two cents. A growl rumbled in his chest, then he gave two sharp warning barks.

Ty put his hand on Rory's head, and he quieted but not without a stomp of his foot to show he was displeased with what was happening.

"I hear you. Okay?" White said. "I'm sorry. I should have passed that by you. My thinking was that you would be more natural if you didn't know."

"But you did it on purpose."

"Ty." She tipped her head to the side and sent him a patient smile. "Look, you have to remember we are tasked with pulling a magic rabbit out of a hat. You have to go from complete stranger to trusted, comfortable, wonderful person with only two more days to go. By Thursday night, you must be invited by Kira onto the Davidsons' jet and fly to the boogieman on Friday. There are more than the normal hurdles to get you there."

"Name one."

"You're a man, and she's a woman. She will be traveling to a Muslim part of the country. It's indiscreet. That has ramifications to her honor."

Ty tipped his head back as he processed. He'd worked in a half-dozen Muslim countries. He knew that there could be backlash against a woman who was seen with, let alone traveled with, a man who was not her relative.

"Kira is stressed. She's overwhelmed. She's imbued in her personal crisis. You have to puncture through that with such a force that she can't ignore you. It will take every manipulation I can conjure up to get you invited onto that plane. And that moment of fear was necessary."

"How exactly?"

When Ty pushed his hips back against the lowboy and crossed his arms over his chest, Rory looked up at him, read the change of mood, sent one more suspicious glance toward White, then lay down at Ty's feet.

"It's a play on social science that indicates that one of the brain systems that affect falling in love is stimulated by adrenaline and norepinephrine. Typically couples stimulate those hormones while they date by trying exciting and novel things together. Let's try this new restaurant. Let's go…wherever. It's the doing of novel things while depending on each other that gets the job done."

"And that's your idea of exciting?"

"Sure, well, she had an adrenaline dump."

"So did I."

"Yeah, sorry. Are you taking the antidepressants?"

Ty tipped his head.

"I'm pretty certain Kira has never been center stage at a dog fight before. That checks two boxes. And I was able to check a third one from a different study. That one says that when things went well, Kira—and you, again, sorry—would produce dopamine. Dopamine is the neurotransmitter that is secreted when falling in love. Oh!"

She clambered off the bed and went to the kitchen cabinet, where she pointed at a white box with a deep rose-colored satin ribbon. It was the same-colored ribbon as the dress and shoes Kira was wearing earlier.

"You said you weren't going to video us."

White opened her eyes wide. "I didn't."

"How'd you choose this color of ribbon?"

"Oh, well, I had a watcher photographing Kira at the coffee shop, so I could cue my helpers to be in place at the dog park."

"Chocolate and love?"

"Chocolate produces dopamine and endorphins." She waggled her brow. "And so does good sex."

He skipped over the sex comment and pointed at the box. "Take that with the rose? It feels like I'm trying too hard."

"Nope, you're right. Rose tonight, chocolates are for the next step."

"Which is?" Ty turned to get Rory's dinner together. He had just enough time to feed and walk Rory, get Rory settled in his crate, and get himself spiffed up and down the road to show up at exactly nineteen hundred hours for Kira.

His heart started pounding at the thought.

"Tonight, let the conversation be warm and comfortable, basic get to know you banter. Remembering you just met her and know *nothing* about her. Also, remember to spend most of the time listening. Ask questions that you're genuinely interested in hearing about.

Kira can read you like a book. And she has a PhD. in book reading."

Rory was watching Ty's preparations with intensity.

"I'm okay with not speaking." He cracked the spoon on the side of the metal bowl to dislodge the meat then rinsed the spoon under the faucet. "Chow now." He set the bowl on the sliver of kitchen tile flooring.

Rory came over and sat in front of his bowl.

"Say grace," Ty commanded.

Rory wrapped his paws around his snout. Ty counted to three then said, "Okay, buddy. Dig in."

"To further trigger Kira's brain to see you as trustworthy and connected, you'll have to uphold your side of the conversation. I'm not worried about that. But I'd like you to be aware of your body. Humans tend to mirror each other—it's a natural inclination. You need to do it consciously. It's believed to help make strong social bonds."

"You don't think that will make her feel…odd?" He leaned back and crossed his arms over his chest.

He saw landmines ahead. Danger signs.

While there was a lot more that White was obviously not sharing, Ty thought she was giving him an extra slice of the need-to-know pie. White surely had her reasons. And it probably had to do with her setting him up to fall in love with a Qatari princess—royal, whatever. He had to understand, and he needed to own this as fact: Kira was *not* for him.

She could *never* be for him.

And if he were to fall in love with her—and boy could he see that as a real possibility—his love would be a burden to bear and nothing else.

He turned and washed his hands at the sink.

Yeah, given his druthers, he'd rather parachute into

a tree, run from rebel rifle strafe, throw himself into a helicopter that might or might not be flyable any day rather than be given *this* particular mission. He'd never been ordered into anything like this position. His job was about intellectual and physical challenges. Emotions had little space on the battlefield.

Ty had been thinking about Kira non-stop since the ice cream scheme. He couldn't wait for his next task so he could spend more time just being near her.

Man, this was going to hurt bad.

"Get dressed," White said. "Outfit four."

Ty went to the closet. There, he pulled out a pair of dark grey trousers and a long-sleeved light blue silk shirt. Belt. Shoes. Quality. Simple. The pants looked small…

He started toward the bathroom.

"Hey, undershorts and socks. Number four."

"Seriously?"

"In case you get lucky."

"Your job sucks."

"At least you understand it's my job and not me." She smiled warmly. "Just like I know you're not a stone-cold psychopath who enjoys killing people. I know that killing people is your day job, and you come home at night and focus on other things."

"Fair, I guess. I'm going to hop in the shower." He pulled the drawer open and gathered the items.

A lot was riding on his ability to pull this off. And—who was he kidding—this was middle school girl jitters. Kira made him nervous in a way that hadn't been part of his world since he was twelve and had a crush on his sister Molly's dance friend Nina.

After he dried off, he opened the door again so they could talk.

"So I don't know what happened from the point you left the dog park until you came back here. Want to catch me up?" White asked.

"She was shaky. I walked her home. She invited me in for a glass of iced tea, showed me the project she's working on, and I left."

"Oh good! You quite literally got your foot in the door. That's an important persuasion technique."

"Do I want to hear this? Sounds like something about vampires."

"I'm...not following."

"Isn't that part of vampire lore? That a vampire can't come into your house and suck your blood unless the person invited you into their home?"

"Oh, ha! Okay. Yeah, maybe in a way. It's a cognitive reflex since she invited you in. Her unconscious decision-making means she wanted you inside and moving to the next stage. Humans don't like to change trajectories. So once we're heading down this path—which you are doing very nicely—unless you somehow screw this up, we'll continue to make strides."

"And that next step? How am I going to get her to ask me to Tanzania with her?"

"We need to scare her about her safety in Africa. Little by little. To make her feel vulnerable. And twice now, she's depended on your protection. Trajectories. It will make perfect sense that in her mind, she'll be safe with you around. You and Rory. To that end, at dinner tonight, you're going to bring up a friend of yours who is traveling in Africa."

"All right. Can I name a name?"

"Nitro is fine. You need to make her feel vulnerable based on what you've heard about what's going on over there. For example, just today, the Italian diplomat to the Republic of Congo was killed with his security forces when a kidnapping attempt went bad. Republic of Congo doesn't border Tanzania, of course, and she knows that. But you could then say that unrest has been problematic, and America hopes those attacks aren't going to cross the borders. Now, caution, if Kira says she's headed to Tanzania, you can't tell her dangerous things about being in Africa. As soon as she says anything about her upcoming trip, you listen, and you ask questions, but you don't tell her she will be in danger. She needs to come to that conclusion on her own. I'll monitor to see what comes of it. If she needs more push, I'll make a plan."

"Give me some other talking points," Ty said as he pulled the pants on.

"I mentioned that Kira holds a doctoral degree in the humanities. Her master's thesis was on Jane Austen and included other Regency writers. The Regency period in England was the time when King George was mentally incapable of the requirements of the crown, so his son, a future King George—and don't ask me which numbers they are, I'm lucky to have held on to these details."

"Okay." Huh. Ty would never have picked these pants off the rack. They were a slim fit, where he preferred the comfort of moving room. He turned this way and that in the mirror. They looked damned good, he'd admit it. And they'd definitely accent that Adonis ratio White told him about.

"The son George ruled England as a regent somewhere in the environs of Austen's writing in the first two decades of the eighteen-hundreds."

"So she likes that." He slid the shirt from the padded hanger and pulled the soft fabric up his arm. It felt like a whisper on his skin.

"What?"

"I'm imagining wealthy men rushing to the rescue of ladies in distress."

White paused. "There might be a bit of that in there, sure. She doesn't need wealth. So it would just be the lady in distress bit. And that picture isn't an accurate one."

"You've come to another conclusion." He was working on the tiny buttons. His calluses were snagging the material.

"Yes, actually. Kira's father had an accident that killed him the winter of her college freshman year. From what I can gather, her dad was comfortable in America and Western models of women's freedoms. This isn't true of her mother, Hamina. Hamina moved to Qatar to be with her deceased husband's family under her husband's older brother Nadir. The same older brother who considers himself to be Kira's protector and is in charge of arranging a marriage for Kira."

"The start of a good Regency novel?"

"Qatar is modern in some ways—women dress modestly but are not required to wear head coverings, for example. Most of the women are college-educated. It's the wealthiest country in the world per capita. Women can own a business and drive, but on the other hand, there's Sharia. How's everything fitting?"

"I'll be out in a second, and you can judge for yourself."

"Kira's dad worked long hours, and Kira's main parental influence was from her mother. Hamina met and married—with Hamina's father's permission—while she was in college. The Taliban in Iraq killed Hamina's family. For Hamina, going against the norm is deadly, and surely, she taught that philosophy to her daughter.

As soon as Hamina's husband died, the brother Nadir came to America, sold her home, packed up Hamina, and moved her to the family compound in Doha to be with her sisters-in-law. Nadir gave Kira permission to stay at Duke and study."

"Big of him." Ty reached down his pants to tuck in his shirt. "And you're tying this into Kira's choice of studies?"

"I am. It's a guess. Kira understood that there would be familial pressures brought against her to conform to the norms of Qatari society. And she's comfortable enough with Qatar, having grown up between America and long family visits there. I think as she studied, she found understanding of women's situations—the obligations to family and to the norms in 19th century women's writings. Perhaps she was trying to find a way to manage her own situation."

Ty emerged from the bathroom as he slid his belt through the loops.

"Very nice," White said with a nod.

"I don't understand why she couldn't get a job in the U.S. and visit her family from time to time."

"Kira's father loved America. He embraced a lot of our culture but balanced it with the traditions he was raised with. One tradition exercised by his family was the separate lives of women and men and that continued in his own home here in the U.S. Another tradition that he kept was being the protector and provider for his family as he would have been in Qatar. His providing for Hamina and Kira after his death would be an extension of that obligation to provide and yet allowed the women to stay in America. Kira could live comfortably on the yearly interest income from her trust fund. But her dad is dead, and her family is insistent."

"What did he do?"

"He was a chemical engineer, and he liked the idea of living on what he could make with his own talents. You know he was a member of the royal family." She held out a hand. "Peripherally. And that's where the wealth came from. In the will, that money was distributed between Hamina and Kira. But the uncle has control of Hamina's wealth, and Kira's future husband would control her inheritance should she ever marry and live in Qatar as her family wishes Kira to do."

"I have to walk Rory. I'll be back in five minutes," Ty said when his eye caught on the digital display on the alarm clock. He didn't want to hear another word about how Kira was going to be exploited. He had no control over any of that.

Ty needed to get into the compound in Tanzania. That was it.

With Rory on his lead, they headed out the door.

When he came back to the room, White looked up from her computer. "Good?"

"Good enough." He signaled Rory into his crate, then Ty brushed his hands over his slacks to remove any Rory hairs.

He opened his drawer to get his vehicle keys.

"Text me if you're bringing Kira back to your room tonight, and I'll skedaddle," White said, sending an appraising eye over Ty. "You look nice. Don't forget your rose."

Chapter 18

Kira

Kira fingered the silks and lace in her lingerie drawer. She could play this one of two ways: She could choose the cotton high rise underpants she wore when she went to yoga, knowing that she wouldn't likely show those off to a lover their first time together, or…

She picked up a pair of indigo satin and lace panties that were her very most flattering—Kira bit at her lips. "I'm doing this, aren't I?" she asked Beatrice.

Pulling out the matching demi-bra, a smile curled onto her lips. She had been curious about Ty in bed since he rumbled his Harley up Elm Street. Yes, it reminded her of her favorite movie, and yes, that movie had a happily ever after that she didn't expect for herself. But still, if this was her last chance to choose her sexual partner, she wanted to bang Ty.

Kira had been with some good-looking men—*but my*

goodness, Ty was spectacular. His muscles, his graceful movements, his obvious intellect, his gentlemanly
demeanor. He was the whole package—the fantasy.

Something about Ty's face seemed so familiar to
Kira as if she'd always known him. And that familiar-
ity made her feel comfortable with him.

Strong and virile, Kira wondered what kind of dad
he would make. Well, watching him with Rory told her
a lot about his calm, steady demeanor.

Even in a crisis, Ty was cool under pressure. Capable.

Instead of working on her book project that afternoon, Kira had primped for their dinner together. She'd
whitened her teeth, deep conditioned her hair, exfoli-
ated, buffed, and moisturized. Now, she needed to find
a dress to wear. Something that said sophisticated and
fun, lady-like but also pick me up and toss me onto my
bed, I'm ready.

Was that too much to ask of one dress?

She opened the drawer on her bedside table and
pulled out the condom box. One lonely condom shook
into her hand. It had been a while since she'd last had a
boyfriend. She checked the expiration date—three more
days. It seemed like serendipity for Ty to show up now.

She laid the condom within easy reach by the lamp
on her bedside table. The last one—she had just the one
shot. She laughed.

Maybe Ty had one in his wallet. Maybe things would
go really well, and he'd run to the pharmacy and get a
whole box.

If Ty was willing, Kira would fill her memory with
pictures of him on top of her, making her gasp with
pleasure.

The evening so far had been wonderful. Their can-
dlelit table for two was set beside an enormous plate

glass window. With the low ambient lights, the diners were treated to the gorgeous sunset over the lake and the sailboats that dotted the dark waters.

Kira and Ty had laughed their way through appetizers and dinner with easy banter. Ty was telling Rory stories, and Kira was talking about some of the crazy experiences she had when she traveled.

"So Kira, I'm wondering how you would describe yourself," Ty said, changing the mood.

Interesting question. So he wanted to get to know her better, was her assessment.

Most people asked this would simply say their school and work background, perhaps list their hobbies. They'd already talked their way through that, so he wanted something deeper, she guessed. How exactly would she describe herself? "Admirable but flawed." She laughed. And not liking that bent to the conversation, she took a sip of her red wine and changed the subject. "Are you reading anything interesting right now?"

"I'm working on two books, *Thus Spoke Zarathustra* and *Frankenstein*."

"Those two works are nothing alike. I studied *Frankenstein* for my master's thesis on Jane Austen."

"Mary Shelley and Jane Austen, do they have anything in common? I mean besides being women writers from the same period?" Ty asked.

"For my thesis, I was actually studying Mary Shelley's mother."

"Also a writer?"

"Not of fiction. Her name was also Mary—Mary Wollstonecraft. She was an English philosopher."

He leaned back in his chair. "I'm familiar with her work. She was an early advocate for women's rights."

"I'm impressed." She beamed a smile at him. Kira

had never dated a man who could discuss eighteenth-century female philosophers. "How it applies to my thesis was that Jane Austen was familiar with Mary Wollstonecraft's writings and incorporated as fiction some of those thoughts. Were you a philosophy major?"

"I'm not a classically educated man. I went to one semester of college, and I knew it was absolutely not for me. I've been in the Army ever since, sixteen years now."

"You're reading Nietzsche. That's rather esoteric stuff." She posted her elbows on the table, laced her fingers, and settled her chin on top. "What's one of your favorite quotes from him?"

Ty smoothed the napkin on his lap and looked out at the waterway. The sun had sunk below the horizon, and the boat lights glowed in the twilight. After a moment, he said, "Whatever is done for love always occurs beyond good and evil."

"Beyond good and evil…" Kira frowned, looking down at the table, processing. "Hmm. I'm going to have to think about that." She brought her eyes back up to meet his gaze. "That's a very male perspective, and I believe most women would disagree."

"I'd like to learn why." He looked concerned. "I was speaking with a colleague, and she mentioned a quote from the writer Margaret Atwood. I haven't seen it written. I think it went that 'while men are afraid women will laugh at them—'"

"'Women are afraid the men will kill them.' Yes, it's true." She let her finger trace up and down the stem of her wine glass. "When you, as a man, go out on a date, you probably think, I hope I have an enjoyable time, and we get along well. Women run through a checklist, have their phones fully charged, call three friends telling them where they are and when they expect to be home. Sometimes they plan check-in times throughout the date. I have a friend who sends me a picture of the guy's license plate, so if she disappears, we know who to send the police to."

"Wow. I... I don't know what to say to that. That's upsetting to learn. Who did you call tonight?"

"No one." Kira blushed. "Normally, I do. This time, it never occurred to me. Maybe it has to do with you showing up wearing your superhero cape twice now." She winked, so he knew not to take that too seriously, though she most *certainly* did.

He had worked his way into her system. She had no fear of him, not even a drop.

Kira couldn't have felt safer.

Time to change the subject away from rape and murder. It dampened the mood, and she had a condom waiting on her bedside table. "You were talking about the books you're reading and mentioned *Thus Spoke Zarathustra*. I have a friend who has that book and has been reading it for five years."

"Yeah? He or she is getting a lot out of it? Five years? Are they writing a thesis on Nietzsche or something? I can only stomach so much nihilism. It's not a philosophy I agree with."

"A thesis? Not even a little bit. He uses it to fall asleep at night. One page and out." She snapped her fingers.

"I lose interest pretty quick if a book isn't challenging me. I'm enjoying this one, but it's not my usual read."

"What is your usual read? Books about K9 behavior?"

"I do that for my job. My reading is for me. I like to build up a 3D understanding of the world. Science, architecture, politics of all bents, government and idea leaders—those that I agree with and those that I will fight with every ounce of my being to stop."

"Those are intellectual fights for you, though, aren't they? I mean, you said you're at Fort Bragg as a K9 trainer?" Sudden fear for his safety wrapped her throat as she remembered how bruised his arms were.

He sat silently, and Kira thought he was choosing his words carefully. "I fight the way the Army asks me to fight. I don't have a lot of say about how and where they use my skills." He reached out and crossed his knife and fork on his plate to signal the server they were finished with dinner. "I raised my hand to be a dog handler. And I'm where I want to be. If the Army asks me to go somewhere, I'll go. I'm proud to do my part in making the world a safer, more equitable place."

"You've been stationed in the Middle East? Does your safer world extend to Muslims like me?"

"I've spent a great deal of my time in the Army stationed and working in the Middle East and Africa. It's not a religious fight. It's a fight against terror and repression. A fight to protect women and other vulnerable people, children, the disabled..." His sincerity was visible in the warmth of his eyes. "No matter where we live in the world, we should all be safe to enjoy our homes, our families, and yes, our personal beliefs. As Americans, we have freedom of religion as part of our Constitution. I believe in that right, or I would never have raised my hand and sworn to defend those ideals." He tipped his head. "Are you of the Muslim faith?"

She took a sip of wine. Under other circumstances, this shift in their conversation might have felt heavy, but here that wasn't the sense Kira was picking up. It was almost like the fluffy first date topics didn't satisfy him. Like Ty wasn't using this dinner as a means to get into her bed. Though, that's absolutely where she wanted him. And he wanted more.

"I'm a bit of a chameleon," she said. "I see the beauty and truth in the warmth of the Muslim faith. I'm not a staunch adherent. My sense of spiritual connection is strong, whether I refer to my maker as Allah or as God or another title." Kira looked around as the server lowered her tray, collecting their dirty dishes and utensils. "I guess I just keep working at being a good person and true to the experience I'm having with this body— gender, health—" Kira concluded after the server went away.

"And beauty."

She sent him a smile. "Looks are to be overcome, aren't they? Good looks can create problems as much as people who struggle with their looks. I have friends who are considered absolutely gorgeous, like my friend London for example. You would think that their looks are a positive, but they all have very low self-esteem. They fear the time when their looks no longer serve them, and they'll be judged on their merits and they feel shaky about being judged for other attributes, like intelligence and skill. It's not voiced, it's something I intuit, and I could always be wrong."

"Doubtful, you seem very tuned-in to me." Ty sat back as the server was back with their dessert. She placed chocolate lava cakes in front of them. "Thank you," he said, and Kira noticed he looked the woman in the eye, and his words were genuine. Kira liked that.

"Tell me more about that idea," Ty said as the server retreated.

She shrugged. "As far as looks go?" Kira picked up her spoon and waggled it over her cake. She wanted to eat it, but she also didn't want to be overly full if this evening led to sexy time. "Sometimes I question my interactions. How people treat me. I want them to focus on the part of me that strives to be a good person, a brain, and a heart, not a face. To that end, I don't often wear makeup. And sometimes, I really like wearing traditional Middle Eastern clothing like I do in Qatar, where my family lives. It's a unifying uniform—perhaps a bit like your Army. But, for me, it also challenges the idea of being an individual. So there's disquiet in my soul about dressing that way. It's why I don't wear the shayla and abaya unless I'm over there, and even then, it depends on where I'm going and what I'm doing. The dress code simply asks for modesty."

"Do you like Qatar?"

"I love my family dearly. I love the food. Oh my goodness, so delicious." She stopped to smile, remembering the amazing buffets her aunts would set out for their guests. "I love many of the traditions. The music. The literature. The Persian Gulf." She fingered the strand of pearls around her neck—ubiquitous to traditionally Southern women in the United States but also important to the Qatari culture. "Yes, there are many aspects of Qatar that I enjoy. But I love the four seasons in North Carolina. I adore the lushness of June when I hike the Appalachians. July here is a bit humid but compared to Qatar's humidity, this is quite bearable." She spooned up a taste of the hot chocolate decadence and closed her eyes as she savored the taste.

When she opened her eyes, Ty was smiling at her with merry eyes and little laugh wrinkles.

They stared at each other for a long moment until Kira suddenly felt shy, blinked, and turned her head toward the sound of a boat horn. She finally felt brave again and turned back to look at Ty. "I do love boating on the Persian Gulf." She looked down at her lap, remembering the princess from Bahrain who had just sent out her hostage video, held captive in her room for two years since her attempted escape on her friend's yacht in the gulf heading toward the Arabian Sea.

Kira folded her hands into her lap, and the animation in her body melted away.

She was firmly wedged between a rock and a hard place.

Meeting Ty was making it tougher on her.

She had prayed all the way through her university years for a deep and abiding love to find her. If she had *just* found Mr. Right, she would have been free of this quandary.

That didn't happen.

Now, her uncle was calling an end to Kira's opportunity to find her soulmate.

Then, as if the universe was laughing at her, Ty landed in front of her.

She could easily see herself falling in love with Ty. Kira could well imagine what life could have been had he shown up oh, six or seven months ago. If they married, she could have lived in her little house when or if Ty went somewhere on an assignment, and she could be with him at the fort, which was just an hour up the street, when he was in town. She'd spend her days working on her literary projects and raising their children.

Ah, make-believe and fiction.

Kira wasn't even sure that if she defied her uncle that William would allow London to be her friend—given his close work with her uncle Nadir.

London was cautious not to displease William since his brain operation last fall and certainly since their baby's birth. Kira thought that there was love between them, but also that London wanted to secure her new lifestyle for herself and for her son. After all, London was something like wife number five—not in the sense that men in Arab countries took multiple wives but as a matter of William's string of divorces.

London's stepdaughter Christen had a mom who fled that uber-rich lifestyle with her daughter in tow.

Christen seemed happy enough.

Kira had met Christen when they were both members of London's bridal party. The woman's strength to do as she pleased with her life had been a source of jealousy for Kira.

And there sat Ty, patiently letting her ruminate. *Focus on the now, Kira. It's really all you've got.*

"I changed the subject on you." She forced a smile. "This started as a conversation about how one's looks affect them. You're by all measures an attractive man." Kira was gratified when he ducked his head modestly.

Most men she knew, when told how handsome they looked, absorbed the compliment as fact. "Do you find it a boon or an anchor?" Her tone turned mildly teasing. She thought she'd done a good job changing the subject from her morose contemplation of what her future held.

"My looks don't really come into play in my life. It's mostly the dogs and me, and frankly, the scruffier and stinkier I am, the better they like me. Old Rory likes me best when I smell like a wet goat."

"Ah, so you showered because you're on leave?"

"I'm on the clock. I'm training Rory to remember his polite company behaviors, and that includes being around people who bathe." He laughed. "You're not eating your cake. Do you not like it? Shall I order something else?"

"We ordered dessert with our meal when my stomach was grumbling. I simply can't take another bite." Oh, she was hungry all right, just not for cake.

Ty lifted his hand to signal for the check.

They were both quiet as they finished up in the restaurant. Ty placed his hands on the back of her chair as she stood; his manners were impeccable.

They took the side door out of the Frog and the Good Ol' Boy. It was her favorite celebration restaurant. How he landed on this particular place almost made him seem psychic. She thought back to him showing up with the single Sterling rose. She wondered if he would have chosen that particular rose if he knew it meant love at first sight.

"What are you thinking?" he asked as he offered her his arm to walk over the wood plank walkway.

"It's a lovely night. I've really enjoyed myself." She stopped, and Ty turned to her. "Would you like to come to my house for a nightcap?" A shiver brushed over her from the breeze coming off the water.

Ty wrapped his arm around her, and she snuggled in, resting her cheek over his heart and absorbing his warmth.

"I'd love that," he whispered into her hair. "But I need to get back and check on Rory."

She nodded but didn't move from her spot.

So much for that condom and its upcoming expiration date. Kira was sorely disappointed. Surely, he knew what she had meant by that invitation. And he hadn't invited her back to his hotel room, probably because he was thinking about her own responsibility with Princess Beatrice.

Maybe he just wasn't thrown head over heels like she was.

Ty trapped her chin in his fingers and tipped her head back. He paused for a moment, giving her a chance to step back if she didn't want this.

She *wanted* this!

He bent, pressing warm, gentle lips against hers. She rose on her tiptoes to meld her body against him, tilting her head so he'd take the kiss deeper.

His tongue slicked into her mouth. He tasted of chocolate and red wine.

His kisses sent tingles racing up and down her spine. Her pretty indigo panties were wet for him.

Ty pulled back and laced his fingers in hers as he started them toward his car. "I don't want our evening to end. But I sadly still have work to do tonight."

Oh, that was better. Not just Rory. Work.

She nodded.

"I take Rory for a run every morning. Would it be okay if Rory and I ended our circuit at your house?"

"Why don't you come for breakfast?" she asked. "Say around eight?"

"I'd really like that," he said as they approached his Land Rover.

He used his key to unlock her door and paused to kiss her again. This time the tingles reached all the way down to her toes. Her system was on fire. Kira could only imagine what it would be like if they were making love.

Maybe tomorrow she'd find out.

Chapter 19

Ty

There was a lusciousness to Kira, her curvy figure.

Her ample ass invited sin.

All the way back to the hotel, Ty had imagined her on all fours, looking around behind her with a hurry up and get it in quirk to her eyebrow. Her hair was long and glossy, and he wanted to wrap it in his fist, tip her head back and rediscover the taste of her full red lips… "And that, my friends, is how your Johnson can get you into trouble on an assignment," he murmured under his breath.

That green light to take a roll with her from the CIA was making his engines race. But he wasn't *that* guy—the elephant in the china shop stomping and crashing around out of pure joy.

Yeah, he was pretty sure he could get himself into the princess's bed.

And yeah, it would probably be a good time.

But he was wielding a very dangerous weapon—psyops could scar a person for life. And he took responsibility for the weapons he held. Ty's decisions made a difference. On his own, if they had met by happenstance, those variables wouldn't have to be worked into the situation. But, damn it, if Kira sent him that *fuck me now* look again, he wasn't sure that he could pry himself away from the opportunity.

When he swiped the keycard and walked into his room, White was rousing herself on his bed. She'd obviously fallen asleep there with her computer resting on her stomach.

Ty knew she was working overtime, working every angle to make sure this mission was golden.

"Darn it," she said by way of hello. "I was hoping to get the call."

"Sorry to disappoint." He put the room card on the counter.

"Things went well?"

"You probably had your spook friends at the table next to us, so you tell me."

White put her computer to the side and slid up the bed to rest against the backboard. "Why do I get the feeling that you could have gotten between her sheets, and you decided not to?"

Ty bent over Rory's crate to check on him, then sat on the couch to unlace his shoes. "Next time you dress someone for the assignment, see if you can't do something to break in the shoes. First the biker boots, now these GQ loafers, you're giving me blisters."

"I see," White said. Which meant she was about to slap him in the face with more of her psychological bullshit. "Falling in love is not hard. So enjoy it. But

Ty, it's temporary. Like having a bowl of your favorite ice cream, but that's all that's available, the one bowl. Once it's gone, it's gone. Once this assignment is over, you won't be in touch with her anymore."

"My understanding is that's not how things happen. The heart wants what it wants."

"Emily Dickinson. This isn't the time for poetry. It's time to stick to the science. Intellectualizing this mission can only help you keep your perspective. Many, many people have gone undercover with the goal to fall in love and manipulate their partners. Some of them marry, have children, have a long life together, and all the while, the mission is the mission. They are still able to bring the bad acting loved ones under the control of the law."

"She's not, though…a bad actor. She's an innocent— a vehicle to an end." He felt himself blush. This was so outside his paradigms and maybe even his moral structure.

"Exactly. And affection, trust, possibly love is the fuel for that vehicle." White dipped her head and raised her brows. "Lives on the line. Innocent lives that won't deal with heartbreak but torture, bullets, psychological agony. You've seen what the human monster can do. This mission has the potential to save lives, possibly thousands of lives. Are you up to this?"

"I'm up to it, yeah. Fall in love, so she picks up on my love through her 1% of the world population intuition-wise and feels she too can fall in love with me. Work the mission, then put it on the shelf."

"*Not* on the shelf. Return to sender. You're done after the assignment. She doesn't know it yet, and I won't explain that to you. She's not available for a future. That should be helpful, too."

"Do you put any of this science to good use in your own life?"

"Of course I do." White pulled herself to the edge of Ty's bed and stuck her feet in her flip-flops. "I know better than to go to dimly lit restaurants with a guy I'm attracted to. Attractions can be enjoyed without the emotional baggage of love connections. Usually," she said, then sighed. "But not in this case. In this case, it's got to be full-on Mr. Darcy shit."

"Who's that?"

"Darcy? A Jane Austen character." White chewed on the inside of her cheek while she thought. Finally, she said. "Things are coming to a head at a disadvantageous time."

"I...what does that mean?"

"Kira was on the phone with her uncle Nadir earlier today. You have to understand that she's lived her whole life with one foot in two very different worlds. Different customs. Different world views. Different laws. There are forces exerting their power on her and equally strong forces that press her away. She's lived with the push and pull, the pressures that have been brought to bear."

"What are they, exactly?"

"Family versus personal sovereignty are how I'd frame them in the most simplistic sense. I don't want to freak you out or anything..."

"Okay. Spit it out." Ty worked hard on his poker face.

"You need to nail this down by tomorrow night. And when I say that I mean it in all permutations of the word."

"What? You want me to... I... My ethics..." He stalled.

"Your ethics aside. You knew this was where this was heading."

"No. That's not what you said. I was supposed to form an alliance. You were basing this alliance on our having an emotional bond. You felt that the fastest and most useful bond was if she supposed herself to have a crush on me. It was never part of any scenario that I would possibly agree to a directive to bed a woman. I won't even entertain such a crazy idea."

"And yet, I never actually said those words. So that's where your brain took you?"

"You're playing psychological games. Stop." He stood up to take the shoes to the closet. "I liked you a whole lot better when you were upfront and straightforward. What did Kira's uncle say to her?"

"*That* I'm not going to share."

"Why not?"

"Because you aren't to know right now, it would complicate things."

Ty suddenly dipped his head as he barked out a laugh.

After he sobered, White said, "Yeah, that was a ludicrous thing for me to say. This is complicated enough. You don't want to sleep with her?"

"Of course, I do. But if I were to…have a physical relationship—"

"Wait. Are you saying your relationship isn't physical? You haven't even kissed her?"

Ty paused. He didn't want to answer. He didn't want to share and take anything away from that kiss. That kiss had been precious to him. It was sacred, personal, and not part of a mission.

"Okay, you kissed her. And I'll walk back what I said earlier. Asking you to have sex with her, if you ever do have sex with her, it has to be a natural continuation of your emotions. It really can't be mission-based. But if I have a good handle on Kira—and I think I do—she should have made a move on you tonight. I hope your chivalry gene didn't talk you out of following through. If she makes the move and you feel desire…" She stopped and coughed. "Ha! I'm chalking this up to one of the more bizarre conversations I've ever had on the job. But if you want her, take her. First, this might be your only shot. Second, she…well, I'm not going to tell you the second. Let's just leave it with my constant reminder that your mission to get to Davidson Range must be successful. Hundreds if not thousands of lives depend on it, and that may well include Kira's."

Fear whipped up Ty's spine. "Is Kira's life in danger?"

"Yes," White said without preamble. "I'm not going to lie. Not on this trip to Tanzania. And not in any way you can imagine. She doesn't fully realize it yet, but Kira has just been tossed into shark infested waters."

Ty held himself very still. He wanted to throw himself out the door and drive to Kira and ask her to tell him what was happening. It was a fantasy. Of course, he couldn't do that and blow the op. Ty promised himself he'd find out, and he'd do everything in his power to keep Kira safe, with or without him in her life.

"We're both tired. Jet lag is a thing, isn't it? I put some melatonin on your sink." She walked toward the door. "This was day two of the four days you had available. Are you seeing her tomorrow?"

"Breakfast at eight."

"Good. Maybe a morning roll would do her some good." She waggled her brows. "I'm not ordering you into her bed. But if you land there, it will move things along much quicker." She put her hand on the knob and turned toward Ty. "That is *if* you think you can make that a pleasurable experience—"

"Wow. Really?"

"Just realize, stud muffin, if you failed to please her, that might be your ticket to Nopesville for the mission. So if you do anything physical, give it your best effort." She sent him a wink and walked out his door.

Ty stared after her as she walked the three doors down to her room. That wasn't a conversation he'd ever imagined having when he signed his name on the dotted line and joined the Army.

Chapter 20

Ty

As he was getting himself together for Rory's morning run, Ty had realized that he needed a plan for going to Kira's house.

A ten-mile would wear Rory out enough that he might calm himself and lie down or play nicely with Princess Beatrice. Ten miles in the high humidity and heat of a July morning in North Carolina meant he'd be ripe.

Ty packed a small runner's backpack, including chew toys for Rory, a change of clothes, antiperspirant, a towel, and the hotel bottles of shampoo and conditioner, so he could clean up respectably.

It felt good to move his body. Stress slicked off Ty's skin and was left behind on the trail as he and Rory set the pace to finish up in an hour. It was a good clip, and he liked that tempo. His mind slowly let go, and he moved into the meditation of a warrior, aware of his surroundings but quieting the inner dialogue.

He found rest in his strenuous workout.

When Ty and Rory stopped in front of Kira's house to stretch and catch their breath, Ty looked up to find Kira in a pretty blue sundress standing behind her glass storm door, smiling at him and sipping from a mug.

He grinned and waved. It felt like coming home. It felt normal and comforting and nothing like a life-or-death ploy to get their hands on one of the most wanted terrorist plotters in the world.

She pressed the door open. "Hey there. Good morning."

Ty emerged from Kira's bedroom, having used her shower. He thought it telling that he was allowed into that private space when she could have directed him to the hall bathroom.

As he soaped his body, he thought about Kira in here doing the same, and his dick jumped to attention. *Yeah, that's not going to do.* Ty turned the water temperature to cold.

He could smell breakfast cooking, warm and aromatic, as he padded down the stairs dressed in one of White's outfits—another pair of jeans, this one without rips, and a black T-shirt.

"I already ate. I hope you don't mind. I woke up ravenous this morning." She gestured toward the table that was set up with a feast. "Please, help yourself."

Ty smiled and went to the table. The meal was lavish with roasted vegetables, eggs, olives, yogurt with olive oil, and some pastries that he didn't recognize. "Thank you, this is amazing."

"I was up early talking with Chef Bruno about this

upcoming event I was telling you about last night. I wish you had been in town a week ago." She gestured toward her counter, where papers were stacked in neat piles with colorful sticky notes. "I'm heading out of town Friday morning, and *this* has to be handled today at the latest." She sat on the stool. "I don't want to get in the way of your day, but I was hoping you would like to just kind of hang out together while I plow through this."

"Is it anything I can help you with?"

"I'm setting up a meeting." She stopped and put her hand on her forehead. "I'm pretty stressed. Last year's meeting was a horrific fiasco."

Ty sat in a chair on the far side of the table so he could face her. "Why, what happened?"

"I had arranged for the group to go out on an orang-utan walk. The head of security nixed the idea as too dangerous, what with bands of robbers who were preying on tourists in the area. Last-minute, I was able to find a different activity and had them hike out to a village inhabited by the descendants of headhunters—I thought it would be cool."

"Yeah? That's what you consider cool?"

Kira pressed her lips together and lifted her brows. "That's not even the thing that went wrong. London's stepson Karl called from the yacht to tell me it was a horrible experience." She huffed out a breath. "Next on the itinerary, I had them take the yacht to go surfing at this internationally renowned and very secluded spot. Some freak storm hit them. They all got back, but they were banged up and in the hospital."

"Wow, that's too bad. But surely not your fault."

"I'm not to the bad part yet. Once they got cleared by the doctors, I arranged for another boat to take them to their island, Davidson Realm. There was an accident—"

"What happened in the accident? They got there by boat? Was it a remote location? Were they able to help the victim?"

"Not quick enough. It was London's stepson, Karl. He was shot in the thigh when his sister Christen was aiming at some bad people who had come onto their island. Marauders. The security guards put a tourniquet on, but it was too many hours to get him into surgery. He had to have his leg amputated."

"Are you serious right now?" That was not how that story went, but surely the Davidsons wanted to keep the truth hidden. "And yet they're still letting you plan the next meeting?" he asked as she swiped her phone and brought it to her ear. She crossed her eyes at him, and it made him laugh.

Kira took call after call, interfacing with the caterer, the florist, the wine steward. The tobacconist. Ty savored his breakfast, content to listen to her planning and her attention to the tiniest details.

London called in, though Ty knew she was in Qatar. It was five in the afternoon, over there. "You want a photographer?" Kira asked as she scribbled over her notes. "That's really short notice. I can go through the contacts and see if I can't get someone. I'll do my best."

She paused as she listened.

"Yes, Joyce Drewby might be good. But it's July wedding season. I had trouble getting her on the books for Christen's wedding celebration. I'll do my utmost, I promise." After another pause for London's side of the conversation, Kira said, "I read the entry visas, it said staff. I'm sure that's how they categorized the pilots and me, but I can't see how adding a photographer would be a problem as far as paperwork goes."

His phone buzzed as he knew it would. White was

nothing if not checking off boxes on her psyops campaign.

He read: You have a friend who was in East Africa and is leaving out of Tanzania. This morning, they heard about unrest along the western border near Lake Victoria, and they're glad to get out of there. Your friend is a man named Mahfud. Erase message.

Ty needed to get into that compound. No matter what else was going on. Damn White to hell and back. He was going to have to frighten Kira and then manipulate her into asking him to come along for the ride. But this photography angle…maybe that might work for him. He could put London and Kira on the plane and stay back as a photographer. That way, he could be there to help his brothers on Echo and Foxtrot take hold of Omar Mohamed Imadi.

He liked that idea. Kira safe. And him zip-tying the terrorist.

Ty scowled at White's text as Kira wrapped up her phone call. *Keep scowling. Wait for Kira to ask what's wrong.*

He moved the message to the trash can.

"Is everything okay?" Kira asked.

He hated this game. He hated lying to her. "Yeah. This text is concerning, is all. A buddy of mine, who's in Tanzania, says he's glad to be heading home because there's some unrest on the western border up near Lake Victoria."

"In Tanzania?" Her hand came up around her throat. "Did he say what was going on?"

"That's the extent of his text. He's heading home." Ty placed his phone back on the table. "He's fine."

Kira's whole body tightened. "Who's your friend?" she asked.

"Mahfud? A buddy."

"What does he do?" Her brows drew in tight with concentration. "Is he in the military like you?"

"Was. Now, he does contract work, risk assessment for companies." He hated all of this.

"Would he tell you more if you asked?" She was kneading her hands in her lap.

"Why would I ask?"

"That's where this meeting is happening. I'll be there with my friend London."

Ty's scowl deepened. "When?"

"I'm flying out Friday to arrive Saturday morning."

"You're heading out to the Tanzanian bush alone?"

She nodded vigorously.

"Where is this on the map?" he asked.

She picked up her computer and walked over to Ty.

He pushed the plates out of her way as she sat beside him. Kira pulled up a search on the Internet, scrolled, and brought the cursor down on the Davidson Range compound's satellite image.

Ty moved his chair behind her, and as she pointed, he gazed over her shoulder. He reached for the mouse and scrolled around. "This is very near the Rwandan and Burundi borders."

"About three and a half hours' drive to either country along this road."

"This is a heavily Muslim country. You're a woman traveling alone? How would Davidson allow that? It puts eyes on you. Possibly a target on your back."

"Yes, I understand it isn't done. When I say I'll be alone, I don't mean that I'll be alone. There will be a pilot, of course, and a copilot."

"These are Davidson's people? They won't be responsible for your safety."

"No. They aren't responsible for me. I'll be on the Davidson jet. They're sending it to the United States as we speak to pick up the things I'll be bringing in, the flower arrangements and food."

"Is that allowed? Aren't there usually prohibitions on plant products coming into their country?"

"On dogs, too. But I have a letter from the Tanzanian government that allows me to bypass the regulations. So, beyond the supplies for the retreat, it won't be a problem for me to bring Princess Beatrice to see London."

"How is it that you got a letter like that?"

"One of the guests going to Davidson Range is the minister who is in charge of the regulations."

"Friends in high places."

"This is William Davidson we're talking about. There aren't a lot of people who say no to him."

"So you get into where? Dar es Salaam?" Ty pointed to the coastal city that was an international hub.

"Exactly. I don't even get off the plane. The pilot gets us refueled, and we fly straight out to the Range."

"Is there an airport nearby his property?"

"The Range has its own landing strip. The plane will be able to taxi right up to the back gate, and the workers will be able to unload."

"But you're afraid."

"Do you ever just get a feeling that something isn't right. That there's danger ahead?"

"It's saved my life out on the battlefield on more than one occasion."

"There, see? I thought you were intuitive. I leave Friday morning." She gestured to the stacks of papers. "Hence all this. From Durham, it's a twenty-four-hour trip with a quick stop to refuel in Spain and again in Dar es Salaam. London gets there on Sunday evening. We leave together on Monday morning to fly to Washington for some meetings. I won't be in Africa very long. It's just that the meeting last year taught me to expect worst-case scenarios."

Ty scrolled the mouse to get a better view of the estate. "That's beautiful."

"Yes, it is and right between the preserve on the west and Lake Victoria on the east." She pointed.

He nodded. "Do you go there often? Are you familiar with the dynamics of the area?"

"I've been there—" she looked up as she thought "—three times."

"I thought you translated literature. What has this got to do with your work?"

"I've been helping London out. She has the new baby."

"Might not be a great time to go there. Let me see what I can find out from boots on the ground." He swiped at his phone, then tapped out a text to White, listed as YT in his contacts. Call me—need info on unrest. He let Kira see it, pressed send, and left the phone on the counter.

No call came through. Ty didn't expect one to.

After a few minutes of silence, she asked, "Why would Mahfud have texted you such a thing?"

"I have teammates in East Africa." He moved his napkin from his lap to the table, then stood to take the dishes into the kitchen.

"Oh." She was staring at his phone as if she were willing it to buzz.

"Not to make you more anxious, but maybe you should check in with the compound's security. I assume your friends have that in place, expensive property like that."

She nodded and rolled her lips in. "I'll ask London. I'm supposed to talk to her again this afternoon. Maybe she has a better understanding of what's going on." She held Ty's gaze for an overlong time.

Ty found contentment being there with her.

He pushed any dark thoughts out of his mind, lest her INFJ could read them as clearly as White said she could.

"Okay," Kira said after a moment. "Back to the planning." She lifted the laptop and made her way to the counter. "Thank you for hanging out. It's nice to have you here. I'm sorry it's not very exciting. What I'd *really* like to do is take the day off and go do something fun with you." She gestured toward her piles. "But I have responsibilities."

Chapter 21

Ty

The morning had come and gone. Kira was pulling ingredients from the fridge to make them lunch.

"We could order in," he suggested.

"Oh—" she turned to him, onion in hand "—cooking is relaxing for me. I need something to occupy my mind so I can marinate some of the details and look again with a fresh eye."

"Then at least let me take you to dinner tonight."

His invitation brought a smile to her eyes. So beautiful. So kind. Intelligent. He'd like to string complimentary adjectives like beads on a necklace and offer it as a gift. Maybe he could think of something, a remembrance he could give her before their paths went in separate directions.

"What was that look?" Kira asked. "You suddenly

look sour, do you not like my cooking? We can call for pizza."

"Breakfast this morning was one of the best I've ever had. I'm looking forward to lunch. My sour look was about this article I was reading. I'm trying to find out more about what's going on over on the Tanzanian border. I sent a follow-up text to Mahfud. He made it to Djibouti and is waiting for transport out. He sent me an article."

She came to lean over his shoulder.

He caught her hand and pulled her around to sit on his lap.

Ty knew this article was about Niger and was nowhere near Tanzania, but the article was scrubbed of those words when White sent it to him.

Tuesday saw one of the deadliest days in decades. A hundred people were killed in two attacks on villagers by Islamist violence.

The responsible group has not been named.

Security sources indicate that the area has seen an escalation in militants' attacks associated with al Qaeda and Islamic State. Officials believe that this violence is part of a broader crisis as rival ethnic communities have embraced jihadist violence amid a scarcity of resources.

These survival resources—food, drinking water, and access to medicine—have spurred revenge killings between groups.

Tuesday's attacks create a grave threat to our communities and our way of life. The government pleads with those involved in extremist groups to understand that Africa will have to work with its allies to survive as the global environmental crisis escalates. Those potential allies are watching closely.

"Your pot's smoking," Ty said, putting his hands on her hips to help her stand.

"When I talk to London later, I'll ask her to speak with her head of security and see what he says. Though sequestered the way they are in the compound, they may be cut off from local news."

Ty followed Kira as she moved to the stove, taking a seat on one of her bar stools at the counter and looking down at lists of menus, times, and instructions. "What's all this?"

"London and her husband William fired their Range chef."

"Oh?"

"Too French."

"I see."

"They have a cook, but they want the food to be amazing. And to them, the most amazing chef is Bruno at their Texas home."

"Do they have a lot of homes?"

"Too many for me to remember them all. All over the world. Each with its own staff. And Bruno has been William's favorite for about as long as I've been alive."

"Big difference in age between you and William?"

"My friend London is younger than two of his children."

"Huh."

"Yeah, they get that a lot. But you know what Emily Dickinson says, 'The heart wants what it wants.' Anyway." She came over and tapped the page. "Bruno's doing the cooking and packaging. The cook simply needs to follow the instructions. Unfortunately—"

"The chef doesn't read English."

"Exactly. I need to get this translated for them. I speak Arabic fluently, so I can guess at what people are saying to me in Swahili. Swahili marries African Bantu with Arabic. It's a mishmashed fusion like Creole in Louisiana."

"I'm familiar," Ty said. Here was another possible road onto that property. "I went to Army language school studying Arabic and a couple of other linked languages. I used it when I was based in the Middle East and Africa for most of my career, including Swahili." He stroked his thumb along his chin. "The compound is on the far west border of Tanzania. There are a lot of lesser spoken tribal languages used out there. Is Swahili the language that her staff speaks? Does she speak it?"

"London? No, she speaks southern." Kira lifted the lid on her pot and smelled the steam, picking up the ginger and adding it in. "And London doesn't talk to the help." Kira put "help" in air quotes to show that this wasn't something she agreed with as she moved vegetable scraps to the trash can. "The main guy who manages the estate grew up in an English-speaking orphanage. So he teaches the workers the basics. If London needs something, she writes it on a pad that she carries around with her, and they take it to the manager for translation."

"What about security? Can her security team speak to her in English?" Ty crossed his arms over his chest and rested his heels on the stool rung.

"The head of security speaks English fairly well." She stirred the pot and added a lid. "He taught his guards basics like how to say 'run, hide.'"

"Run and hide? Is that necessary there? Are there secret places to go? Secure rooms?"

Kira shrugged. "We never needed to know that. It's so far away from everything. It seems very safe. The main concern is when the elephants come and rub their backs on the security wall. There's fear that they'll crash the walls down, then all of the wild animals would get in, and the workers' flocks would get out. Here." She moved her computer closer to Ty and flipped through the pictures. "London sent me these photos of the newly refurbished rooms, so the florist and I could pick complementary colors for the arrangements."

Ty moved forward and backward through the photos devising a way to send these to White while Kira wasn't looking. "I see four guys in the corner sentry booths."

"Yeah. There are a lot more than that. The Davidsons pay them very well by Tanzanian standards. They're all very loyal. The staff comes from a local tribe that has lived in the area for, I don't know, a thousand years? And they want to stay on that land. They're safe within the compound, have lovely servant's quarters, all of their needs are met. I can't imagine them allowing anything bad to happen there and upset that apple cart."

"I'm not sure I'm following you."

"If the tribal peoples let anything happen to the Westerners there…well, their lives would change for the much worse. Their children's too. London hired three teachers for their workers' children. A primary teacher, middle, and secondary school. She's set up college scholarships for the students if they pass their entrance exams. She's very generous."

"She sounds like a good friend."

Ty dragged her computer closer. This was the first time he was getting eyes on the compound. Foxtrot and Echo would have even better satellite imagery. But Ty was interested in getting a feel for where he was heading—*hopefully* heading.

"I've never heard of unrest in the area. The animals are the real issue—the elephants, keeping the monkeys out, and snakes." Kira turned and focused, skidding the cookie sheet of vegetables into the oven.

Ty surreptitiously slid a memory stick from his pocket and started downloading the photographic files. There were a lot of details in here that would be very helpful.

As he moved from photo to photo, Ty realized that the Davidsons' place had the same feel as the U.S. Diplomatic Mission in Benghazi, Libya.

Ty had been in Africa that September eleventh when Benghazi lit up. Not in Benghazi, Libya, but Niger. Ty had merely seen pictures. But these photos on Kira's computer brought up memories of that night.

It had been a hellish event, and he had Delta Force brothers in the mix.

With the news being broadcast on all channels back home, his parents heard the name "Ty" over the news and panicked.

He and Tyrone shared a shortened name—Ty...that had hit Ty's mom hard.

Ty couldn't imagine the heartbreak of families who had lost loved ones that night and having that horror projected over the airwaves. He did know what it had done to his own family.

In the wee hours of the morning, in Niger, Africa, Ty was pulled from a sound sleep to the buzz of the phone. His dad was on the other end. "You have to help your mom," he'd said.

"Look. Look, Pauline. He's on the phone. Ty's safe. He's fine." His dad held out the video connection for his mom to see.

Ty's mother was lying on the floor in the foyer, bunched in the fetal position, her hands gripping at her heart.

"Talk to her, Ty. Keep talking."

So he did. He recalled memories of the family. He talked about how he'd been accepted into the K9 handler training course and that he'd be home in the U.S. learning his new responsibilities.

The scene was overwhelming—to see his mom fold like that. She had always been a rock, his biggest cheerleader, and this... He couldn't wrap his mind around how her fear for her son's safety had put her on the ground.

"Keep talking, Ty," his dad had whispered. "I have the ambulance on the way just in case, but I think this is an anxiety attack." Then his dad got down on that cold slate foyer with his wife, wrapping himself around her.

Ty hadn't noticed until then how white his parents' hair had grown, how hard it was for his previously athletic dad to get down on the floor to comfort his mom.

When had they gotten old?

He wasn't a talker, but Ty rambled on in the soft, soothing voice that was trademark for Unit operators. He had no idea what would help. He kicked doors. He drank beer and fired up the grill. At home, he was a good ol' boy who hung out on the outer rim of the party. Watched. Enjoyed. Was part of and yet not. He'd always been that way.

And there was his mom, so upset when the news had said "special operations forces" and "Ty" that he thought he could very literally be breaking his mom's heart.

She eventually got up off the floor, returning to her steady self. This was a new side of her he'd never seen before. Perhaps she had a public side like a sweater she pulled on, the thing that people would see—comfortable and warm. Underneath that, though, was terror.

Ty had seen that with his own eyes.

His mom was one of the few people in this world who knew what Ty did for a living—a dog handler for one of the most secretive specialized units in the world.

It was a burden he'd thrust on her.

That was a decade ago, and he'd taken that lesson to heart. He'd sworn to himself that he'd never ask a woman to live every day what he'd seen of his mom's anguish that night.

Ty lived on a street at Fort Bragg with some of his Echo brothers as neighbors. He saw their wives. They were good actors, just like his mom.

Echo's job. Their lifestyle. It put those he loved into distress and sometimes even physical danger.

Just last January, though, the Unit was in the cross-hairs of a terrorist plot—a painstakingly laid out terror attack against Delta Force where they lived in Fort Bragg.

When the families were targeted, his friend Storm Meyers, now with the DIA, had discovered the plot and protected the Unit's wives and children.

If Echo hadn't saved Storm's life, what would have happened to their own families these many years later?

Fierce. Strong. Level. Ty had run missions with Storm for years when she was still with the Army. Trained well enough to operate with special forces, Storm acted as translator. She patted down the women when the soldiers could not without putting the women's lives at risk for allowing a man who was not their husband to touch their bodies. She talked to the women, gained their trust *and* their classified information.

Ty had been there at the end of her military career.

Out on a mission, Storm was the victim of an attack on her convoy and knocked unconscious from an explosion. Omar Mohamed Imadi—who was still Abu Musab al Khalil at the time and had already been listed as an HVT (high-value target) by the Pentagon—took Storm captive. The mission to save Storm and the three other captives had been circulating in Ty's mind and blood stream since White posted the pictures of Omar back at the base in Djibouti.

He couldn't clear himself of the remembered sights and smells.

Of the horror and devastation.

For days Echo hunted the captured soldiers.

When they found the camp, Ty was the one to pull back the tent flap and found Storm bound, on her knees, with tears and vitriol in her eyes. They were trying to get her to read a poster. Anti-American, anti-troop, she'd refused.

Ty's gun was fast. The blade at Storm's throat was faster. With Ty's triple tap, the terrorist collapsed forward on top of Storm. Ty was at her side in a split second, pulling the terrorist off her. The terrorist's dagger had pierced through Storm's throat, the hilt had crushed her airway.

And while Storm blinked up at Ty, thinking that she had taken her last breath, and Ty was the last person she would see, Ty stabbed his own knife into her throat. It was a last-ditch effort—a Hail Mary.

His actions had contained zero thought.

There had been no time for deliberation.

The bullets whizzed over his head as he crouched over her. He used the tube from his camel water bladder to make a trach tube. Holding it in his fingers, sticky with gore, the taste of copper filled his mouth as he smelled the old penny tang of blood.

Now, Omar Mohamed Imadi was within reach.

Imprisoned, he could never plan and train his terrorist thugs to hurt people like Storm ever again.

Was Ty the kind of person who would put an untrained woman, tender and kind—someone like Kira—would he put a woman he *loved* into a position of fear and to possibly become a target like that?

The idea was a surgical assault. No one would even know Echo and Foxtrot were there. The silent warriors. It required data and planning.

He *would* keep Kira safe.

If he wasn't going to Tanzania on that plane, neither was she. He'd figure out how to preempt her trip if and when the time came.

If he was on that plane, getting the details his team needed, then he'd make sure Kira was clear before she was anywhere near a Delta operation.

Had he just thought "the woman he loved?"

Ty did *not* love Kira; he worked to convince himself. It was a mirage, not a future marriage.

Just psyops fiction.

Ty had been warned to keep that both within his awareness and tucked away so that gentle, soft, intelligent, empathic Kira didn't sense his duplicity and steer clear of him and his goal to get to the compound.

Ty needed to keep his head on straight.

He was here in Kira's life for the sole purpose of manipulating her and taking down Omar Mohamed Imadi. Period.

Chapter 22

Kira

Ty had sat quietly at the counter, working from his phone while Kira had finished making lunch. They'd eaten companionably, then Ty had taken Rory out for some exercise.

Kira was starting to appreciate that Beatrice only needed the one walk and a few tosses of the ball in the afternoon.

Malinois were high-energy dogs.

She'd straightened up from their meal, having batted away Ty's offer to do it himself.

And now, Kira was standing in the middle of her cleaned kitchen, watching Ty toss a ball in the air and Rory leaping over Ty's head to snatch it from the clouds.

Those shoulders. Those thighs. That smile.

Kira's libido had come to a simmer.

By the time Ty turned and headed back into the comfort of her air-conditioned home, Kira's desire had come to a lusty boil.

When Ty walked through the door, he found her standing there with her fists balled; her arms were straight and rigid by her side, her eyes fierce and haunted. "I love having sex," she announced loudly as if that thought had started as a pinprick that exploded a balloon.

The vehemence in her voice startled her, and her body jerked.

Ty stood very still. His muscles banded and rigid. His focus on her intense. She noticed it wasn't the sexual intensity that she'd seen in men's eyes in the past when she'd said, "Let's go." This felt…she'd characterize as soldier mode—protective and fierce.

It confused her, and tears sprang to her eyes. "Is it too soon for us to have sex?"

Ty said nothing. His eyes bored into her as if pulling away the packaging to see what was buried inside the present she offered.

It was the gift of her body.

Though, honestly, that was the way she'd thought about her sexuality *before*. She was sharing herself, her body, her emotions, her care—sex *was* a joyful gift. *Had been* a joyous gift experienced by both Kira and her boyfriend at the time.

To think that this might be it. That Ty might be *the last* pleasurable sexual experience of her lifetime was cataclysmic. As Ty just stood there looking at her, the full ramifications of the loss hit her, and tears streamed down her face.

Ty turned and shut the door.

Kira moved out of his line of vision, trying to tamp

down on those thoughts, to dam the ugly crying back for a later time when she was alone.

Incredibly, *this* was it.

She'd be flying to Tanzania the day after tomorrow. Her uncle would be there, and she would be required to tell him what she'd decided to do—marry the stranger or lose her family.

She *couldn't* lose her family. The thought was devastating.

Ty followed her into her living room, where she'd curled onto her sofa.

"I'm sorry." She stretched her fingers wide. "Please—"

Ty sat down beside her, reaching out his hand for her. Instead of taking it, Kira moved into the open space made by his lifted arm.

He pulled her into his lap, tightly up against him, wrapping her in his arms—not sexually—protectively. He skated a hand down her hair. "It's not too soon for us to be together, Kira." His words were a warm whisper in her ear. "I want you in my bed. But it doesn't seem to me like you're feeling horny. This is something else."

What could she possibly say to him?

"Ha!" Play it off. "I'm stressing out about the event. *Obviously.*"

"What's really going on?" He repositioned so he could see her face, but she burrowed into his shoulder. She wanted to hide away from her destiny, and this felt so good.

No, I can't tell you, Ty—well, I could tell you, but I won't. I can't imagine that you'd go to bed with me if you thought I "belonged" to another man.

"Oh, a bunch of things coming to a head all at once." She swiped at her damp face. "These tears have *noth-*

ing to do with you." She laced her fingers and squeezed her hands. "I really enjoy your company. Honestly, I've wanted to be with you since you saved Beatrice at the ice cream shop. The kiss last night on the boardwalk. And watching you outside, I thought that I'd really enjoy being with you." She realized she looked like she was praying or a supplicant. That was the wrong image to offer. She released her hands to her sides.

"Same. But why are you crying?"

She reached up to brush another tear away. "I'm just overwhelmed that everything for me will be changing. I'll be moving to Qatar soon." There, she'd said it. It had been the truth for these last ten years, but until this moment, she hadn't acknowledged that this was her future, and she'd have to adjust.

"That's quite a sea change." He tipped his head to the side, his brows bunched with concern. "When will that happen?"

Kira cleared her throat. "I'll see my uncle in Tanzania. I'm sure he'll tell me then what my family wishes for me to do." Her mouth pulled hard into a frown; she couldn't fight the corners of her lips into a neutral position. "And I'm terrified to go by myself—to Tanzania, that is."

"I thought you were meeting London there." He reached out and wrapped his hands around her shoulders, peering into her eyes. "What's going on, Kira. Tell me the truth. How can I help?"

"You can't," she said with a shake of her head. "But I appreciate your listening to me. I just feel vulnerable, is all. I'm heading out to this remote place alone. My friend Lula has been sending me articles about unrest and attacks on Western women. She's worried. And then, what you shared this morning… It should be okay.

I won't be out in the public sphere. Once I'm at the Range, I'll hear my family's wishes, as I said, about when they want me to move." She looked around the room. "I bought my little house with my inheritance and have lived here for ten years while I was working toward my degrees. I've loved my house." She raised an open palm. "It's a lot to give up." Then she laid her head over Ty's heart.

"Do you have to?" Ty stroked his hand over her hair; it soothed her. "Could you not just go on extended visits?"

Kira was very still. No, she couldn't travel back and forth. She would be married to a stranger of her uncle's choosing, and she would be under this stranger's guardianship, which meant, for the most part, that compared to her freedoms in the United States, she would be in a child-like position, again.

"Kira?"

"I am constrained by duty." She looked up. "You have a duty to the Army and the United States. You go places you'd rather not go and do things you'd rather not be doing for the greater good. Mine is not such an obvious sacrifice, but it's the same. I'll move for my family's sake."

"Okay, I get that." He put a finger under her chin and gently tipped her head back so he could look her in the face. He dropped a light kiss onto her lips. "Nothing I can do about your Qatari move. But perhaps there's something I can do about Tanzania."

Her brows pulled together.

"You said that you'd fly in, set up, host the dinner when London gets there, then you and London are flying back?"

"Yes, then home to the United States. No matter what

my uncle asks of me, I still have my affairs to wrap up." She blushed hard at her word choice. "I have to sell my house and most of my things. Paperwork. Finances. I need to conclude my life in the U.S. *Again with the tears?* she reproved herself. Though, she couldn't make them stop.

Ty laid his hands on either side of her face and swiped the moisture from her cheeks with his thumbs. He held her gaze steadily. "I can come with you."

"What?" Did she hear that right?

"To Tanzania. I have time. It's just another passenger on the plane. You could call me security or translator. Can you get the paperwork changed to include my name? I could apply for a visa."

Her voice was barely a whisper. Kira was afraid if she were too loud she'd realize this conversation was a fantasy. "A visa wouldn't be necessary. It's on the paperwork, me and my staff, food, flowers, and companionate dogs."

"So Rory could go."

"I don't see why not." She swallowed past the lump in her throat. "Are you really offering to join me?"

"Yeah, sure. Why not? It's an adventure." He sent her a grin, but Kira knew that was for show. He was worried. And there was something more…

Her hands came over her mouth, she pulled her body in tightly. "Seriously?" she whispered.

Ty's laughter was full of warmth. He seemed…bemused and charmed by her response. "Yeah, sure. Rory and I are up for an adventure."

Kira wrapped herself tightly around his neck. *Clingy*, an inner voice warned her. But this would be her last relationship, her last opportunity to feel free and happy. Kira *would* cling to every moment possible. Drink every last drop of this heady brew. She would store every moment as a precious memory to carry her forward.

Ty lifted her hair back and smoothed it away from her face. "No more tears?"

"No more tears. Thank you. I would feel safer if you were there as my security. But once we're in Tanzania, you have to understand that we can't have a physical relationship. A Muslim area of the country and being unwed—"

"That's right. This conversation started with you announcing how much you loved sex." He chuckled.

She planted a kiss on his lips. "I *do*!"

A slow grin spread across Ty's cheeks. "So do I."

Chapter 23

Kira

Ty wrapped his arms around Kira as he stood. Slowly, he slid her down his rock-hard body until she felt the carpeting under her bare toes.

He touched the diaphanous skirt of Kira's sundress, lifting the hem, then letting it fall. It was a whisper across her thighs.

"I want to hear about this love you have for sex." The words were a silky breath against her neck. "Tell me what you like."

Though her lips longed for a kiss, she resisted. Kira stretched her body up taller, standing on her tiptoes, brushing the tips of her nipples against his chest, her chin tilting back, making her neck long and graceful. She gave herself a moment to respond. She'd never been asked that way before. "I like to feel feminine. And soft." She ran her nose along his jawline. "Desirable. Lush."

Ty's hands rested on her shoulders and drew down her arms. His calloused palms made her feel delicate and very female. She turned her hands so she could lace her fingers into his, but already he was drawing the tips of his fingers back up her arms, her neck, and into her hair. He captured the long black waves, pulling her hair lightly in his fist, dragging her head back. His lips hovered over hers. "Tell me more. What makes you feel feminine and lush?" His lips wrapped around the words, caressing them into warm honey.

The tug of her hair was novel. And amazing. She liked it. And she liked that Ty had asked. If only she knew, had a list, a road map. Go here then there, then the big bang, and you finish up.

Was it strange no one had asked her what she wanted before? Her mind searched through the times when she'd felt the most turned on. Ty knew she'd be remembering past encounters to answer him; her past didn't seem to daunt him. His ego. "Strong muscles. Silky fabrics," she offered.

"Mmm, hmm."

"I like to be—" She was too timid to say it aloud. The pause went on too long.

"To be?"

"Manhandled."

A grin spread across his face; she could feel it brighten the air. "I see." There was a knowing crinkle of pleasure at the corners of his eyes. "Kira, you have to say yes before we go any further. May I make love to you?"

"Yes." She wrapped her arms around his neck and stood on her toes so she could reach his ear and nibble the lobe.

"You have to promise me that if you change your mind or you feel at all uncomfortable, you'll say no."

"No."

"No, you won't?" His hands splayed across her lower back, holding her against him—his hard-on pressed against her stomach.

Who could possibly say no to Ty and his hard cock? "Yes, I will—say no, that is. But I don't want you to stop."

His hands cupped her ass, squeezed, released, squeezed again, and her breath caught. "We need an in-between word then," he said.

"Are you asking me if I have a safe word?" Her words were laced with a bit of incredulity. The men she'd been with had been very vanilla—sweet and lovely. But dependably the same. A roll in the bed, sometimes in the shower, once in a car.

"Kira, you were crying. I won't take advantage."

She was suddenly worried that his gallantry would stop him from making love to her. She had to have him. Wanted him in her now. "I've fantasized about you since we met. My desire isn't springing from this moment. It's been a slow simmer since you licked your ice cream." Her fingers curled into his shirt. She swayed her hips against him.

"All right, we'll use the stoplight. Right now, we're on green." He danced her back a couple of steps, turning her so her ass was against him. His fingers traced down her curves, taking her wrists and moving her hands up behind his neck. "Leave your hands there. You're not to move them."

She nodded.

He gathered her hair, twisted it around his hand, and tugged until her lips were on his. "Beautiful." His fingertips traced her jawline down her neck. "Delicate." He kissed her slowly…gently. "Delicious."

She panted as his fingers swept inside the neckline of her dress, traced along her clavicle. His hands explored down her torso, sliding in at the waist, resting on her hip bones, and tugging her against him.

His moan was the most decadent, arousing sound she'd ever heard.

Ty used the silk fabric of her dress to brush her skin, like a firefly flitting through her consciousness, lighting her nerves. "Yes." She sighed, letting her head lull against his broad chest muscles.

Ty's fingers traced over her breasts, around and around her nipples until they hardened.

Button, by slow button, he moved along the bodice of her dress. His patience was driving her mad. Kira needed this to go faster. She wanted the warmth of his palms. She started to reach down to rip her clothes away.

"Hey, now." Ty pressed her elbows, gently reminding her to leave her hands behind his neck.

Another button.

The last.

He drew his thumbnails from the edge of her waistband up her quivering stomach, peeling the bodice to the side.

With her back to him, there was nothing for her to do but receive.

He stepped forward three steps, guiding her ahead of him, until she stood in front of her living room chair with its solid back and padded seat.

He reached down again, capturing her skirt between his index and middle finger, dragging it along her thigh. The whisper of silk made her gasp and shiver. "Put your hands in the air, Kira."

And she did so instantly. Her name on Ty's lips was

reverent. She felt cherished. He pulled her dress off and flung it out in front of her, where she could see it, a puddle of color against the cream-colored carpeting.

Ty reached up to her hands and interlaced their fingers, then wrapped his arms so warm and strong around her and held her there. Kira looked down at his arms and wondered once again how and why he was covered in bruises and healing welts. Somehow, she knew he wouldn't be able to tell her. That he'd been doing something dangerous.

That thought sent a shiver through her system. She was both immensely proud and, at the same time, fearful for his safety.

Ty tapped the back of her knee, pressing until she lifted it onto the seat of the chair. Then the other.

Kira stuck her ass out and wiggled it saucily.

He gave it a playful spank. "Behave." He took off her bra, letting it drop with her dress in a pile of silk, lace, and ribbon.

Though her house was a comfortable temperature, as he slid his hands down her bare arms, surely, he felt her shiver with excitement. He lit her senses on icy fire.

Taking up her wrists, Ty pressed her hands onto the back of the chair. "Leave your hands there. Do you need something to remind you? Shall I tie them in place?"

Tie? She shook her head. She'd never been asked before. She'd never considered it before. That was probably the most erotic thing that had ever been suggested to me.

She felt a rush of desire that took her breath.

"Was that a yellow light or red?"

"Yellow." It was a maybe. "I think this time I'll just hold onto the chair on my own."

"Good." He kissed the back of her neck with approval. "Now, what color?"

"Green."

"Leave your hands where I put them."

She licked her lips and gripped the back of the chair. This was glorious agony.

Ty left a strand of kisses along the indentation of her spine. She arched. An ache between her legs. Her panties moist with need.

She could feel his lips smile against her skin between his kisses.

Kira desperately wanted to turn and slide into the warmth of his arms. But she was too intrigued by these new sensations to deny herself this experience.

Kneeling behind her, Ty's tongue lapped at the back of her leg. Her toes curled. His hands. His mouth. It was exquisite. Luxurious. Decadent. "Ty," she groaned his name.

He nipped at the lace that circled her thigh.

"Ty," she exhaled, having lost all other words.

His fingers slipped under the sides of her panties. "Kira?"

"Yes."

Slow. Excruciatingly slow, Ty drew the wisp of nothingness down Kira's legs. His thumbnails' scrape was gloriously bright against the gloss of satin until the panties reached her knees. "Kira spread your legs for me. As wide as you can." He captured her hips with his hands and lifted her slightly as he nudged his knee between her legs.

She shifted her weight from her right knee to the left, unsure how to accomplish what he asked.

"Spread your legs, beautiful." He lifted her by the hips enough that she could stretch her panties as far as the elastic would allow. She arched her back until her ass curved up into the air. Her hair swept down over her breasts.

She was electric.

Behind her, Kira heard Ty shuffling around as he undressed. Kira was desperate to see him. His muscles. His cock. "Fuck," she whispered.

Ty chuckled.

The silken head of his dick teased her thigh as he slid his hands down her arms and over her breasts. She pressed her hips back into him, trying to angle closer to the head of his cock.

"Kira, you're interrupting my manhandling." There was a smile in his voice.

She grinned in reply, though he couldn't see.

Ty knelt behind her, licking her thighs, getting closer and closer to where she wanted him. She tingled, anticipating the roughness of his tongue on her clit. She winced, hoping this wasn't a tease and that he'd stop.

And then, *oh*!

He was there, his mouth on her.

She lowered her forehead to the back of the chair and closed her eyes as she focused her attention on the sensations. Waves of warmth rippled through her system. "Oh…oh…" She tipped her head back, her jaw-dropping. "Ah."

His tongue ran along the sensitive flesh of her vulva, and he slipped a finger inside of her.

"Kira?"

"Yes."

Two fingers slid into her, thick and sure. They curled, stroking her G-spot. It was a lot. The sensations overwhelmed her. Her shoulder dipped down, trying to find stability on the back of the chair as her knees went weak. She reached her hand back to smooth over his hair.

"My instructions, Kira—"

She immediately put her hand back on the chair.

His tongue returned, warmly lapping at her. His fingers had never stopped. She hoped they'd never stop. Never—oh, *so* good.

Her stomach clenched, held. She exhaled but then couldn't bring herself to drag air in. She was dizzy and confused. Her muscles trembled. And then, with a gasp and a cry, she shattered. Her pussy gripped and pulsed around his fingers. She felt Ty push to standing behind her. He took her weight as she heaved a breath out.

"Be still." He let her go, leaving her cold.

She strained to hear what was happening. His jeans were lifted from the floor. There was a tear of foil. A condom. She was about to get what she'd wanted since she'd seen him giving that ice cream cone to Rory, sitting in the sidecar of the motorcycle.

She'd been masturbating to those images ever since.

"Kira?" This time, his voice was strained as if he were holding himself back, as if doing so was costing him.

"Now, Ty. Now!"

She'd expected him to slam inside of her. She'd braced her elbows to take the impact, but no. He glided into her slowly, reverently. His breath was ragged as he pulled back out.

"I wish you could see what I'm seeing, Kira. How sexy it looks for me to slide into you." He pushed into her. "Can you feel me, Kira? How much I want you?"

"Yes," she whispered. "Faster. Harder."

"Patience. I want to relish you."

She couldn't help herself; she pressed her hips back until his cock filled her, and she ground herself against him. "So good. Ty."

His hands on her hips, her pussy still quivering from

her last orgasm, he let her find her pleasure, riding him. Harder. Faster. Sweat slicking her back and stomach. Her hands gripping the back of the chair for balance. She pulled and pushed her arms, rocking herself along the thickness of his cock. "Please," she called as she climbed toward her second orgasm. She wanted him to go over the cliff with her. "Come, Ty! Come!"

She arched her back as he slammed into her. Once. Twice. The third time he gripped her hips and held himself deep, deep inside of her.

Their gasps and moans melted together.

Ty wrapped one arm under her hips to hold her up and lowered his head to her back, gulping for air.

Kira trembled with joy and exhaustion. If he let go, she'd slide to the floor.

The next moment, Ty slipped his arm under her legs and lifted her into his arms. She curled into his chest as he walked her up the stairs to her bedroom and tucked them under the covers.

With their limbs tangled together, they fell into a deep and recuperative sleep.

He was right there with her, and in this moment, her life was bliss.

Chapter 24

Kira

Kira had absorbed every moment of that sexual encounter. As she lay in a sleepy stupor, she relived it. She wanted to keep it fresh and whole, so she could take it with her into her new life.

The smack on her ass had been playful. There was zero malice or misogyny in it. It was a man wanting to bring her pleasure. And doing a damned good job of intuiting her needs. She'd never had a sex spank before, and she *loved* it.

Manhandling was indeed achieved.

She realized that he had asked her what would make this experience—their first—good. But she had not asked him, not even once, what he wanted.

What titillated him?

What did he fantasize about?

Kira wished she had time to explore and discover,

but she only had today and tomorrow. She'd have to ride these waves for the rest of her life.

Imagining for a moment what was heading her way in her contrived marriage, Uncle Nadir had said that he was choosing one of his business partners. They'd set a date for her to be in Qatar. The man had to be old. With any luck, he was flaccid and didn't care to take little blue pills to get his aging dick to stand. She pushed those thoughts away. She wanted nothing to mar this time for her.

"Tell me, Ty…"

"Yes, my pearl."

That stalled her. Caught her about the throat. She tipped her head back. "Why did you call me that?"

"As a pet name? It reminds me of you. Should I choose something else?"

"No," she said, tipping her chin down to cozy into him again. "I like it. I'm just curious as to why you chose *that* one."

"Pearl?" He dropped a sleepy kiss into her hair. "I don't know. It just came out that way. But I think it's fitting. Pearls are understated sophistication. They can dress up or be casual. Much more versatile than gemstones." He drew a finger down her arm. "And the sheen is somehow voluptuous, isn't it? All other gems—diamonds and emeralds—are hard-edged and cold looking to me. There's a warmth, a glow to a pearl."

"Yes?"

"I remember reading something about them." He turned her hand over and brought it to his lips and kissed it. "A pearl warms against the skin." Ty kissed her pulse point and massaged his thumb over her forearm. "It stores that heat in the layers of nacre." He kissed along her arm up to the crook of her elbow. "The structure of the pearl allows the heat to re-emit. What it takes from the wearer, it returns in kind."

"And I'm absorbing warmth to release again?"

"You glow with your inner radiance."

Kira threw her head back and laughed. There was joy in that laughter.

Ty pushed up on an elbow so that they were nose to nose when she faced him again. "You don't think so?"

"I…" She shook her head. "No one's ever said anything like that to me before. Though, it's interesting that you should choose pearl." She wiggled down the bed until she could tuck in against Ty and pillow her cheek on his chest. She let her fingers trace down his washboard abs and play along the dark curls of his goody trail. She looked at him through her thick lashes.

More bruises, here. A belt of black and blue. She simply couldn't imagine how this could have happened. A seatbelt? A car accident? She knew in her bones that he didn't want her to ask as he wouldn't be able to answer her truthfully, so she kept her concerned curiosity to herself.

"Qatar is known for its pearls," she said, coming up on her elbow so she could read his face. "It was one of the main industries there a century ago until, of course, it was replaced with oil and helium."

"Really?"

"And beyond that, I told you that my master's thesis was on Jane Austen. Do you know her books?"

"I read one in high school, *Mansfield Park*, I think it was called."

"Yes, that's one of her titles."

"I read another one by Steinbeck, *The Pearl*. But as I remember, that one had a ruinous outcome, which has nothing to do with us. So pearls and Miss Austen?"

"Yes, well, in the U.S. version of the movie that came out some years ago, Mr. Darcy—that's the hero."

Ty's lips twitched at the corners of his mouth, and Kira thought he was holding back the smile that warmed his velvet brown eyes.

"Mr. Darcy tried on an endearment that Elizabeth didn't like."

"Why didn't she like it?"

"It's what her father called her mother when he was displeased."

"Yes, that would be bad. Did your father call your mother Pearl?"

"Never. He called her Sparrow. I don't know why. At any rate, Darcy wanted to know what Elizabeth preferred as a pet name."

"All right. And what did she choose?"

"She said to use her given name on weekdays, my pearl for the Sabbath, and when he wanted something for a special occasion, he could call her a goddess."

"Goddess, then."

"Only for special occasions." She batted her eyelashes.

"It's Wednesday. That seems special enough. Do I really need to reserve 'my pearl' for Sundays? You're not Christian. That wouldn't make any sense."

"The Muslim holy day is Friday." When she said that, Kira quickly moved her hand away from Ty's abdomen and put it on her own hip.

An internal line was crossed. Kira would not speak of religion when she was touching Ty.

This was actually a difficult problem for her. Kira had been sexually involved with men since she thought she was in love her senior year of high school. But as a woman who was not a virgin—she could be charged in Qatar under Zina laws. Sexual intercourse between a man and woman outside of a legal marriage meant she could be punished beyond bringing shame to her family. She could be jailed, or worse. In the Qur'an, Zina is punished with a hundred lashes.

If and when she married the man her uncle had chosen, she would have to be very careful about how she approached their marital bed. If he was a good man, kind…or even someone worried about having such a crime associated with his name, Kira might be safe. If he were a brutal man, her life could be in danger. She could act the virgin. She *could* turn any aversion she had toward the stranger to make it look like bashfulness. Her revulsion could be read as innocence and inexperience.

It was just another layer of considerations she needed to weigh.

She risked her life if she agreed to the marriage. She risked her life if she *didn't* agree to the marriage.

But how could she go the rest of her days without the family she loved?

Kira flapped around restlessly. Her breath caught as anxiety squeezed her ribs down tight against her lungs. She tried to hide her reaction by climbing from the bed and pulling on her robe.

"Are you okay?" Ty pushed up onto an elbow. "Have I upset you?"

"No, no." She gathered her hair from under the collar and let it fall down her back. "I just need a moment." She pointed to the bathroom and went in. Kira shut the door and leaned her weight against it. She looked at her face in the mirror.

She'd gone white.

Her eyes held too wide.

Kira felt like Ty was her lifeline, and she should grab at it. Grab at him. But wasn't that a literary trope? The princess in dire straits in a foreign land, depending on the strength of body as well as the heart of the knight in shining armor to save her from her dragons?

They shouldn't be dragons.

She should trust her uncle to have chosen someone that would be a good match for her. But Uncle Nadir was an ambitious man. And he knew her little as she spent most of her visits in the women's area of the compound.

She was chattel.

And she was on her own.

Kira took a deep breath and left the bathroom. She had today to be happy. She wasn't going to let her worries rob her of this joy.

Chapter 25

Kira

Kira had just emerged from a hot bath.

While she soaked, Ty had gone out to get some things for Rory, so they could spend the night. He would also grab dinner from the Thai place around the corner.

Now, dressed in loungewear, Kira was sitting at her kitchen counter, a video chat open with London.

"What do you think of this dress?" London asked.

"I don't love you in yellow. It's hard for most people to pull off, and with your blonde hair, it makes you look sallow. How about the blue?"

London turned to pick up the lapis-colored gown.

"So I was asking if you saw the reports," Kira said. "There have been some attacks on Westerners."

"Why would you be concerned?" London asked, pressing the dress's bodice to her and swishing the voluminous skirt as she considered the choice in her floor-length mirror. "You speak Arabic. You look like that Disney princess."

"Cartoonish?"

"Funny."

"Actually, this *isn't* funny. I love you. But I'm not willing to be part of tribal unrest or terrorism. You remember what happened last summer in Ngorongoro. You're the one who told me about it—all of those tourists killed in the bombing. All of those international workers who were hostages were taken west toward the Range."

"Not toward our Range. They were northwest on the other side of Lake Victoria. Hours away. That's like saying that you are in particular danger in North Carolina for something happening in, I don't know the exact distance, but up in Pennsylvania or something."

"London, I'm scared to come. Let me send a man. Jordan maybe?"

"To set things up with an artistic eye? To explain things to our chef? To make sure all is exactly correct and comfortable so my husband's friends will have a seamless stay? Jordan can't do any of those things. I'm depending on you. You *promised* me."

"Yes, but that was before I knew this was happening. It's right there on the Tanzanian border."

"Four hours away. And if we hear of anything happening, pile on the plane and take off."

"How would I know?"

"You wouldn't," she admitted. "But neither would they. Honestly, you're flying in. You're off-grid. No one knows you're there. The people who work at our Range live in the domestics' quarters. They don't interact outside of the compound. Delivery men, that's all."

"Are you sure about that?"

"Who would they tell about you? Why would any-one care that you're there?"

"I. Don't. Know. But London, I'm *frightened*."

"You will be gone again in almost no time at all. We fly in. You greet us. Twelvish hours later, we're on the plane heading for Washington. The pilots already know it's an immediate turnaround."

Kira didn't respond.

"I can't send you my security. I need them where I am to protect me because of the baby. Can you hire someone there? Call Omega, tell them you need a man." London snorted. "Sorry. Sorry. That wasn't nice."

"I didn't like the Omega guys. I didn't trust them. They felt…wrong to me."

"Do you know someone who would make you feel comfortable about doing this? I'm not being a bad friend. I hear your concerns. I want you to feel safe. If not Omega, I'm not sure whom to suggest."

"I'll think about it. But if I find someone, I can bring them?" Ty had offered, but if she just came out and said that to London, it might get back to her uncle, and her uncle might ask her pointed questions about her rela-tionship with Ty.

It was better if this idea came from London.

"As a paying gig? I'd need to know how much. It has to be reasonable. And they have to follow all of the laws. I'm not digging them out of prison." She re-jected the blue gown, tossing it onto the pile on her bed. Standing in her bra and panties, she pawed through her closet for another option. "Do you want me to ask your uncle for a name or have him put someone in Tanzania when you get here?"

"No! Promise me you won't bring up my name with my uncle."

"Fine. Just let me know what you decide to do. Only thing, please, please, please don't decide to not come. I'm depending on you. Figure out who's flying in with you, give me the guy's name, and William will make a phone call and get that put into place with the customs guards, so your close protection guy can bring a sidearm. Normally, the laws say no handguns in Tanzania. Oh, but it's no problem to bring rifles if he says they're for hunting." She paused to examine her fingernail then focused back on Kira. "Anyway, you'll have the paperwork tomorrow if you can get me a name before you go to bed."

"Thank you, London."

"Now, where's my pooky-wooky precious princess?"

Kira leaned down and scooped up Beatrice.

"There you are, lovie! Mama misses her cutie pootie. You're going to see Mama on Sunday, sweetums." She made kissing noises at the screen. "Thank you, Kira. I appreciate you bringing Bea along. I need to give her some mama snuggles. It's been way too long. Love you, Kira. Find a good man!" She laughed, and finger waved, then the screen went black.

Oh, Kira had *definitely* found a good man.

But finders keepers wasn't a game she got to play.

Ty had picked up Rory's food at his hotel and had brought some clothes back to Kira's house.

With the food growing cold and forgotten on the entry table, they had sex in the foyer.

Sex on the couch.

They had played Mr. and Mrs. Clean in the shower, but Kira had gone to her bedroom to pull on a negligee while she let Ty have some privacy to brush his teeth.

It felt natural. They fit like puzzle pieces. If only he

had shown up last year at this time, her life might have taken a very different trajectory.

While Ty was out gathering things from the hotel and getting some take-out, he must have stopped at the pharmacy and a high-end gourmet shop. There was a new box of condoms on her bedside table next to a box of Belgian chocolates, tied with a rose-pink ribbon that exactly matched the color dress she had worn to the park yesterday when he and Rory had protected her from the aggressive rottweiler.

That had to have been a conscious choice, didn't it?

Seeing those boxes together had sent a woosh of hormones flooding through her system.

She got another tidal wave of horny hormones when Ty emerged wearing a pair of sleep pants that rode low on his hips.

Bare-chested. He was an Adonis. Kira had never seen such a desirable man.

Oh, the bittersweetness. Well, as Jane Austen wrote in *Pride and Prejudice*, "A lady's imagination is very rapid; it jumps from admiration to love, from love to matrimony in a moment."

Yup. It had been just a moment since she and Ty had met, and yet she couldn't remember not knowing him, and she couldn't imagine him only lighting the shadows of her memories.

Before grief wrapped too tightly around Kira's heart, she pushed those thoughts away to focus on Ty.

He lifted a framed photograph from her dresser. "Are these your parents?"

"Yes. That photo was taken at our neighbors' house just before Dad died. I like it because they look happy together which was rare."

"What brought your parents to America?" He set the photograph back exactly as he had found it.

"Education and opportunity. Dad was a chemical engineer. He met Mom at university. She studied physics." Kira looked over to the corner at the bed she'd made of cushions and blankets where Rory slept in a protective circle around Beatrice. His tail was thumping against the wall as he saw Ty come into the room.

"Smart," Ty said as he went over to give Rory some attention and make sure he'd settled in.

"Very. I didn't get any of the number genes. My mind likes words."

"So a compliment to their talents."

"Their brains were a world apart from how mine works. They kept giving me science kits—build a robot, mix chemicals to make them explode. All I wanted to do was curl up and read the day away. I got in so much trouble in school because I'd hide my novels in my textbooks. The teachers would figure out that I was just a little too intent on my schoolwork. They'd walk around behind me and then—punished."

"That seems so wrong, to reprimand a child for reading when it's their job to instill the love of literature."

"Maybe," Kira said, plumping her pillows and wiggling under the covers. "Or maybe they were using reverse psychology. They wanted me to feel like I was a rule-breaker by consuming books while in the class."

"Did it work?"

"No. Oh, definitely not. I have an internal punishment system. If I feel like I'm doing the wrong thing, I'm quite hard on myself."

Ty stood up and went to wash his hands. Kira assumed it was so that he didn't smell like dog when he touched her. That thought sent a rush of *yum!* through her system.

When he came back to her room, he walked straight to the bed and under the covers, reaching his arms out for her. "I'm glad your parents' science didn't deter you from studying the subject you love." He kissed her hair.

"I think we all have to justify why we're here on this Earth. I think I'm here to preserve the voices of the women who came before me, so they can be heard. Who knows, perhaps my life trajectory is taking me to Qatar to better understand the voices. While their social structure isn't a replica of the 19th century, many of the mindsets are similar. I'm conflicted by my move, but aren't we all?" She licked her lips, sorry that this conversation was so bleak. "I have the pressures of my heritage sitting on my shoulders."

"And if you didn't?" Ty smoothed the hair from her face, looking her in the eyes.

"One could either say I was unmoored as in set adrift. Or one could say that I had the opportunity to explore. As you know, words have meaning, and how one frames a situation changes the brain and the way one perceives a situation."

"I'm not sure I understand what we're talking about here."

"Duty. Honor... I don't know where I fit in. It's an existential question, isn't it? I wish I was one of those people who was sure. Where they live is where their roots run deepest, and they *belong*. Family... Let's change the subject."

"Okay." A twinkle came into his eyes. "Changing the subject, did you find your chocolates?" He pointed to the box on her bedside table.

"I did." She smiled. "I'm looking forward to both the chocolates and the condom box. Thank you for both."

"I was hoping to play a game tonight."

"Game?"

"Pirate." He quirked his brows.

"Pi—what?" She laughed. "Seriously? How does that go?"

"I'd like you to show me your treasure chest. Do you play with toys?"

"You mean sex toys?"

"I want to watch you pleasure yourself."

"*You* please me," she said emphatically.

"I'm glad. Would you let me watch? *Because* that way I can learn what you like. And I find it erotic."

Kira felt pink tinge her cheeks. She liked that Ty knew what he wanted and wasn't bashful about asking for it. He was a straight shooter. Kira grinned, as she didn't miss the double entendre of her thoughts.

Climbing from her bed, Kira reached underneath for her embroidered satin box. She didn't think it would be traveling with her when she went to Qatar. It was a shame; she had some very expensive and very arousing toys that she used when she was alone.

Ty's wanting to watch her made her horny as hell, yet another sexual discovery.

Too late.

Chapter 26

Ty

Kira was sleeping with her round ass pushed up against his hips. If he hadn't made love to her three times in quick succession, his cock would be loving this, but his dick was taking a nap.

He pulled the blanket up and tucked it under her chin as the air conditioning cut on and chilled the air.

Today was their last day in the United States.

He was on his way to accomplishing his mission of climbing on that private jet, winging over the Atlantic Ocean, and getting his eyes on the inside of the compound.

His focus was on getting past the compound security and putting hands on Omar Mohamed Imadi.

And yet, here he was. The most pleasurable assignment of his time with the Army was about to become one of the worst.

White was right—he'd fallen in love.

It was a sensation he'd never felt before. And yet, undeniable.

Maybe he should go ahead and start White's antidepressant meds to get them going in his system as soon as possible.

No, Ty wanted to feel every nanosecond of this, wanted to revel in his feelings for this woman—he hadn't understood what love could mean to his mind, body, his very soul.

It wasn't part of his vocabulary to even explain these sensations. He was humbled by this experience.

Yeah, this mission was going to fuck him up.

He just hoped that for Kira, anything she felt for him was quickly overcome.

When Kira came awake, Ty closed his eyes to hold on to this moment, wrapping Kira in his protection for as long as he could.

She lifted up and turned to look at him. Then turned back and buried her head in her pillow. Her body trembled as she cried.

Now, Ty had slept with enough women in his lifetime to know that orgasms were stress reducers. Sometimes, as the top layer of stress sloughed off, another layer bubbled up, ready for its release, and that manifested as silent tears. The first time it had happened to him, Ty thought he'd hurt the girl he was with—it was a horrifying thought. But luckily, she had calmly explained that was just something she did, especially after a bad day at work. She was letting it all go so she could sleep.

That wasn't what this was.

Ty opened his eyes so if Kira looked again, she'd know he was there, supporting her. He thought if he said anything, she'd wipe her tears and move on with her day. He didn't want that. He wanted the truth.

When Kira reached out for a tissue to blow her nose, Ty smoothed a hand down her back.

She curled herself into his arms, dabbing at her eyes and letting him stroke his fingers through her hair.

I will go up against anything that is coming to harm you, he thought—the beast of male power swelling his chest.

"Ty," Kira's words whispered over his skin. "You should know that I am… I'm enjoying our time together."

Ty was surprised by the tone in her voice. He recognized it as the one he used to color his own words when he had "the talk" with a woman he'd been seeing. It was the "let me set clear expectations with a velvet glove" tone.

On the one hand, he was glad to know what she was experiencing.

On the other hand, White had told him that she was under immense pressure to succumb to her uncle's directives. Ty was afraid this meant she was about to tell him that she was giving in. He'd done a little research on Qatari women. It seemed that in some families, the male head of the family was the one to pick a woman's spouse. Sometimes, the woman didn't even meet the guy until she showed up to sign the marriage contracts. It was a different way of life. It was Kira's choice.

But his heart was hammering in his chest.

He was surprised by what she said.

"Sometimes, I feel like humans aren't making a lot of progress. I've spent a decade studying words written by women two hundred years ago. Time doesn't really change much in the human condition. I share with the characters many of the same struggles. There's a passage that's coming up for me right now."

In the Unit, words were precise, straightforward, and linear. Challenging subjects were faced head-on. This was a learned skill that was built on trust.

Ty had found that kind of honesty and straightforwardness wasn't part of most people's communication styles. Most people he knew filtered their conversations through the prism of social correctness.

Kira was that way, societally polite in dealing with stressful subjects.

White had told Ty to pay attention to the literary stories that Kira mentioned in conversation. White explained, though they often seemed to come from left field, Kira expressed her inner machinations through literary metaphor.

Literary Rorschach tests, White had called it.

"What novel are you thinking about right now? Any scene in particular?" he asked.

She peeked up at him through her insanely long thick lashes and laughed softly. "Don't let this freak you out—"

He shook his head.

"It was a scene from *Pride and Prejudice*."

Ty nodded for Kira to continue.

"The main character is a woman named Elizabeth Bennet. There was this dreadful man." She straightened her arms to lift up and look him in the eye. Her eyebrows raised, making her eyelids pull wide. "This has nothing to do with you. It's about the general position I find myself."

Ty nodded, not wanting to distract her from telling him what was going on.

She tucked back down into his arms. "This dreadful

man proposed to Elizabeth, and she turned him down. Her mother was furious and exhorted Elizabeth to do the right thing by the family and marry him. Her father—remember this is a male-run society, the expectation was that the daughters would follow their father's directives."

Ty clenched his back teeth, making his jaw bulge. He didn't like where this was going, and he hadn't read that far in the book yet, so he wasn't sure if the dad had forced the situation on his daughter.

"'From this day, you must be a stranger to one of your parents,' Mr. Bennet had said. 'Your mother will never see you again if you do *not* marry Mr. Collins, and I will never see you again if you *do*.'" She swallowed. "That scene keeps bubbling up in my mind."

"The dad was opposed to her marrying for the sake of the family?"

"And it was easy enough for him to do. You see, Elizabeth, her mother, and her sisters would become homeless as soon as the father died. It was part of the way the will was written to leave the property and money to a male heir. Elizabeth marrying Mr. Collins would be the economic security that they needed for the future. As long as the dad was alive, they'd be fine."

"So the dad would never suffer the consequences, and he was okay with his family being destitute when he was gone?"

"He wasn't the most ethical and loving of parents."

"But why are you thinking about that?"

"It's not exactly the same state of affairs for me, but I've always been drawn to this novel for that very sentence. My dad, when he was alive, wanted America for me. In fact, when he died, he left me with enough money that finances would never be a reason for me to make my choices. My mother wants Qatar for me. She feels that beyond finances, my fortunes, and the family's security lies there. So my dad is dead. He suffers nothing from my choices. My mother is alive, and she would face repercussions for my actions."

"Where is she now, your mom?"

"So in Qatar, it is often a thing that families live in community. After my dad's death, Mom moved into the family complex to be near her sisters-in-law, and to make sure that our family's honor wasn't tarnished, her being a woman without male supervision here in the States."

"And…?"

"And, as I've told you, my family wishes me to return to Qatar now that my education is completed."

"What do you want to do?"

Kira didn't answer.

Because of this assignment, Ty was listening to her in a way he'd never listened to any of the women who had moved through his life. She was a tactical puzzle to be solved. Everything she said was essential to mission success. He had to focus and listen and learn from her.

He *liked* to focus, and listen, and learn from her.

This was a revelation.

She intrigued him.

Ty asked, "The mother's reaction to Elizabeth was, 'marry the man, or I will never speak to you again,' making her basically an orphan?"

"Yes, exactly. And rudderless."

"Kira, what do you want for you?" Ty held his breath. What he realized he wanted at that moment was for her to look him in the eye and say, "You, Ty. I want you. I want an us."

He wasn't at all surprised when he concluded that's

what he wanted for himself, as brief and as manipulated as their time together had been.

Wasn't that just another man putting external pressure on her? He didn't want Kira to move to Qatar and lead that life, but he also acknowledged that he wasn't from that culture, didn't understand it, and wasn't in a position to make judgments.

"What do you want to do?" Ty repeated.

"I want to find peace." Her face drooped. Her shoulders sagged. It was as if Ty was watching her melt into the pillows with no energy to keep herself erect.

In his mind, Ty was both singing a song of gratitude to Johnna White that she'd put him on a path that would cross with Kira's, and he cursed White for the same reason.

Joy and pain were strange bedfellows.

"Ty, I'm sorry. I want nothing more than to cuddle in bed with you all day." Her lashes veiled her eyes, and she didn't look at him when she murmured. She glanced at the clock.

Six a.m. He'd have to take Rory out for a run soon.

"This is my last day before we leave. I have to finish getting my ducks in a row and get packed."

"Kira, meeting you has been wonderful," he said. "I know you have a heavy decision in front of you." He reached for her hand. And though it cost him, Ty said, "Whatever you choose, I support you." He glanced over and saw the edges of her lips twitch momentarily up.

"Is that funny?"

"Literature parallels."

"More Austen?" he asked.

"I'm thinking of an earlier work. Some scholars attribute the story to Chaucer, some to Gower, but a question was posed to King Arthur by a hag who had the power to help him or allow him to be killed. There's more to it, but in a nutshell, to leap the hurdle, he had to answer this question: What does every woman want?"

"You're a woman."

"Thanks for noticing." She looked over at him, and her mood seemed to shift.

"Sarcasm, huh?"

"Deserved." She laughed as she crawled from under the covers, and he immediately missed her satin warmth against him.

"So every woman wants the same thing? That's not possible any more than every man would want the same. Every K9, cat, or kangaroo—"

Kira walked immodestly naked around her room, gathering her clothes for the day. "Within their species and gender."

"Exactly." Ty slid up the bed to rest against the headboard. He laced his fingers behind his head, enjoying their banter. "That any group would be homogenous that way is absurd."

"Ah, but is it?" She went into the bathroom and left the door open. It might have been an invitation to come and shower with her again, or it might just be so they could converse. He'd wait and see if he was offered an invitation.

"I'm running through my lists, and I'm coming up with," he said, "every woman wants air to breathe, food when she's hungry, shelter from the storm."

Kira called past the running water. "Storms take various forms."

"Granted." He reached out to Rory and Beatrice, who jumped onto the bed.

"Isn't that what my mother chose by moving to Qatar? Shelter from the storm?"

He was scratching behind both dogs' ears. "Is that what your mom said when she moved?"

"It's what I intuit," Kira said.

"Do *you* need that kind of shelter?" Ty regretted those words immediately. He tried to shift back again. "What is it that Arthur told the hag?"

"It wasn't Arthur who answered. It was one of his knights. Are you sure you want to hear this?"

"When I was growing up, my dad was in the Army. I always knew that was my career trajectory. In school, I focused on the things that I thought would best help me with being a successful soldier: science, math, foreign language, history, ROTC. I wasn't big into my English classes. I thought reading all of those old books was a waste of my time. But when I was stationed in Afghanistan, I discovered reading. It helped me pass the time. It gave me fodder for new thoughts and for conversations that got stale really fast when I was with the same people day in and day out, month after month. I love to read now, and I'm trying to broaden my horizons. When you talk about literature, I'm really interested. Intrigued."

"All right, the story of the hag. The hag says she'd give King Arthur what he needs, but in return, she says that she wants to marry a knight from the round table. Now when I say hag, I mean hag—an old wrinkled, stooped woman with arthritic hands and scraggly hair. Arthur is horrified that he made that promise. He's married to Guinevere, so he can't fulfill the obligation himself."

"Did he lie to the woman about following through?"

"Arthur returned to the round table to explain what happened to his knights. Sir Gawain says he'll do it. He'll marry the hag."

"That's brotherhood. I wouldn't do that even for my brothers in my unit."

"No?"

"No."

"Well, Gawain's ready to throw himself on the proverbial grenade. That's when Arthur explains that actually the hag is the most beautiful woman in the realm but for only half the day."

"Twelve hours of beauty and twelve hours of ugly?"

"Exactly. And here's the kicker: he could choose which time she was ugly. For example, she could be ugly all day long and beautiful at night when she was in his bed or beautiful to look at all day but ugly at night. Which would you choose?"

"This is a trick question. First, you can make love at any time of the day or night, so why would that matter? Normally, I'd say love is blind, and he sees her inner beauty no matter the time of day—but he doesn't know her and so doesn't love her, that would make a difference. At night, her beauty would be in the dark. If she were ugly during the day, she might be poorly treated. But that all seems to be missing the point. It sounds like Gawain is supposed to answer that question from a place of his own comfort without weighing in or giving precedence to her. I don't think it should be his choice. It should be her choice because it's her body and her life. And he can either discuss it with her and come to a shared decision, or he should leave it to her and adapt."

Kira stood in the bathroom door, a towel hugged to her. She blinked at him. "You haven't read this before?"

"Not that I recall. Why? What did he choose?"

"Well, the hag was obviously under a curse, and the curse would be lifted—"

"Is this like the frog thing? The prince is a frog until he can convince a princess to kiss him?"

"Beauty and the Beast tropes? Yes. Someone has to see the cursed person with a kind heart and not be deterred by appearances. That was the same in this passage. Gawain couldn't see with a selfish heart. He had to put her first. So Gawain basically says, 'You choose what works best for you.' And when he said that, answering the question, what does a woman want most? It's to have her own way."

"As do we all."

"So true." She sighed and moved back into the bathroom, raising her voice to be heard. "When she was told it was okay for her to choose her own path, she was released from the spell and was always beautiful. She lived the rest of her days happily with Gawain."

It might be wishful thinking on his part, but could it be that Kira was asking him to give her space and trust that she could find her own way to the happily ever after of fairy tales?

Was there really a choice?

He was here on a psyops mission. When he'd mapped the compound and given the intel to his Unit, Ty's contact with Kira would be over. They'd each part ways and go about their lives. He didn't see a way that a relationship between them was possible. Especially after he manipulated her the way he did. He was complicating her life. If she felt for him at all—through science or alchemy or the fates themselves—like he felt for her, he was going to hurt both of them.

He would do what he was ordered to do. He was a soldier who risked everything for the good of his nation. His heart was one thing—he'd been warned. But he'd failed to truly recognize and appreciate the impact this might have on Kira.

Shame washed over him. Ty was glad Kira was in the adjacent room and couldn't see and intuit what an asswipe he truly was.

Chapter 27

Ty

Ty had told Kira that he was going to run Rory and end up back at his hotel room for a meeting.

She asked him to pack his bags and bring his things back to her house, so they were ready to go in the morning.

They had one more night to sleep together. Once they were in Tanzania, his posture toward her would have to change for everyone's safety.

Just a few more hours.

Once he was on the jet, he was on his way to taking down a major terrorist plotter.

"How's it going?" White asked as she trailed him down the hotel corridor and into his room.

"Did you know that she's moving to Qatar?" he asked once the door shut and he'd thrown the bolt.

"That's a new detail from a recent conversation with her uncle. Did she tell you that's what she's decided to do?"

"I can't say she's a hundred percent. Does this have anything to do with this mission?"

"Yes. And I won't say more on the subject." White dropped her briefcase by the dinette and pulled out a chair.

"Is she part of the enemy?"

"She is *not*. I can promise you that." White sat down, angling herself toward Ty. "We talked about her psych evals. I will remind you there is a perfectionistic piece to her personality. People with INFJ self-punish with *enormous* anxiety if they believe they have done something wrong, their inner voice is punitive."

"I think I saw that these last two days," Ty said as he took the lead off Rory.

White held her hands in the air as Rory went over to sniff at her. "Tell me more."

"We were having a conversation about her moving to Qatar. That's enough, Rory. Load onto the bed." He paused and waited for Rory to comply. "Good boy." He turned back to White. "It was like watching her dissolve in front of me. This is a weird analogy, but it made me think of the Wizard of Oz scene where Dorothy threw the bucket of water on the Wicked Witch, and the Wicked Witch melted. Though, Kira is the opposite of wicked. So take that piece out. It was like circumstances were thrown at her, and…yeah. I don't know if that information is helpful to you."

"She has family obligations."

"Can you tell me what they are?"

"I can tell you, but I won't. You're not involved in her life other than getting on the plane with her and flying to the Range. I will remind you again, you were chosen for your personality profile. Do *not* get attached to the idea of a future beyond Monday. You cannot help her. *Cannot*."

"So she's in danger." Ty's tone was carefully emotionless. He picked up Rory's bowl to clean it out and get him fresh water.

"That's not part of the scope of this mission. Now, we need to take next steps. Here's the thing I want you to know. This mission is high stakes. There are a lot of international relationships on the line—Qatar, Tanzania, Saudi Arabia, Japan, among others. There's a high potential for blowback. No matter what, you will remember that this mission falls under your security clearance. If you ever discuss this mission with anyone—and by anyone, I mean Kira—other than to say that you are there to protect her and make her feel safe, it's a problem. If any of the methods we have used are shared—including the how and the why of you showing up in her life—you'll have a long time to think about them sitting in solitary in prison."

He set the bowl carefully on the ground. "Why do you feel the need to threaten me?"

"I chose correctly," she said. And to her credit, she seemed unhappy about the situation. "You've fallen in love. Your conscience will make you want to whisper the truth to her. You are an ethical, forthright, respectable man. You'll want to tell her that your relationship is built on duplicity. But you'd be wrong."

"How's that?"

"Ha! See, you didn't deny you love her."

"I love her. You're right. I see no reason to deny my feelings."

"See how quick that can go when you apply science?"

"White," he said sharply. He wanted her to cut the crap.

"Your relationship was chosen through science. I gave you some skills to apply. But when people date, that's what they do. They think about how they can best attract the person who has caught their fancy. Where to take them on a date. What outfit they will wear. What they can talk about. It's all part of the dating game."

"This is life or death, not Go Fish."

"Still, all that happened was we applied science to get you on her team. It worked. But your feelings were not constructed out of thin air. They came from your natural affinity for each other. You fell for each other. That's happenstance helped along by science and my excellent people skills."

He moved farther into the room to sit at the table with White. "I'm going to agree with you because, selfishly, that makes me feel better."

"And she won't be in your life for much longer. You have the pills."

"Let's change the subject.

"All right. If you didn't put it together, Davidson Range belongs to D-Day's father. It's her pop's safari hangout for when he and his buddies want to do some large animal hunts and to take their mistresses, but we needn't go through all that. No women who aren't living there as domestic workers will be there at the time Echo goes in. From London's descriptions to me, the domestic staff is housed on the opposite side of the compound. They'll be at a safe distance."

White pulled out a map and laid it across the table.

Ty scooted his chair closer beside her, leaning over to take in the terrain.

"The photos you supplied and the video tour from London's interior designer were helpful. Though, obviously not enough information. It was still a good step forward. You arrive on site Saturday. You'll have a little over twenty-four hours to gather all the information you think will serve your unit. Most importantly, we need to know where Omar is sleeping. The Davidson group will arrive on Sunday in time for cocktails. Kira will host the evening. You're there in the guise of bodyguard, correct?"

"Yes."

"That's good because your ideas for filling the roles of photographer or translator won't get you the tour with their head guy of security. We anticipate the strike Monday night, depending on the decisions made by Echo and Foxtrot. You won't be there. Monday morning, you're back in the air. When you get on the plane, you will already have sent off your reports to your Delta Force brothers. The jet is off to Dar es Salaam for refueling and then a return flight home. Everyone will stay on the plane during refueling. It's part of the agreement with the Tanzanian interior department, and it's because of the dogs and possible Western foods and flowers. A twenty-four-hour trip, and you're back to the States. I'll send you a thumbs-up when the Unit successfully bags our guy. No message with it. It's just a courtesy until you get to the Echo hot wash to talk through the mission."

"Who's on the plane?"

"You, Rory, Kira, Princess Beatrice." She dipped her head while amusement twitched her lips. "London and Archie, the pilots."

Ty tipped his head. "Archie?"

"London's infant."

"Wait." He leaned forward. "There's going to be an infant involved in this scenario? Kira mentioned London had a new baby, but I didn't think she'd be bringing him along with her." Ty's posture became rigid; kids in harm's way set his system on fire.

"No, the baby won't even be on the same continent. You're flying out before the attack." White looked him in the eye and waited for the answer to sink in. "After you leave, the when of the operation is the commander's to figure out. I'm just the intelligence."

"Smartypants?"

"Ha!" she said with a grin, obviously liking the label. "So Archie was born in April, that makes him somewhere around three months old. Expect a screaming infant to interrupt your sleep." She paused. "Is Rory okay around babies? I really should have asked that earlier, though we can always handle that differently at that juncture."

"Rory tends toward the macho. He has identified women and children, especially babies, as his to guard once he thinks they're part of his pack. If they're not part of the pack, he ignores them."

"What happens to make Rory think they're part of the pack?"

"If I hold them."

"Ah, yes. Well, you'll have to decide how that best suits the mission."

"I haven't said this to you," Ty said, placing a hand on his heart. "But thank you, sincerely, for giving Echo this opportunity. Man, I'd love it to be me with Omar in my crosshairs."

"Put it out of your mind. That's not going to happen." She paused and waited to catch his eye. "Look, I've read through your files. I know who this guy is to you. I know that you were the operator in the tent with Storm. I liked her—a lot. When I was new in the field, I got an opportunity to be on a team with her. She was fantastic."

"Still is." He felt his hackles start to rise.

"I'm sorry. I said that poorly. What I want to say is that I understand you want to be the one to pull the trigger. But—and Ty, this really is a major *but*—you fit a need. You're the right pick for this leg of the mission. As a matter of fact, your doing this well means the difference between getting our mark or not. The CIA has been trying for nearly a decade to line up our sights with this guy's forehead. I *want* this. I've been laying the groundwork for this mission for two years. *This* is my shot. I planned this out meticulously within my power. I've come to the end of my capacity to help and have to live vicariously through the Unit. But that's par for the course with my assignments. Now you get a taste of the flavor of my work. Not being there to see it through can be frustrating. We can do this—you and I. You. Mostly you."

"No pressure."

"Oh, you're not afraid of a little pressure. I have faith in you." She turned her attention back to the map. "The interesting thing here, as you can see, is that, once you're there, you're there. The national borders hem movement in this way. The water hems you in this way. The refuge, which has very strong laws about entering, is in this direction."

"Are there lions and things?"

White reached over to her computer, pulled up a list, and read them off. "*Indigenous wildlife includes ver-*

vet monkeys, sitatunga, bushbuck antelopes, and genets. Chimpanzees, elephants, giraffes, black-and-white colobus monkeys, and African grey parrots. Sounds lovely." She stopped and smiled. "If only you had time to go on safari."

"I'm on my own safari. I'm hunting a trophy."

White put her finger on the map. "Not that you need this information, but I'd like you to see that once Omar is at the Range, he's trapped. The escape would have to happen along this single road out. If he were escaping overland, the kinds of wildlife that he might encounter could be deadly. There are a couple of small day sailboats at the dock here for a water escape. But I assume that would be a last-ditch scenario."

"There's no motorboat?"

"Not according to Foxtrot. There are hippos in the shallow waters and crocodiles.

"Huh. Yeah. That wouldn't be a good exfil."

"Besides the sharp teeth, there are other dangers to keep someone away from the water. Omar would catch diseases if he got in there: diarrhea, cholera, dysentery, typhoid, polio, bilharzia. To be clear, I don't care what takes Omar out, us or nature. It's all good. You're up to date on all your shots?"

"I don't know. What shots?"

"Knowing the Army, you have them all. You're a K9 handler, so you've had your rabies vaccines. That's good. Just, if anything bites you, try to identify it. And we'll get you dosed up. There's a long list of deadly vipers in the area. Just do what you can with identification. Best if you can take a photo."

"Wonderful."

"I'm told Foxtrot has antivenom with them. Let's not

let it get to that because you could blow your cover and the op if Foxtrot needs to swoop in and save your ass."

"Let me just take some notes." He picked up his pen and scribbled on his notepad: Try not to get bitten by the deadly snakes.

White circled her finger on the map. "I want you aware, you're kind of trapped within the walls of the compound, so I'd keep track of that pilot, make sure he's healthy, happy, and has a good rapport with you. I'm trying to find out more about him to give you areas of interest that you share and maybe a special treat that you could offer—cigars or scotch… I told you how gifts work to create a debt. I haven't discovered anything useful yet."

"Yes, ma'am. Weather?"

"Clear skies. Low wind." She popped her eyebrows at him to say that she'd learned about the parachuting adventure when they stole the Russian helicopter. "Daily high temperatures are around 71°F, lows around 56°F. I have your wardrobe packed. I've added some fleece."

"No sticky notes this time?"

"I think you can figure it out. Once you get there, the wooing is over. You're in combat prep mode."

"What are Tanzania's threat levels?"

"I put together a risk matrix for you. I've emailed that to you, but as a general rule of thumb, there are always the risks of violent crime and crimes of opportunity in the populated areas. Terrorist groups continue plotting possible attacks in Tanzania. The State Department tells tourists that terrorists may attack with little or no warning, targeting embassies, police stations, mosques, and other places frequented by Westerners. We're watching some unrest that's been bubbling up along the border, where the leadership vacuum created by Momo Bourhan's death has escalated clashes between various Islamic radical groups. Foxtrot hasn't seen anything on the ground that is a specific cause for alarm. Also, members of the LGBTQI community have been targeted for harassment and arrest. And oddly, those detained under suspicion of same-sex copulating could be subject to forced anal examinations."

"Is anyone in our party from the LGBTQI community?"

"Your pilot is transgender. He/him."

"Noted. All right. That pilot is our way out, so I'll keep close tabs. And this section on the map. You said that's carefully watched."

"Watched with high-power guns. No one is allowed in this area without permission. They'll assume you're a poacher if they see you. Though, if you were going to be here with London for a few days, she would definitely take you here. It's one of her favorite spots. Coffee?" White stood up and moved toward his kitchen area.

"You can drink caffeine this late?"

"I don't have a clock that tells me it's late. I have a clock that tells me my work isn't done." She ran the tap to fill the carafe. "For example, London Davidson's eight hours ahead, and she likes to chat in her afternoon, which is middle of the night for me. She's tired. Her nanny's taken some sick leave, and London doesn't trust others with the male heir. So for the first time, she's taking care of her infant all by herself."

"I see."

"She's also sad because she loves the preserve because of the orphaned elephant calves. She goes over and feeds them their bottles and her quick turnaround time negates that. She has to be in D.C. to plan Christen's celebration thingy. And she's not feeling warm and fuzzy about that. Expect her to be a little passive-aggressive. She is normally, to some extent, but this series of events has turned up the heat on this particular coping mechanism. I know that's one of the things that you dislike, so that's your warning."

Ty pointed at the map. "What's going on in this space over here?"

"The other preserve to the east of the Davidsons' Range is called *Rubondo*. It's on that island out in the lake, and you don't want the party to go there even if, for some reason, it's suggested. It could mess up our mission trajectory by some unforeseen accident. This group's last meeting was broken up when Christen shot her brother Karl. I applauded that outcome. But on this mission, we don't want to miss our opportunity because of crocodiles."

"And hungry hippos."

"Right. Keep track of Rory. He's the one I'm most concerned about."

"And Omar shouldn't expect help from the people in the area because they'll think he's a poacher and kill him."

"Omar shouldn't run in that direction. But again, if he's mistaken for a poacher and the rangers shoot him dead? I'm fine with that. Though I'd really like to interrogate him, then watch him sit in his max prison solitary cell. Not your worry. You'll be flying in to protect the lady, so she doesn't feel distressed. You'll recon and send the info to Echo. It's on them to figure that all out. London comes in with the party of her husband's associates. She gives them a welcome dinner, one more sleep, then the eight of you—two dogs, a baby, a pilot, a copilot, two women, and you fly to Dar es Salaam.

Flying back to the U.S., you tell Kira nice knowing you, you've been called out on deployment, shake hands, and move on from her."

As if Ty ever could.

Chapter 28

Ty

Kira was staring hard at her phone. Her face had gone still. Holding her brows high and rigid, the blood had drained from her cheeks. She looked like the proverbial deer in the headlights, paralyzed by what she was seeing.

Ty pretended not to be aware.

She laid the phone on the seat next to her then said, "Excuse me," as she made her way down the aisle to the back of the jet.

They had taxied out onto the runway in Spain where they'd stopped for refueling. The pilot said he was just waiting for the all-clear, and they'd be in the air on their next leg to Tanzania. They had brought a third pilot along, so they could swap out and grab some shut-eye over their long flight. One of the copilots was waiting for them to get into the air, then he was headed toward the bedroom to take a nap.

Kira slid past him on her way to the bathroom.

With a quick glance to make sure no one was watching, Ty reached for the phone, where he read the text.

London: I know who it is! I happened to be walking by William's office and overheard a conversation William had with Nadir. The guy is called Omar. I haven't met him, but he'll be at the Range. Kira, because I love you, I'm sharing this with you even though it would probably make William very angry with me if he found out I did this. Make sure to erase this text immediately. And when you meet Omar, you can't show any reaction. At least this way, you can get to see him without having to act like his intended. I found a picture of him. He's the one on the right. The guy on the left is an English oil friend of Karl's. That guy isn't involved with our event. Remember shhhhhh. I'm trusting you.

Beneath the text was a picture of none other than Omar Mohamed Imadi.

Intended. *Shit*.

Rage roiled Ty's blood.

Obviously, if London had to identify which man it was in the picture, Kira had never met the guy. Surely with her INFJ extrasensory intuition, when Kira did meet him, she'd know that her uncle had set her up for a horrific future.

Ty had been right. Kira was heading to Qatar, where her family would arrange a marriage for her. He'd met wonderful families where that was how the couple came together. Heck, look at Kira and him. That's precisely what they were, an arrangement. The goal wasn't marriage, but someone who knew them both, with careful planning and meticulous intervention, had brought Kira and Ty together.

But Omar.

White had said that Kira's uncle was the money and brains behind many corrupt events that impacted the world market. Nadir had been one of the orchestrators of the helium crisis last year that put computer manufacturing as well as MRIs and other medical equipment at risk.

Shrewd and without a moral compass, Nadir still could have held his family as sacred and protected them.

Nadir *had* to know who Omar was.

He *had* to know what a sick, twisted, dangerous son-of-a-bitch Omar was.

And he was offering Omar his niece?

Ty felt physically ill.

He vowed he'd never let Kira get trapped in a marriage with a vicious terrorist no matter what else happened.

Echo had this. Kira would be safe.

Underneath that, a voice in the back of his awareness added, *she's mine.* But Ty distracted himself from those thoughts.

The future part of this equation didn't matter right now.

The goal was the same: capture or kill. Move forward.

Ty placed the phone back precisely the way he found it.

Kira came back a moment later. Ty didn't think he could handle the sadness he read in her eyes. He'd hold her and comfort her, but the crew would see, and they worked for William Davidson. He would do nothing to mess up this operation.

The pilot announced they were ready to take off.

Sitting down in her seat, tugging her safety belt into place, Kira gathered her hair and pulled it to one side. She leaned back in the padded leather chair, closing her eyes until the plane had reached elevation and had straightened out.

Once the pilot announced they were free to move about the cabin, Kira pulled her file box around, opened it, and extracted a photograph file.

"What are those?" Ty asked.

"The guests. On each of the guestroom doors, there's a picture frame for the occupant."

"That's interesting."

"It helps the drunk guests get back to the right room."

"I see."

"It also helps the house staff. If a guy with a mustache brushes by a staff member and says 'I need fresh towels,' the staff member can get that taken care of without memorizing all the guests' names and corresponding rooms. It's a trick that the designer came up with, and it seems to work well."

She pulled off a sticky note from Omar's room and exchanged it with one for another man whom Ty didn't recognize.

"Rethinking room assignments? Can I see?"

Kira placed the photographs in Ty's outstretched hand. As he flipped through, Ty found a picture of himself that Kira had taken outside of the restaurant on their first date. According to the sticky note, his room was next to hers. That made sense from a security point of view. It would be hard to guard her if he was anywhere else. Still, knowing she was on the other side of the wall, and she'd never sleep in his arms again, was a stab in the heart.

After Kira's room in the lineup was the Davidsons, and Omar had been the next down. Now, Omar was as far from her as she could make him.

Echo had to get their hands on that guy. Had to take him off the world terror stage. Had to keep him far, far away from Kira.

"Are you okay?" she asked.

"I was just thinking that this was a really good idea, the photographs." He passed them back. "But I'd prefer that your picture and mine are not on our doors, for security's sake."

"Oh, okay. I'll leave those off if you think it's best. Is that true for everyone?"

"Davidson has his own security staff that can make those decisions. Your safety is my responsibility." Ty watched her put the photos back in their place. "Kira, tell me how you got involved with the Davidsons." Though White had told him about Kira and London's history, he wanted to know how Kira would describe their relationship.

Would London help protect Kira if need be?

Kira looked at Ty for a long moment, then angled her head up as if she were pulling up a memory. "London and I were freshman roommates at Duke. We got along because we're both introverts." She sent him a distracted smile. "London comes from an upper-middle-class family. She had nice clothes that she got from her aunt, who works in the fashion industry up in NYC, which helped her fit into the more affluent crowds. Her family had *nothing* like William Davidson's wealth."

"Or your wealth?" Ty asked.

"I don't need to work to live comfortably, very comfortably. I live simply. I prefer it. A rather Zen existence, though London calls it bleak."

"Why are you helping London then if not as a paying job?"

"Old loyalty? When I went to visit my family, London usually went with me. She loved the idea of being jet set, though she couldn't afford it. My family paid her expenses so that I would not be traveling alone as an unmarried female." Kira stopped.

White had told Ty that silence was fine for Kira. Let her have her space to gather her ideas. Just sit quietly and wait. White hadn't been wrong yet. Besides, Ty was completely comfortable not rushing Kira. She could unfold her story the way she liked.

"I'm the one who introduced London to William." She smoothed her hands down her pants' legs. "He was visiting my uncle in Qatar when they met."

"Does she love him?"

"Hard to tell. Probably even hard for her to tell. She was gobsmacked when they met. They married after a very short time together. Is she enamored of the life or the man? It isn't easy to separate that out. Especially since the financial future for her looked like she'd end up a barista making complex coffee orders for minimum wage and tips."

"Why's that?"

"She was a fine art major. London originally went with me to Qatar because I told her there was a VCU art school there. VCU is one of the best schools in the U.S. for fine art."

"I see. So she decided not to go?"

"She planned to go, yes. She was accepted. We were talking to my aunt Fatima about suitable housing for London. At the time, London and I had been going back and forth to visit my family for years. We were both on the slow train in college. We both understood that the other side of the diploma looked grim."

"Why is that true for you?" Ty looked over at the dog crates where Beatrice was chewing on her rubber chicken, making distracting noises.

"As long as I was in school, my uncle would allow me to continue my education. Education is extremely important in Qatar, even for females. We have excellent education systems."

"And Sharia."

The airplane bobbled in the turbulence and Kira pulled her belt tighter across her lap.

"Yes, and Sharia. London had no idea what to do after her master's degree, so we both slow-rolled our classes, taking just enough credits each semester to maintain our full-time status. She had a wedding instead of going to her graduation ceremony. They mailed her master's diploma to her."

"And you went on to get your PhD."

"The problem for me concerning William and London…it doesn't matter. I'm not married to him. Those are London's choices."

"But she's your friend. What worries you about William?"

"My family is part of the royal family. But William thinks he is as well."

"Interesting. How is that? Not through marriage. So…"

"In America, there is a group called the Assembly."

"I read about them in the paper. Was it two years ago? A massive computer dump exposed some of their illegal actions. Some were imprisoned, others publicly shamed. A lot of mistresses."

"The way William explained it to me is along the

lines of the historical way that royals were seen as demi-gods. They think that God put them in a place to rule, and the royals were God's voice on Earth. By deifying royalty, the royals maintained their power. The heads of state were revered. Laws applied to the serfs. Royals do whatever they want without repercussions."

"Davidson sees himself as a king?"

"An Assemblyman, so yes. But there was that scandal you mentioned. It messed things up a bit for them. The group took up residences in other countries like London and William do. They're rarely in the United States now. They fly in and fly right back out again. The Assembly core stayed strong. I think they're just biding their time to make a comeback, letting memories of bad actions fade. London has tried to find me a husband amongst the Assemblymen—William's friends."

"As if you'd need help finding someone."

"London is not the same person that I've lived with for almost a decade. I sense that she's been radicalized since she's married William. She thinks that the Assembly beliefs are true." Kira frowned and stared at her hands resting on her lap. "I love her. She's been a dear friend for all my adult life. This is the *last* time I will help her like this. I have some major life changes... I just don't know. Our friendship..."

"Tell me what you mean about her being radicalized," Ty said.

"So I was studying this."

"Why?" Ty asked.

"I had some decisions to make about me—my life. I was watching London and was confused by the changes in her ethics and beliefs. If only life came with an instruction manual. I wish I believed in palm reading and astrology—that someone could look in their crystal ball and tell me."

Ty rubbed his hand across the back of his neck. "You're making my hair stand on end. I'm a soldier, that usually only happens when I'm in someone's rifle sights."

"I don't know what that means."

"It only happens when there's mortal danger."

She looked down. And thought for a moment. "Danger for you?" she asked.

"Or my team."

"Do you think of me that way? As a teammate?"

"You?" He laughed. "Hardly."

When she pouted, Ty reached over and covered her hand with his, squeezed, and waited for her to look up. "It's crazy that we've only known each other for a few days. You have become precious to me, my pearl. I'm here to keep you safe. And when we're back on American soil, we need to have a very serious talk about us." Ty was sorry the moment he said that. Grief filled her eyes. So he changed the subject back again to London.

"At work, we take classes on radicalization," Ty said. "It's hard to unwrap once it's in place. How do you think London came to be radicalized toward her husband's beliefs? Do you think they're dangerous beliefs?"

"If someone is convinced that they're above the rules, above the law, above ethics or scrutiny, then they can't help but be dangerous."

"Do you think she was radicalized on her own, or do you think William has threatened her in some way?"

"London is sequestered by William. He keeps her moving from one place to another. He's had numerous other wives, and I think he's figured out how to keep a wife from up and leaving him."

"Destabilized from lack of roots and strong support system."

"Right. Keep the people she comes into contact with all telling her the same thing. She has no outlet, no other perspective to balance."

"What about you? You're a counterweight."

"Me, no. I have no sway. London sees me as Qatari. In Qatar is Sharia. The Assembly and Sharia are very much the same things."

"Are you considering subjecting yourself to Sharia law?" Ty had to tread softly here. "You would have to if you were moving to Qatar, right?"

"Yes, that's right. That's right… It's complex. There are ramifications for my actions and my inactions."

"I don't understand. You're American through and through—"

Kira interrupted him. "You don't have the same penalties to pay."

"What exactly are we talking about here?" Ty leaned forward, resting his forearms on his thighs, bringing his eyes down level with Kira's.

She scratched her brow. "Well, it depends. On the family. On the individuals. I don't know how to answer you." She stilled. "I showed you the novels that my aunt Fatima's friend sent me to preserve."

"Yes, beautiful. You said you were enjoying it though you haven't made much headway."

"In the first novel, the woman followed her family's wishes, and it's going very badly for her. The husband was vicious."

"The character told the authorities?"

"Men can do as they wish to their wives."

"No," Ty said insistently. "They *can't*."

Kira lifted her brows with incredulity. "No?"

"Well, in America—"

"Women in the U.S. are brutalized and murdered by their husbands all the time. When a woman comes forward and says she's being abused, people don't protect her. They ask what she did to deserve his anger. Or they ask her, well then why didn't you leave? Or they say, well, if you had just done this or that, he wouldn't have hit you. Or they think she's lying or being hyperbolic. Or any other reason to blame the victim instead of the perpetrator. It really takes a great deal of effort and sheer luck to get a man to have repercussions for their behaviors."

"That shouldn't be," Ty said softly.

"No. It shouldn't be—not anywhere in the world. But, frankly, some places are more dangerous for women than others. In some countries, women who are victims of rape, for example, are stoned to death. In other countries, the rapist can evade prison by marrying his victim."

"Surely, the victim would say no."

"Surely, it doesn't matter what she says. In India just this morning, the news said a father beheaded his daughter in an honor killing."

"I was in Iraq—" he pointed to Rory "—with the dogs. I didn't like how widows were begging in the streets, trying to get food for themselves and their children. We were told not to approach them, lest we bring anger toward them for talking to men, especially American men. The Taliban would kill them. Yeah—" he looked out the window "—I hated that."

"You have to be careful to honor the community that you're in and not step on their social norms unless you know you will truly be helping. Sometimes thinking you're doing good and actually making a positive difference aren't the same. Qatar isn't like the Iraq that you knew. It's very metropolitan. Very international. I can speak to men. I can wear what I want—as long as it's modest. But there are rules. And the rules must be followed lest you disgrace the family. And that," she whispered, "would never be allowed by my uncle. He's too worried about anything happening that would disrupt his plans."

"Which are?"

"World domination." She said it sarcastically, but there was a bright note of truth to her quip.

Chapter 29

Ty

"Kira." Ty gently swept a hand over her hair until she roused. "We're landing."

She pulled in a deep breath then looked out the window.

"See the giraffe herd?" He pointed at a distance.

Kira thrust her head forward, squinting at the landscape. "Oh!" She gasped. "Look at them running, so graceful." She turned to him with a little frown. "Our plane probably frightened them." She reached down and tightened her belt, yawning to help her ears equalize the pressure.

The tires bounced down. She turned to Ty with a forced smile. "This is it."

"Are you okay?"

"Stresses. I told you how bad things got the last time

they had this meeting. Karl getting accidentally shot by his sister…"

"Fresh start."

When the pilot lowered the stairs, Ty and Kira descended to find the staff lined up to greet them.

"This is Tumo. He manages the property," Kira said. She placed her hand over her heart and gave him an ever so slight bow. "Jumbo! Tumo."

"Miss Kira, welcome back to Davidson Range. We have all prepared for your welcome."

"Thank you." She turned to Ty. "This is my head of security, Ty Newcomb and his security K9 Rory." Kira juggled Bea in her hands. "And this is London's pet Princess Beatrice."

Tumo gestured to a man in a ranger-like uniform, who advanced to stand side by side with his colleague. "Mr. Newcomb. Please meet the Range Head Security Officer Moses."

"Jumbo!" Ty said, shaking the men's hands.

Rory sat at attention, letting nothing miss his observation.

"Tumo, there are fresh flowers on the plane. Each arrangement has a flower pick in the vase, indicating which room it should be placed in. We kept the air conditioning cool on the plane, so they are crisp. Have your staff look them over. Anything that's drooping should be removed."

"Yes, Miss."

"In the plane's hold, you'll find the food, as we discussed. Ty has translated the instructions for the kitchen staff. The chef should read them over and ask any questions he has about them today. Ty and I will only be here until Monday morning. Once I leave, everything is to run smoothly without any mistakes."

"Yes, Miss."

"Once everything is unloaded, please come find me so we can go over the plans."

"Of course, Miss."

"Our pilots are exhausted. If you could please show them to their rooms and ask if they would benefit from a massage. Make sure they are well cared for as our guests. They need to be ready to go pick up Mr. and Mrs. Davidson and their party in the morning."

"Yes, Miss."

"Moses." Kira turned.

Ty was seeing Kira in her element. She was obviously well respected. She was clear and authoritative, gentle and detail oriented. This was the kind of life Kira led.

Ty thought of his own life on base. It wasn't like tier-one operators made any kind of money. Even with imminent danger pay, they made enough to meet bills, but not much beyond. And to think that in some dark recesses of his brain, he had imagined Kira coming home to his house at the fort, sharing his bed every night he wasn't out on a mission.

"Miss." Moses repeated the gesture Kira had made earlier, placing his hand on his heart and offering her a slight bow which she returned in kind, treating the men as professionals.

"I would like you to take Ty on a thorough tour of the Range. You are to apprise him of how everything works security-wise. What your concerns are, especially about groups in the area and any troubles you've noticed, even if they haven't risen in your estimation as a concern. He is to know everything about everything. He's here to determine risk management." She skated her hand out. "Which is a task I'm performing for Mr. and Mrs. Davidson to see if you need anything else to keep the Range safe. His being here doesn't reflect in any way on you or your job performance. Ty has techniques and systems that might make your job an easier one."

"Thank you, Miss." Moses turned to Ty. "Sir."

"Ty's fine. No need for sir."

Moses bladed his hand to indicate they should head through the gate.

"Just one second," Ty said in Swahili. "I want to grab my bag."

Moses showed Ty to his room and pointed out the window at another building. "This is where my office is. Once you're settled, if you will join me there, I will show you our operation." Moses flipped back and forth from English to Swahili.

Ty continued to use the native language, hoping that Moses would see him less as a good idea fairy that fluttered in to make his life more difficult—or worse, to make him feel like his job was endangered. It was all about posture and tone.

Now that Ty was alone, he opened his equipment bag. Ty attached microphones and pulled on the baseball cap with the integrated camera system. The camera would pick up a one-hundred-degree wedge in the direction he was looking. Recording everything for his team to see and hear was the simplest way to share the information without it coming from his sole perspective of what was important.

Delta Force was a unique group because they drew their operators from all branches of the military. Though Ty came up through the Army Rangers, T-Rex had been a SEAL, Nitro had been a Marine Raider. There was a lot of expertise that sat around the table when they reviewed a mission. Different eyes, different perspectives, all coming together to develop the plans with the highest opportunity for success.

Getting his connection in place, he looked around the room. "Testing. Testing. Testing. Echo-zero-two to Echo-zero-one."

A soft voice in his ear said, "Receiving clear audio-visual. Over."

Ty let his eye sweep over his room. Under his breath, he oriented the team to where he was and what he would be doing as he jogged toward the security office.

"Moses," Ty said as the man, wiry and lithe, opened the door to him. "I watched some of your men walking perimeter with two rifles slung over their backs while we were still in the air."

"Yes, one rifle, one BB gun. The rifles are for large predators. There have been some cats in our area because of the big migration. It's the time of year when we must be more vigilant."

"And the BBs?"

"The curiosity of the monkeys, especially today. They will be drawn in by the bright colors of Miss Kira's flowers. We do not wish to hurt the wild animals, simply to deter them from coming into the Range. Even with the rifles, it is the noise that scares them away. If the cats become a danger, then we get the preserve rangers to come and decide how to best handle the situation."

"What is usually done?" Ty asked curiously.

"Sometimes the animals are sedated, given tracking collars, and moved to a preserve. Sometimes, the cats approach humans because the animal is unwell. You see, Tanzania gets most of its preservation budget from selling special hunts to those who have the money to pay for such things. Animals who become a danger to humans or others are marked for such a hunt. Many animal rights groups frown on such a model. I have seen with my own eyes a bull who killed three endangered cows because he was crazy in the head. Had the hunters killed this bull, they would have saved three. They would also have had about a hundred thousand dollars with which to pay anti-poachers' salaries to save more animals of their kind. Luckily, I am not in the business of managing such things. We merely tell the rangers, and they take actions."

"Has your staff seen wild cats recently?"

"Not in a fortnight. Things are calm here."

"Tell me about concerns in the area in general. You mentioned poachers."

"Poachers will stay away from the Range. They know that the owner is wealthy, and so the government would act harshly against them. In Congo, some groups have been gathering under the Islamic Extremist flags. We know that they have been creating issues along the Tanzanian borders as they move through the surrounding countries. This is particularly true since there was oil discovered under Lake Edward. There's an anti-Western—if you will excuse me—sentiment."

"I'm looking for facts. I'm not concerned with my feelings."

"Yes, there is a lot of anti-Western anger. England is claiming that oil. Russia wishes to take control of the oil. This is African oil. It should benefit the African people, not those from a different continent. The militias have felt emboldened in the last year since the successful terror attack at Ngorongoro Crater."

"And Mr. Davidson is an oilman."

"This he is." Moses chewed on his back teeth, making his jaw muscles bulge.

"And is that a problem when the Davidson family is here?"

"More so now than in the past. Mr. Davidson's oil business and his buying such a large parcel of land as a foreigner has raised security concerns, most definitely. Once we learned of this meeting, and the people who would be attending, we have increased our normal security measures."

"Did you hire more guards?" Ty asked, worried that without proper vetting, they might have brought in a spy.

"No, we prefer to depend on our own warriors. I have extended their hours of duty during this time. They carry more ammunition with them. Once the guests have arrived, our guards will wear bullet-resistant vests and helmets as part of their uniforms on the exterior of the retaining walls."

"So you have that kind of equipment?"

"I will show you our storage room. Mr. Davidson wishes us to have what we deem necessary for securing his home."

Ty followed along beside Moses as they moved past a fully equipped gym to their supply room.

"Mr. Davidson and I have discussed before that it is preferable for the family to drive to the Range. Everyone for miles around can see his jet coming in. They will know he is here."

"I see. And he decided not to pay attention to your counsel?"

"It is an uncomfortable drive both in time and with the road conditions. Mr. Davidson will do as he sees best." Moses bladed his hand toward the door with a "SUPPLY" sign.

As they entered, Ty noticed the care and precision of the room. The guns and ammo were in a caged space with a padlock. Moses showed Ty that he carried the key on a cord around his neck.

Ty took his time in that room. He made sure that every item was seen for his team to catalog. If Echo and Foxtrot dropped in, and security was aware, these bullets could be aimed at his team. They needed to know exactly what they were up against.

"Come, let me show you our security plan. I can see we are of the same mindset. Perhaps if Mr. Davidson hears your own assessment, he might reconsider. All of our people would be involved should anyone grow interested in Mr. Davidson's presence."

Ty liked Moses. He was an intelligent, capable man.

As they continued on the exhaustive tour, Ty learned that Moses had been part of security at Ikulu, the Tanzanian president's White House. Moses said the same architect for Ikulu in 1922 had also designed Davidson Range. "Though of course, it had a different name in the past."

Security was probably as tightly enforced here at the Range as it was at Ikulu.

Echo and Foxtrot didn't have an easy job in front of them, that was for sure.

Chapter 30

Ty

That evening, Ty, Kira, and the heads of staff ate at the large kitchen table.

"Thank you, Nen," Kira said to the chef as she spread her napkin across her lap. "I always describe my time here in Tanzania as a paradise with fruit." She smiled. "Everything looks and smells amazing."

Ty noticed that their meal was traditional Tanzanian food and not a single dish that Bruce had sent over, for which he was glad. Plain, honest food was much more to Ty's liking.

They ate, then Ty accompanied Kira back to her room. "How are the plans coming?" Ty asked her.

"The staff could not have been more ready. Everything was so easy, thanks to their help." She looked pointedly at Ty. "I placed the photographs the way I had planned on William's guests' rooms but left them off of ours as you suggested." She looked at her watch. "We'll be gone again in thirty-two hours." Kira looked impatient for the time to pass and to head back out again.

"The flowers and food are all squared away?"

"They are. And I wanted to ask you, as I imagine you travel long distances for short periods with your job. Do you have a best practice for being bright-eyed and bushy-tailed? I'll admit, the flight left me exhausted, though I slept. Tomorrow I need to be on my toes."

She'd be meeting her "intended" tomorrow. White had said that exhaustion played a role in how we were perceived. If Kira was tired, she might let her guard down. Her face might shine the truth that London exhorted her to mask. Kira needed to be running on all cylinders.

"I have some sleep medicine with me. If you take them now and curl up with a book, you should wake up in the morning feeling acclimated to this time zone."

They had reached their bedrooms. As Kira waited for him in the hallway, Ty dug through his bag for the pills found in every special forces' operator kit. "These are going to knock you out," he said as he emerged again into the hallway.

"Thank you, that sounds perfect."

"May I have the key to your room, so I can check on you?"

Kira looked up from the bottle in his hand and their eyes caught and held.

"I don't think that's a good idea, Ty. Uhm. Tanzania. Already, placing your room next to mine is questionable. But the key might look concerning."

"I don't really need a key to breach a lock." He said it jokingly, but he was dead serious. There wasn't a door that could keep Ty away if he thought Kira needed him.

"You'd break down the door?" There was a laugh that twitched Kira's lips.

They stood across the hall from each other. Kira's hands behind her back; Ty's arms crossed over his chest. "Kira, do you think anything would stop me from protecting you?" He held out the pills. When she stepped forward to accept them, he whispered, "It's going to be hard for me, knowing that you're in a bed on the other side of the wall. When we get home to America, I'll show you how much I missed holding you."

She accepted the pills with downcast eyes and no response to what he'd said.

Ty could already feel her trying to pull away from him as she transitioned to her new life. What she didn't realize was that Omar's time on this planet would either be spent in an American prison, or his life expectancy was counted in hours instead of days.

Kira opened her door, turned to him, came to some conclusion, then handed Ty her key.

That felt huge to Ty. Symbolic that she trusted him to think of the broader picture, not just his immediate needs.

Ty and Rory went to his room next door. He lay down to power nap. At midnight, he was going on a recon to figure out how the security functioned after dark. How many were on duty? Where were they positioned? What weapons were they carrying? What communication systems? The last thing Ty wanted was for Moses or one of his guards to be injured in the operation Monday night as the Unit descended into the complex to capture or kill Omar Mohamed Imadi.

As Ty lay on his bed, waiting to fall asleep, he remembered on their mission to Uganda to steal the Russian helicopter that Nick of Time had brought up this place. D-Day had said she'd never been here. As adventurous and bold as D-Day was, it was hard for Ty to imagine her passing this up. It had to have something to do with family dynamics.

It was mind-boggling to Ty that this was D-Day's background. A more down to Earth, straight shooter he couldn't imagine. That her background included this level of over-the-top decadent wealth? D-Day sounded like the opposite of Kira's description of William and London.

Ty listened to the herds of sheep and goats that the staff maintained in the south pasture. When Ty was on that fateful mission last year to save CIA's John Grey, the mission that had bought Echo their ticket onto this Omar Mohamed Imadi ride, D-Day had been their pilot.

Forced to the ground by RPG fire, as the pilots worked to develop a way out of their dilemma, Ty was lying in front of them with his eye on his rifle scope. D-Day and Nick were spreading a camo net over their Little Bird to hide it in the landscape, hoping the enemy wouldn't spot them.

D-Day had been talking about the movie about Benghazi—*Thirteen Hours*. She'd mentioned a scene where they were trying to decide what was going on with the sheep herd, was that the normal sheep behavior, or were terrorists using the sheep as cover?

Benghazi was twenty-four hundred miles from here.

But the unrest on this continent was palpable.

Anything could happen at any time.

Chapter 31

Kira

Despite being designed by an Englishman, Davidson Range was in a country with many devotees of Islam. A minaret had been included in the exterior wall design. The imam for the tribe proclaimed the call to prayer as the sun set.

Kira took her prayer rug to the women's area in the courtyard and moved through the Maghrib with those at the Range of the Muslim faith.

While she didn't often perform the ritual prayers, on occasion, Kira took refuge in them.

Tonight, she needed Allah's help.

Though the plane had been delayed getting to the Range, soon London and her guests would arrive, and amongst them would be Omar, her intended. And with her would be Ty, the man she loved.

It seemed like an ugly joke that fate had worked out this way.

Ty was…

Everything.

He was everything she respected with her mind. Everything she craved with her body. Everything her heart wanted.

When Kira was with him, she felt valued and appreciated. She felt like she was enough just the way she was, that he didn't want to change a single hair on her head. The connection was a belated miracle. And Kira knew…she just knew her loving Ty would be forever.

If only he'd come a month ago before her uncle had offered her to Omar.

Now, more than ever, if Kira refused her uncle, he would not only deny her access to her beloved family, but he would seek revenge. That was the kind of man he was. He would feel if he didn't aggressively punish her, he would lose power in some eyes and be embarrassed in front of his colleague. Who knew the ramifications for that?

For Kira, turning Omar away would mean a lifetime of looking over her shoulder, flinching at shadows.

She was stuck. If only Allah would bring her peace. Even a tiny sliver of respite from her fear while she was here at the Range. She would deal with tomorrow when tomorrow arrived.

But for London's sake, she needed a serene face to provide a warm welcome.

She couldn't expose her friend to backlash for her help, warning her about Omar.

Overhead, Kira could hear the jet approaching.

With her ritual complete, Kira rose, rolled her prayer rug, and started back to the villa.

Ty was in the shadows, watching over her, taking his duty seriously. That made her smile.

"Ready?" he asked.

"Ready." She wished she could slip into his arms and walk together to the plane. But this was on her. She was about to meet her future husband.

When they arrived at the jet, London was just disembarking. "Oh, look at the sunset," she sighed out as Kira pressed up to kiss her cheek and the top of Archie's head.

Kira turned to look. The red sun was sinking behind the horizon. The last gasp of the day, then it disappeared. "Did you make a wish?" she asked London.

"No need." London smiled over at her husband. "My life is perfect."

As the guests arrived at their sides, Ty stood back out of the way. Close enough to help her if needed, far enough away that he wouldn't cause her grief.

"Uncle." She smiled and touched her heart.

London announced everyone's name as they greeted her, though Kira had memorized the names on the photos. She was glad, though, to have them pronounced for her.

The last in line was Omar.

In truth, he wasn't a bad-looking man. Salt and pepper hair had been carefully styled, and he was wearing European labels instead of a traditional thobe. Maybe there was hope that he also embraced more Western sentiments about women. She touched her heart and welcomed him with the exact same tone and facial expression as everyone else, she hoped.

Her stomach churned with a hot, greasy sensation. When Omar touched his hand to his heart in response, Kira noticed that his pinky had been amputated, and she wondered how that had happened.

A blur of action at the corner of her eye pulled Kira's head around.

Rory raced forward and came to a halt in front of her, sitting on her toes and giving Omar a death stare.

"This is your dog?" Omar asked. "He seems quite protective."

"This is Rory. And yes, he is very protective of me." Kira felt no need to tell Omar that Rory was with Ty. "Shall we go in?" Kira gestured. "I have evening cocktails and hors d'oeuvres set out on the veranda while the staff delivers your luggage to your rooms. Dinner will be at eight-thirty. I hope everyone brought their appetites."

That was met with chuckles of anticipation as she started up the stairs.

London was beside Kira leading the way for the guests. "Where is my princess?" London asked. "Is she afraid of this dog?"

"Rory? Oh, no, Beatrice adores Rory. And Rory is very protective of Beatrice. As a matter of fact, some huge rottweiler tried to eat Beatrice, and Old Rory here leaped an eight-foot wall to get between the bad dog and Beatrice. I'm not sure what would have happened if he wasn't such a good boy."

"You saved my precious?" London crooned to Rory. "Thank you. I'll tell cook to find you a big bone to gnaw on."

Rory ignored London but slid his head under Kira's hand, and Kira rubbed his ears. "Did you hear me tell London that you're a good boy? You are. You're a very good boy." She turned her attention to London. "Beatrice is in your room in her crate. Some vultures were flying around earlier, and I was afraid that bitty Beatrice might get scooped up in their talons. Since I was running around getting everything set up, I thought it would be prudent to keep her safe."

London bumped her hip into Kira and raised her brows. Kira knew that London wanted some clue about what she thought of Omar. Kira pretended she didn't understand and just kept walking.

"Here we are." Kira lifted her palms welcomingly and added a lilt to her voice to help create a festive mood. She had music playing. It was gorgeous, the food was light but delicious. As she watched, everyone unwound from the journey, drinks were tipped back, laughter rang out.

London was off being London, and she didn't seem to notice that Kira had shrunk into the shadows.

Soon a staff member arrived at the veranda door with a little gong and mallet in his white-gloved hands. He struck the instrument, and everyone quieted to hear him announce, "Dinner is served." He turned and left.

"If you'll follow me," Kira said, glancing into the shadows where she saw Ty standing. Rory was still at her side. "Rory, go find Ty."

Rory ignored her.

Kira raised her brows to Ty, but Ty did nothing to help.

So off she and Rory went, leading the guests to the dining room.

Archie was displeased with the change.

As soon as he crossed into the villa, he began to scream. London sent a frown to William. "It's near his bedtime."

"And?" William asked.

Kira scooped Archie into her arms. "Why don't I go

give Archie his bath and get him ready for bed while you enjoy your guests? Is his formula in his diaper bag?"

"But Kira, dinner," London said, though she didn't stop Kira from taking Archie, who shook little balled fists and projected his anger in a voice so loud that it was hard to believe it came from such a tiny frame.

"I had plenty at cocktails. I'll stay with him. You enjoy dinner."

Kira could feel Omar's eyes on her watching her every move. She thought that he was pleased with her taking the baby. She wondered if he was annoyed by the screaming or if he imagined her holding his son. Nausea slicked up the back of her throat.

She turned and walked away.

Kira, with Archie in her arms and Rory plastered to her side, moved toward the stairs to the bedrooms. There stood Ty, waiting for her.

"Hey," she whispered.

"Are you okay? You look ill."

"Thank you, I'm fine. To be honest, I'm happy Archie's furious. It meant I could escape."

"Kira…" There was an intensity around Ty that she hadn't experienced before.

"Did you send Rory over to me earlier? What was the command…hold the fort?"

"I didn't. He went on his own. You should know that Rory is very instinctive. You can *always* trust Rory's judgment."

"Isn't that interesting."

"Do you know that man?"

"We met just now." Kira knew that Archie's screams echoed through the villa. "He needs a bath and a diaper change, a bottle, and some sleep."

"I have a meeting. I'll be in my room if you need

anything." He turned. "Keep Rory with you," he called over his shoulder as he opened his door.

That Rory came to safeguard her on his own was meaningful.

It told Kira that Rory was sensing that Omar was a person that she needed to be protected from. It wasn't her nerves but her intuition that was telling her to run from Omar.

Yes, if Rory made the call to come and get between her and Omar, out of self-preservation, Kira needed to say no to her uncle. And find a way to stay safe.

If she were to marry Omar, she would be his to do with as he wished, take her to Saudi Arabia, lock her in a tower like the Bahraini princess.

Marrying Omar did not guarantee that she would have any contact with her family.

Now, face to face with that destiny, Kira knew that she *couldn't*.

She *wouldn't*.

Kira sent up a prayer of thanksgiving to Allah for putting Ty in her path. She might not have come to this conclusion had she not met Ty and seen how much she'd be giving up.

Chapter 32

Ty

Ty popped open his computer on an end-to-end encrypted channel. "It took me a minute to get away. What's the situation?"

T-Rex sat in front of the screen. "You've got problems, brother."

The view turned to a split-screen—T-Rex on the left, satellite imagery on the right with little white boxes around moving vehicles.

"Incoming," Ty said. "What is this?"

"Eight transport trucks, standing room only, we believe twenty per bed, three in the cab. Two hundred or so militants are converging on your location."

"Foxtrot?"

"Echo isn't close enough to be of assistance. Foxtrot is managing an overwatch drone that they sent up.

They fielded eight guys. They went in lean for recon. They're not equipped to stave off a militia."

"Neither is security here. The men are trained and have experience. They're well equipped. But not for an attack of two hundred. Has Foxtrot seen them up close? What weapons are we looking at?"

"Visible? Rifles and khat."

Khat leaves had been used in Ethiopia and Sudan, but the use was now spreading across Africa. Chewed, the leaf gave the consumer a sense of excitement and euphoria, hyperactivity, and manic behaviors.

If the militants were all high on khat, their behavior would be erratic and illogical. There would be no way to talk them down, especially if they were spiraled into a frenzy by their leaders.

"What have you got there in the way of transportation?" T-Rex asked.

"A couple of golf carts. A delivery truck."

"How many women and children?"

"In the visiting party, two women, one infant. From the residents: thirty women, say about forty children. We can start by moving the children and the mothers with babes in arms to the preserve."

"They won't let them cross the gates," T-Rex said. "The rangers' job is to protect the wildlife. If they think that you're drawing two hundred militants in their direction, they will bar you from entering."

"Rightly so. We just need to not let the militants know we're coming in. But London Davidson is keeping that place afloat with her donations, so with her in the cab, they'd have to open the gates. I'll get the rest of the women and the elders in the golf carts or walking in the right direction. Once I get the first group unloaded in the preserve to hide, I'll go back and gather the rest of the women. How much time are we talking about?"

"At their present speed, forty-seven minutes."

Ty pulled out his phone and pressed the quick dial he had loaded in earlier on his tour. "Moses, this is Ty. I need you in the Davidsons' suite stat. There's a major security breach spooling up."

He turned back to T-Rex. "Can't air support handle this?"

"You have eyes in the sky, and that's all that Tanzania will allow. Those men are not Tanzanian. The host government doesn't want Americans to explode their relationships with their neighbors. They're afraid of another Benghazi. Their military is being deployed. They'll get there. We're just not sure how fast. Foxtrot has been ordered to pull out. They'll continue to monitor and advise, but per the new communications with our host nation, Foxtrot is not to shoot."

"No one said I couldn't shoot, right?"

"My understanding is that you are close protection for a private citizen. Omar's there?"

"Yeah. Once I have my precious cargo protected, I'll hand the truck keys over to one of the others and let them continue with the evacuation. Do you think the militants are after Davidson or Omar?"

"Intelligence is telling us that the flags on the trucks belong to a group that is in opposition to the cells Omar inherited from Momo. Omar is probably the main target. We can't let them take Omar. Not only will we lose track of him and not be assured that he's been dealt with, but that might escalate the factions. Command prefers that we maintain control of Omar's timeline."

"Wilco."

"Good luck. Out."

Ty could hear Moses thundering up the stairs. Ty went two doors down and threw open the door to the Davidsons' suite.

Kira was rocking a sleeping Archie. She looked up, startled.

Ty pointed at her. "There's a security issue. Call London and tell her to get up here now. Put the baby in his crib. Then go change your clothes. Black everything. Tennis shoes. Fleece against the cold night. You have three minutes. Go."

Kira startled, stared, and taking in Moses out of breath and obviously in go-mode, she nodded and rolled Archie into his crib. She pulled out her phone and was calling London.

Ty turned to Moses, opened his computer, and showed Moses what was heading their way. "Anywhere to hunker down? Safe rooms?" Ty had asked earlier, and Moses had said no, but Ty would have said the same. He'd never reveal safe rooms to a stranger.

"They weren't built into the architecture. There's the wine cellar. The guests can hide behind the crates."

Ty went over his plan for the women and children. When Moses brought up the same concerns T-Rex had about the preserve allowing them in, Ty simply said, "London's money is our golden ticket."

"These men in the trucks have no morals and no mercy," Moses said, his phone out. "They will rape, destroy, and slaughter. Do you have any help?"

"No. I'm sorry. I only have information. This is my plan."

As Moses made a string of phone calls, telling everyone to keep their activity calm and quick, London burst through the door to her suite. "What? What's happening? Why did Kira tell me to come up here immediately?" She peered down at Archie, placing her hand on his back and feeling him breathe.

Moses caught Ty's eye and then hustled out to get his security in place.

"London, there's about to be a breach on your compound. I need you to change your clothes to go to the preserve. Pack a diaper bag for Archie. Comfortable, warm clothes, shoes you can walk a long distance in. Change now."

Kira came back in the room dressed as Ty had requested. She had a daypack on her back. She looked at London. "Get dressed!" she yelled at her friend.

Kira moved to the diaper bag and started filling it with Archie's requirements.

London looked at Ty as if he should leave the room for her modesty. Ty couldn't care less about the woman's privacy. As she realized this, with shaking hands, she pulled out an outfit and started to change.

"We need to get the household staff together and tell them to fire their rifles and make the men in the trucks go away."

"Ma'am, those trucks are gunning—and I choose that word specifically—for someone who came in on that jet. My goal is to get the women and children to safety in the preserve."

"No." London stopped dressing, one leg in her pants. "William. He must come, too. And our guests."

"Women and children first because they face the greatest danger. Finish dressing, London." Ty's voice was calmly authoritative.

His command animated her again.

"Do either of you know how to use a gun?"

"I've seen it in the movies," London said, working on her socks. "How hard could it be? Point and shoot, right?" Just like for Kira, adrenaline made her hands shake to the point of being ineffectual.

Ty hated to lose time this way. "No, not right. If you don't know what you're doing, you're going to flinch and aim away from the danger, putting everyone under mortal threat. You either know how to hit the mark, and you've practiced, or you're arming the bad guy as you stand there quivering and unable. That'll get you killed."

"Give me a gun, Ty. I'm paying your salary. You respond to my commands. I'll shoot them in the leg, then they can't chase after us," London said, zipping her pants closed.

"Kira, are you ready with the bag?"

Kira nodded.

"Let's go then." Ty made his way over to the crate and got Beatrice out, thinking that having Bea along would help soothe London into complying. He snapped a lead onto her collar and handed her into London's outstretched arms. "You don't seem to understand what adrenaline can do. Shoot him in the leg. You're dead from his bullet. The thought that you could be that precise under stress with a weapon you've never fired before? Ma'am, that's just delusional. Rory will stay with Kira. Rory." He caught his K9's eye. "Flank Kira. Let's move."

"No!" yelled London.

Kira slung Archie's bag over her shoulder, wrapped the baby in a blanket, pressing his pacifier into his mouth as he sucked on it anxiously, and moved into the hallway, Rory plastered to her side.

"But William." London's voice was shrill. "I have to talk this over with him."

"Moses already took William and your guests down to the wine cellar."

"Then that's where we should go, too."

Ty knew that London had to be on the transport to get the women and children into the preserve. So he said, "I *will* throw you over my shoulder if I have to. But that means you have to leave Beatrice here on her own."

Glowering but silent, London followed after Kira into the hall.

With every second that ticked by, the militants were drawing closer, and their chance at safety dwindled.

Chapter 33

Ty

Ty slid momentarily into his room and grabbed his backpack.

Putting his hands on the women's elbows, Ty steered the group down the staff staircase toward the back exit and the truck.

"Won't the headlights give us away?" Kira asked. The back of the truck was filled with mothers positioned around the circumference of the cargo space and the children piled in the center, older children with the younger ones in their laps, everyone squished in tightly.

"You're right. We won't be using them," Ty responded, accepting a rifle from Moses and a MOLLE vest of magazines. "Thanks. I'll be back as soon as I can."

"How will you drive?" London's voice was high-pitched with fear.

Ty handed Kira his phone with a topographical map to their destination. "Night vision." Ty pulled his helmet from his pack and strapped it under his chin.

Moses handed Ty a paper map. "This is the preserve. Here, there are shelters for the poacher patrols. They aren't known to many. Hide them here." He moved his finger over to the north. "Here is where you will go in. They should be safe from the militants there."

"And the wildlife?"

"This may be an issue, but we will hope that all will be well."

Moses reached up for the hand of one of the women who leaned over the side. "Be safe, wife. Protect my son. I love you," he told her.

"Moses, cut all lights once we're out the gate," Ty said.

"Yes." Moses raised his hand, the gate opened, and Ty rumbled the truck forward.

Ty tapped his chest where his comms unit lay under his shirt. "Echo-zero-two to TOC."

"Go for Echo-zero-one."

"I'm heading to the preserve. Twenty minutes out."

"That's cutting it close, brother."

"Can Foxtrot meet us at the gate and go in to protect the evacuees?"

"That's already in play. A five-man team will meet you at the gate and walk in with you. I want you back on perimeter. The other three are pushing for the compound."

When the lights went black at the Range, Ty pulled his night vision into place.

"This is so spooky," Kira whispered as they drove through the black of night.

"I can see well enough, Kira. I'll keep you safe."

"There's no reason for us to be afraid," London said, manically stroking Beatrice's fur. "We're good friends with the president and the government. They know us. We've been invited to their homes. I've spent time with their wives and children. Just call them. They'll send help."

"Ma'am, they have been contacted, and they're sending forces. They're an hour away. The militants are thirty minutes away. A lot of terrible things can happen in a half-hour. By the time the military can get on-site, you'd be captured."

"Captured not killed."

"Yeah, well, you may wish you had been," Ty muttered under his breath.

"Kira!" London said. "Kira is part of the royal family. She could call someone. She could reach out to the heavy hitters in her family. They can help."

"From Qatar, ma'am?" He pursed his lips.

A pall settled over the cab.

Ty did his best to drive gently over the landscape. He knew that the women and children in the back were taking a beating from the bumps. He also knew that time was of the essence.

Moses decided that the golf carts were too dangerous to use to transport those fleeing toward the preserve because the lights would illuminate their path and bring attention from the bad guys. Moses only had enough night vision for his men on the wall and couldn't spare any of the devices for drivers.

The elders and the women who were not able to get onto the truck were moving off toward the tree line to the south to take shelter. Ty would take one of the Foxtrot unit members with him as he drove back to rescue the others. Then, Ty would try to get eyes on Omar while his brother helped evacuate as many as they could to the relative safety of the preserve.

Rory was curled on the floor at London's feet, his chin rested on Kira's lap, sniffing the baby. "Rory," Ty said. "I'm depending on you."

Rory responded with a sharp bark. He took his responsibility for Kira seriously.

They were met at the preserve gate by a band of armed rangers, standing shoulder to shoulder and looking determined. Ty simply pulled up and shined a penlight on London's face.

After a moment of indecision, they peeled back.

As they did, Foxtrot rose from the ground pulling their grass-covered ghillie suits off.

To say the rangers were startled that they'd been standing there without seeing the soldiers was to put things mildly.

Ty leaned out his window. "Echo-zero-two," he identified himself.

"Foxtrot. Our orders are to help secure the evacuees."

Ty handed them the map and the location Moses had chosen. "I need one man with night vision to go back with me to drive the next group out. Go ahead and get everyone unloaded."

A stir of activity ensued.

A kiss from Kira. She whispered, "I love you. Thank you. Be safe."

She loved him.

"You do what you have to to make it through this. Stay safe. You have Rory." He pressed his lips against her forehead and whispered back, "I love you, too. We'll figure us out when this is over. I promise."

A Foxtrot brother had helped London from the cab and reached out to assist Kira, with Archie in her arms.

Rory stumbled out after them, shook his coat, and looked Ty in the eye. He'd do his job.

Driving away from Kira had to be one of the hardest damned things Ty ever did.

Chapter 34

Ty

Outside of the compound, his Foxtrot brother had filled the truck with the second group of refugees. The women had wrapped provisions in blankets and rested them on their heads to make room to squeeze all the people on.

The strafe of rifle fire lit up the night as the truck turned and headed back to the preserve, leaving Ty off as they passed closer to the Range.

Ty was alone as he made his way back to the compound. He dialed Moses, who answered him breathlessly. "What is your status, Ty?"

After quickly catching Moses up, Ty then requested an open door to come in and help.

"This is too dangerous," Moses said. "We cannot stop the breach, there was a small band who got in already, using a boating hook. The best we can do inside is hide and hope the military arrives quickly. I've placed each of our guests in a different space, so if one is found, they aren't all found."

"Good plan. I have to get in, Moses."

"All right, on the south-facing wall, we will lower a rope."

"Yes, do that."

The whipping whir of a helicopter rotor buzzed in the distance coming from the northwest.

Ty hunkered at the wall waiting for a rope to drop. "Echo-zero-two for TOC," he said into his comms.

"Go for Echo-zero-one."

"Who's in the sky?" Ty asked.

"That's not us. It's not an exfil. I repeat, we are unaware of friendlies. It is not an exfil from the Unit."

The rope popped against the wall. Thirty feet high, two feet thick, it was enough to keep the animals out, but wasn't secure from militant hordes. Ty wondered why those that already climbed the wall hadn't simply opened the gates for their friends.

Ty reached out to grab the thick rope and put his weight on it to see if it would hold. It felt solid enough. Ty tugged on his tactical gloves and climbed.

By the time he reached the top, the helicopter had landed at the Range's front wall on the west. Luckily, they were still outside the compound.

How long would that last?

Maybe those that were inside were waiting for their commanders before they acted.

Stooping, with his rifle swinging from its strap and his bag on his back, Ty ran along the top of the wall and flung himself down at the top of the northwest corner.

Focusing through his rifle scope, Ty watched a group

gather, looking jubilant, smacking each other on the backs, raising their rifles in the air.

Moments later, the front gates swung open. *Yup, waiting for their leader.*

A spotlight from the helicopter focused on the group who emerged. The militants were shoving Omar out in front of them. His hands on his head. Blood dripping from his nose. He tried to shield his eyes from the bright light with his elbow.

One of the men jabbed his rifle's stock into Omar's back, and he crashed face-first into the red soil.

The men laughed and spat at him.

"Echo-zero-one. Omar is being exfilled on the helicopter. Please advise."

"That helicopter is not identified as friendly. You are cleared hot."

As Omar climbed to his feet, Ty was thinking again of *The Last of the Mohicans*. Omar was on his way to his torture session with his rivals. Ty was not lining up this shot to save Omar from those just deserts; he was lining up this shot to protect innocent lives.

Ty drew in a breath, exhaled halfway, and with his crosshairs between Omar's brows, Ty squeezed the trigger.

His shot rang out, loud and echoing against the night sky.

The world stopped spinning.

In the absolute silence, Omar slipped lifelessly to the ground. Shocked faces searched to understand this change in events.

Those who had come on the helicopter jumped back on.

The heli took off toward the north.

Ty lay there in the black of night, his heart racing.

Abu Musab al Khalil, reinvented as Omar Mohamed Imadi, White's white whale, could no longer terrorize the world.

And Omar would *never* be given a chance to harm Kira.

They were on the jet back to the United States. London was asleep with Archie in his car seat strapped in next to her and Beatrice on her lap.

Ty had both arms around Kira, and she was nestled against his chest.

It was going to take a while for him to absorb the idea that she was safe.

Davidson and the others from their meeting were still back at the Range carrying on as if nothing had happened.

Mind-bending.

Kira placed the flat of her hand on his chest. "My uncle wanted me to marry a terrorist. I won't even consider marrying anyone my uncle chooses for me. What a terrible thing he asked me to do."

Ty petted his hands over her hair to soothe her.

"And you," she said. "That was a setup, wasn't it? You knew that was going to happen."

"No. I would have protected you, told you not to go if I had any idea that would happen. I did know that Omar was going to be there. I can't tell you more."

"My knowing you was a setup," she insisted. "Your being here was no accident."

"That's correct." His hand continued the rhythm.

"Thank goodness." She pressed a kiss into his shirt. "I'm imagining what would have happened if you hadn't been there. Think about it. If you hadn't been there, I would have met Omar and I would have convinced myself it was okay to do what my family wanted even though he made me sick to my stomach when I met him. I would have chalked that up to anger and nerves. And that's *if* the other terrorist group hadn't come to get him. If everyone had still been in the lodge when the bad men came in the helicopter, I'm convinced that once they took Omar away, that their leaders would have allowed the men in the trucks to come in and destroy everything and everyone." She pushed herself up so she was looking Ty in the eyes. "Your being there saved me from either hellscape." She laid her head back on his chest.

Ty bet she could hear his heart racing.

She was right.

That would have been a horrific nightmare of a scenario.

"I'm sure there will be more to process in the days ahead." It sounded like she pushed the words past the nerves constricting in her throat. "How much of what you told me was a lie…but in this moment, I'm still a bit in shock." Her fingers curled into his shirt. "I'm deeply, deeply grateful. To you, and of course to my Rory who never moved an inch from me as we hid in the wilds of the preserve."

Rory lifted his head and placed his chin on her knee so she could rub between his eyes.

"You said you loved me when I was going into the preserve," she whispered.

"I do. My emotions about you—our being together… our physical and emotional connection—are my truth. I'd never lie to you about something like that. My only act of deception had to do with meeting you on purpose. That purpose was to go to Tanzania and see inside the Range. Nothing else. Just getting information so America could capture Omar. I deeply and truly love you, Kira."

"I love you, too."

Ty dropped a kiss into her hair. *She loved him.*

"Now that I'm free from feeling an obligation to my uncle, I'm free to make choices for myself. I can't tell you what a burden has been lifted from my shoulders."

"And what do you want to do with your new-found freedom?"

"I want to live in my little house. I want to enjoy preserving women's stories." She leaned her head up to receive Ty's kiss. "And most of all, I want to see if our own crazy story is a true romance."

"Oh?" He tipped his head. "And how will we know?"

"Oh, a romance always ends with a happily ever after."

Epilogue

Four years later...

Kira stood at the podium, smiling out at the audience. "I want to thank all of those who are celebrating with me this evening. This prestigious award from the Library of Congress is a true honor." She smiled as she lifted the plaque. "I am with you tonight because of the bravery of my husband First Sergeant Tyler Newcomb, who is here with his parents, Roy and Pauline Newcomb, and his sister Molly Newcomb…my family." She held out a palm to indicate where they sat.

Kira waited for the applause to come to a stop.

"While I am very excited to move forward with the next book in this incredible discovery brought to me by my beloved aunt Fatima in Qatar, I would like everyone to know that soon I will be taking some time off from the project, as I'm working on a little project of my own." She stepped from behind the podium and turned sideways, smoothing her dress over her rounded pregnant belly.

The audience clapped their congratulations.

She stepped back to the mic. "I hope, though progress will be slower, I will be able to make strides in revealing the richness of these works. And though we aren't sure who wrote the four novels found hidden in a wedding album, we do know that she was a woman of great intellect. Witty, strong, bold even. And her voice needs to be heard. Thank you again."

Kira carried her plaque from the stage and walked down the steps to slide into Ty's arms.

"I am so proud of you," he whispered into her hair.

"I'm so grateful to you," she said, leaning back to accept one of Ty's kisses, destined to keep her smiling for the rest of her days.

* * * * *

Get 4 FREE REWARDS!

We'll send you 2 FREE Books plus 2 FREE Mystery Gifts.

FREE Value Over **$20**

Both the **Harlequin Intrigue**® and **Harlequin**® **Romantic Suspense** series feature compelling novels filled with heart-racing action-packed romance that will keep you on the edge of your seat.

Get 4 FREE REWARDS!

We'll send you 2 FREE Books plus 2 FREE Mystery Gifts.

FREE Value Over **$20**

Both the **Romance** and **Suspense** collections feature compelling novels written by many of today's bestselling authors.

YES! Please send me 2 FREE novels from the Essential Romance or Essential Suspense Collection and my 2 FREE gifts (gifts are worth about $10 retail). After receiving them, if I don't wish to receive any more books, I can return the shipping statement marked "cancel." If I don't cancel, I will receive 4 brand-new novels every month and be billed just $7.49 each in the U.S. or $7.74 each in Canada. That's a savings of at least 17% off the cover price. It's quite a bargain! Shipping and handling is just 50¢ per book in the U.S. and $1.25 per book in Canada.* I understand that accepting the 2 free books and gifts places me under no obligation to buy anything. I can always return a shipment and cancel at any time by calling the number below. The free books and gifts are mine to keep no matter what I decide.

Choose one: ☐ **Essential Romance**
(194/394 MDN GRHV)

☐ **Essential Suspense**
(191/391 MDN GRHV)

Name (please print)

Address   Apt. #

City   State/Province   Zip/Postal Code

Email: Please check this box ☐ if you would like to receive newsletters and promotional emails from Harlequin Enterprises ULC and its affiliates. You can unsubscribe anytime.

Mail to the Harlequin Reader Service:
IN U.S.A.: P.O. Box 1341, Buffalo, NY 14240-8531
IN CANADA: P.O. Box 603, Fort Erie, Ontario L2A 5X3

Want to try 2 free books from another series! Call 1-800-873-8635 or visit www.ReaderService.com.

*Terms and prices subject to change without notice. Prices do not include sales taxes, which will be charged (if applicable) based on your state or country of residence. Canadian residents will be charged applicable taxes. Offer not valid in Quebec. This offer is limited to one order per household. Books received may not be as shown. Not valid for current subscribers to the Essential Romance or Essential Suspense Collection. All orders subject to approval. Credit or debit balances in a customer's account(s) may be offset by any other outstanding balance owed by or to the customer. Please allow 4 to 6 weeks for delivery. Offer available while quantities last.

Your Privacy—Your information is being collected by Harlequin Enterprises ULC, operating as Harlequin Reader Service. For a complete summary of the information we collect, how we use this information and to whom it is disclosed, please visit our privacy notice located at corporate.harlequin.com/privacy-notice. From time to time we may also exchange your personal information with reputable third parties. If you wish to opt out of this sharing of your personal information, please visit readerservice.com/consumerschoice or call 1-800-873-8635. **Notice to California Residents**—Under California law, you have specific rights to control and access your data. For more information on these rights and how to exercise them, visit corporate.harlequin.com/california-privacy.

STRS22R3

Get 4 FREE REWARDS!

We'll send you 2 FREE Books plus 2 FREE Mystery Gifts.

FREE
Value Over
$20

Both the **Love Inspired**® and **Love Inspired**® Suspense series feature compelling novels filled with inspirational romance, faith, forgiveness and hope.

YES! Please send me 2 FREE novels from the Love Inspired or Love Inspired Suspense series and my 2 FREE gifts (gifts are worth about $10 retail). After receiving them, if I don't wish to receive any more books, I can return the shipping statement marked "cancel." If I don't cancel, I will receive 6 brand-new Love Inspired Larger-Print books or Love Inspired Suspense Larger-Print books every month and be billed just $6.49 each in the U.S. or $6.74 each in Canada. That is a savings of at least 16% off the cover price. It's quite a bargain! Shipping and handling is just 50¢ per book in the U.S. and $1.25 per book in Canada.* I understand that accepting the 2 free books and gifts places me under no obligation to buy anything. I can always return a shipment and cancel at any time by calling the number below. The free books and gifts are mine to keep no matter what I decide.

Choose one: ☐ **Love Inspired**
Larger-Print
(122/322 IDN GRHK)

☐ **Love Inspired Suspense**
Larger-Print
(107/307 IDN GRHK)

Name (please print)

Address   Apt. #

City   State/Province   Zip/Postal Code

Email: Please check this box ☐ if you would like to receive newsletters and promotional emails from Harlequin Enterprises ULC and its affiliates. You can unsubscribe anytime.

Mail to the Harlequin Reader Service:
IN U.S.A.: P.O. Box 1341, Buffalo, NY 14240-8531
IN CANADA: P.O. Box 603, Fort Erie, Ontario L2A 5X3

Want to try 2 free books from another series? Call 1-800-873-8635 or visit www.ReaderService.com.

---

*Terms and prices subject to change without notice. Prices do not include sales taxes, which will be charged (if applicable) based on your state or country of residence. Canadian residents will be charged applicable taxes. Offer not valid in Quebec. This offer is limited to one order per household. Books received may not be as shown. Not valid for current subscribers to the Love Inspired or Love Inspired Suspense series. All orders subject to approval. Credit or debit balances in a customer's account(s) may be offset by any other outstanding balance owed by or to the customer. Please allow 4 to 6 weeks for delivery. Offer available while quantities last.

Your Privacy—Your information is being collected by Harlequin Enterprises ULC, operating as Harlequin Reader Service. For a complete summary of the information we collect, how we use this information and to whom it is disclosed, please visit our privacy notice located at corporate.harlequin.com/privacy-notice. From time to time we may also exchange your personal information with reputable third parties. If you wish to opt out of this sharing of your personal information, please visit readerservice.com/consumerschoice or call 1-800-873-8635. Notice to California Residents—Under California law, you have specific rights to control and access your data. For more information on these rights and how to exercise them, visit corporate.harlequin.com/california-privacy.

LIRLIS22R3

HARLEQUIN
PLUS

Try the best multimedia subscription service for romance readers like you!

Read, Watch and Play.

Experience the easiest way to get the romance content you crave.

Start your **FREE TRIAL** at
<u>www.harlequinplus.com/freetrial</u>.